# Elephant

# Elephant

## David Grant

# This edition 2022

Refreshing Words Press
www.refreshingwords.co.uk

First published 2007, Burning House Books

A catalogue reference for this book is available from
the British Library.

ISBN  978-1-7392350-0-0

Cover and book design by Paul Fulton.
www.paulfulton.co.uk

*To C, D, H and R – it ain't you babes.*

# 1

# Spellbound

The alarm clock shrieks eight inches from my left ear, but it doesn't wake me. I have been lying here seemingly for hours anticipating, feverishly, its battery-driven announcement of the official start of yet another fabulous day in the life of James (in more dashing days, Jamie) Gallagher: publisher, father of two dysfunctional teenagers, husband to Harpy-in-Chief and truly fucked-up forty-six-year-old.

I don't remember the last occasion I had cause to be woken – I haven't needed any alarm for a couple of years as I am usually awake at 4am due to excess worry, minor depression (as yet clinically unrecognised), bowel problems and alcohol abuse. Even now, lying here, I have a mouth like a prioress's gusset. I feel a hangover developing, like some army amassing at a border, waiting to pour in and overrun the unprotected country next door that is my wellbeing. But old habits die hard – faithfully, I set it nightly, hoping either that I will sleep soundly for a change, or that I will die in my sleep and the pain will cease.

OK, dear reader, a caveat just two paragraphs in – if I have a weakness it is for maudlin self-pity, so please excuse me. Oh, and while we're in the confessional, I'll admit now to gross vulgarity, self-delusion and towering arrogance, just to save me the trouble later on.

Helen snorts slightly in her sleep beside me. There was a time a few years ago when I would have cuddled up to her, my fingers stroking her back and shoulders in the near certainty that I would be packed off to work with a damn good shag. But not today. In fact, not for some time – if you want to know the sticky detail, last time out was a year ago in the Dordogne, following a particularly lovely couple of bottles of Bergerac's finest.

Nope, our relationship, such as it is, seems to be based on me working myself to a premature but almost welcome heart attack, her finding more and more ways to spend exactly 10 per cent more than I can possibly earn, while at the same time moaning like a fucking fishwife at her sorry position on God's earth.

All of which must sound, dear reader, like the self-pitying whingeing of a sad, middle-aged loser, and whilst I resolutely object to the term middle-aged, the rest of that sentence just about sums things up. I am in a marriage which can at best be described as cold, at worst moribund. I have a house, two cars and two children, none of which I can properly afford. I hate my job, my coterie of so-called friends bore me fucking rigid, I drink way too much – and to cap it all and to complete the full set of reasons to be cheerful, it is another bloody Monday morning.

I arise, she stirs and moves into the warm space I have left – at least that level of contact with me doesn't revolt her. I head for the en-suite bathroom in the guest room (Helen insists on this when we are guestless – which is most of the time currently – as she does not like me polluting her bathroom) and I ablute. I will spare you the details, gentle reader, as my story should not be classified as of the horror genre – and start to shave.

I look at the jowly figure in the mirror – bloodshot piggy eyes, surrounded by pink pouched flesh – staring back at me, and I want to cry. You would not believe this now, but once I had a reputation as being a bit of a dish. I would have women glancing at me in the street, smiling at me in restaurants, working their way through a crowded room at a party to engage me in conversation. And now? The only glances I get are off the visually impaired, or the truly desperate.

I wash my face in near-scalding water, determined to achieve a really close shave today, despite the contours of jowl and chin. I note that once more my ears have sprouted thick bristles that would a grace a boot-scraping ornamental hedgehog at the back door of a farmhouse.

I hate getting old.

Working the foam with the brush over the two days of growth on beard and upper lip, I begin.

Strangely, my eyes, despite the bloodshot, the fear, the disappointment, look at me as if they belong to the person I was 20 years ago. It is like being spied upon by oneself. The eyes, as they do every day, seem to be asking me: 'Jamie, what the fuck are you doing with your life?'

I can see myself, 20 years ago, in those eyes. I was full of hope, joy and energy – and a determination to live my life to the full. And bloody hell, those eyes disapprove of what I have now become.

'You'll learn,' I say to my young eyes, 'you'll learn.'

And then I painfully rip a zit off my chin with the razor, and the conversation ends. My little self-dialogues have been going on for some time now, and strangely I do not fear for my sanity. Indeed, I am convinced that they are helping to keep me sane. My morning chats are the closest thing I get to interesting conversation these days.

I wash my face again, and watch with disbelief as the tufts of greying beard appear from the folds of skin that my podgy face produces. And then the bleeding starts, the nicks and grazes which have topped the numerous spots and moles of my face,

4

and I seep blood like a colander holding raw liver. I look at myself in the mirror, and despair. 'You fat bastard,' the eyes say. I strip, and walk across the plush pink carpet towards the power shower.

I catch sight of myself in the full-length mirror, and despair some more. I have breasts large enough to ruin a supermodel's career. I have a stomach that looks as if it is being leased by a fertility clinic. My legs are fat and stubby, and I am certain I have shortened over the years. I have no neck, my head just growing straight out of the top of my shoulders.

And to make matters worse, my privates appear to have shrunk in the same proportion as everything else has grown. Forget meat and two veg – think slug and two cherries.

Amongst all of this horror, there is one saving grace – I still have my beautiful luxuriant hair. At present it is sticking up ludicrously, but it is there in abundance. It is greying a little, but I consider this to be a sign of maturity which brings dignity and *gravitas*.

I think baldness would truly necessitate me taking my own life. I mean, you can't hide baldness, you can't run away from it. OK, I'm currently carrying a few more pounds than I should be, but I can – I will – lose those. I'll go to the gym again. I'll jog, cycle, I'll get off the sausage-roll-and-chip diet that I've embraced so vigorously of late. But baldness

– there's no way back from that awful abyss. Like Alzheimer's – there's nothing you can really do about it. Wigs are just a vehicle, quite rightly in my very humble opinion, for ridicule. Every kid you see on the street will make some reference to your rug and a wig-wearer never truly gets eye contact from another person. The modern tendency – to shave it all off leaving the hardman bristle look – is brave and bold, a little like those northern football fans you see without their shirts on in the crowd in the middle of a Yorkshire December: brave, bold but utterly, utterly pointless. Hair replacement treatment costs a fortune, looks great to begin with, but after a year produces a patchy, wispy look reminiscent of the elbows of a crap fur coat in a jumble sale.

So, just to establish one fact here: my hair pleases me.

I get into the shower and begin to wash thoroughly. I'd like to sing – the acoustics provided by this perfect tiling are splendid – but my 'Elvis Costello: the early years medley' at this time of the morning is not welcome, I have learnt from experience.

I dry myself (avoiding the mirror), deodorise, and leave the bathroom for the guest bedroom, where the night before I have left out my uniform for the day. It's my Cerruti suit – perfect Italian cut for the fashion conscience fat bastard with a wife who thinks £800 is a bargain in a sale – my pale blue shirt (handmade, £80) and Boss tie (£75). I have become the man who knows the cost of everything and the value of credit-card balance transfer offers.

You see, I have an Important Meeting today, and I have to Look The Part – it goes with the territory. And because it is my old-fashioned American boss who's flying in to see me specially, I can't get away with the rakish suit and casual shirt I normally sport – no, I have to be booted and suited.

I dress. Despite my size, I look and feel good. I pull my hair back – combing and drying it ruins the windswept image that I am desperate to portray. Finally, I put my tie on loosely, but will not tighten it until I reach the office – rebel yell, indeed.

I leave the bedroom, and stop for a minute on the landing. The house is silent – it is another hour before the kids have to get up, and Helen will prolong her stay in bed for as long as she can before the necessity of giving them breakfast forces her to rise. And then what for the consumate lady of leisure? Probably the gym, shopping with her girlfriends (Helen's friends are, in my opinion, too old to be called girls with their average age of 45, but hey, that's just me being catty), followed by yet more serious damage to my perilous finances as she goes out shopping with one of my myriad credit cards.

There was a time when I loved the feeling, the smell, the very texture of the family house – that was before we moved into this chintzy, nightmare executive pile. When the children were little, I would stand on the landing outside their rooms, and hear their sniffles, their sleeping grunts and groans, and it was as if the house itself were alive. I imagined I could feel the membrane of the walls breathe at the same time as the children.

And before I left, I would go into their rooms, kiss them gently on the forehead and say, 'I love you,' in a whisper, hoping my love would reach them through some kind of osmosis for the rest of the day. And then I would visit Helen, kiss her gently goodbye, and invariably she would try to lure me back into bed for a quick grope, or hurried sex ... We were real, regular, passionate lovers for the first few years of marriage, as I recall.

How things have changed. Last week, I'd forgotten to lay out my socks or boxers or whatever, a heinous crime I am the first to admit, that would in most civilised countries be met with extreme corporal, nay capital, punishment. I tried to sneak back into the bedroom without waking her. Of course, I bumped into a dressing table and some twee designer knick-knack she's decorated the bedroom with – a two-hundred quid brass ballerina or some such – thumped to the floor. All I heard, as if from the silk-printed duvet itself was: 'You selfish bastard, I'm trying to sleep!'

Talking duvets, voices in my head – it's like fucking Hogwarts this place – without the suspension of disbelief.

Anyway, this morning all is in order and I complete *ma toilette* without further incident or interference. I'm running a wee bit late so I slurp down three paracetamol to stun the impending hangover at least temporarily and an espresso (the product of our gleaming Italian coffee maker which appeared last week, and which will be paid for over the course of the next five years at credit card interest rates – buying a fucking Kenyan coffee farm would have been cheaper) and head towards the front door, sleek leather briefcase in hand.

It is still dark outside. I hit the button on the keyfob of the BMW, and the sleek monster that is my new car blinks and lights up. I sling my case casually onto the back seat and climb into the front.

On turning the ignition key, the dashboard lights up like the control panel of something NASA plan to have in active service in 2050. There is an electronic hum as the components come to life. I strap myself in, and consider whether to have a news programme on the radio, or some music, during the short but delightfully stressful journey to the railway station car park.

This car costs as much as a row of houses in the Welsh valleys. It's my new company car. I drive an average six miles a day in it, get taxed to buggery for it and it costs me a fortune to put fuel in to it. Why do I bother?

I bother because it is part of the package. I loved the old Honda I used to drive to the station in, with the suggestion of moss growing on the rotted rubber window seals, and the rear-view mirror that would fall off without warning and land on exactly the same spot on my knee, causing my eyes to water. And the radio that would only tune to Radio Nottingham and some Dutch phone-in channel.

But I loved it because it was mine, and different to what every other fucker drove. Now look at me.

I decide on the musical option. The iPod's docked and I hit the shuffle button.

As I swing out of the gravelled drive of my executive pile, past the small Greek statue that cost three hundred bloody quid and which I think is indescribably shit and tasteless, 'Rock the Casbah' booms out.

There is a little part of me – despite the crap house, and the naff statue, and the coffee maker – which remains, and will always remain, a windswept rebel of a man. Sadly it only manifests itself by my playing old punk and new wave music at top volume.

George opposite is leaving for the city. Oh, how proud Helen was when we took delivery of the new car, bigger and more sparkling than George's. She even briefly considered going out and washing it the first weekend we had it, just to engage the neighbours in conversation and elicit their envy, before deciding that she was much too posh for scrubbing cars – that's what working-class car valeters were for.

I could let George out first, but I don't – no fucking way. It is every man for himself on the Wild West cut-throat roads of the commuter route to London. Let someone out in front of you, and you may miss the lights at the High Street, then the lights on the main arterial road and before you know it you are five minutes behind and 50 cars away from the car park exit nearest to the railway platform and disaster – the train arrives and you've missed your spot on the platform and your usual cosy seat. All because you let some captain of fucking finance out first.

So, I sweep in front of him, and The Clash are rocking big time. I wave imperiously as I do so and begin the drive through the village.

Village – an exaggeration, I accept. There are no true villages any more in the South of England, just big or small towns. Thirty, even twenty years ago, this was a village with a local pub, and shops where the shopkeeper would know all of his customers. People would work locally, some even on the land, and spend their income locally. Now all that's left are dormitory towns – the perfect description. People return to them every evening after a hard day trading currency or stocks and shares in polluting petrochemical businesses or landmine manufacturers, and do nothing there but sleep. Then they wake up and do exactly the same thing the next day.

I reach the Chinese takeaway and the Happy Poacher Steak House – which used to be a charming pub called the Kentish Man, with a real fire and good food and a curmudgeonly old bastard of a landlord until it was bought by a PLC and bedecked with plastic trout and rabbits. The traffic has started already. I grind to a halt, and we lurch, stop, start, along the High Street, gleaming car after gleaming car carrying stressed men on their way at 6.50 on a dark Monday morning to the only thing that defines them – their work.

I glance in the mirror and see George eight cars behind me already. That, rather pathetically I accept, offers some small compensation.

I reach the end of the High Street where the traffic lights, in conditions like these, separate the big hairy testosterone men from the boys. I resolutely prepare for the First Big Battle Of The Day.

It's a two-lanes-into-one situation here. It takes nerves of steel, the bravery of a lion, a gladiatorial soul and a disregard for one's paintwork to win. The wimps play it safe, stay in the inside lane and eventually pass through the lights safely, if three phases later than the real men, men like me, who go for the outside lane and force themselves in.

It's urban warfare and only the strong will come through victorious. And I am Master of the Universe when it comes to this challenge. I even function with just one hand on the wheel, the left involved in an array of gesticulations that over the years have accused approximately seventy-five per cent of the county of excessive masturbatory (if that isn't a contradiction in terms) activity. As a result of this exercise, I have abnormally large muscles in my left arm. Oh, the simple beauty of the circle made by thumb and forefinger, as it is waved languidly in response to an angry toot of the horn. Truly this is the most fun you can have at this time of the morning whilst still in a Cerruti.

Today I shine, forcing in front of a crap Ford, waving at the driver condescendingly, as I push my way in at least five yards further than I have any legitimate right to attain.

And so on to the roundabout which is jammed solid as usual, but no real challenge to me, the nerveless man of steel, this morning. I go for an impossible gap and make it without even so much as a mouthed 'Tosser!' from the driver of the white van I nearly kill. He obviously respects a noble adversary when he sees one.

The sun is beginning to rise over the misty fields and the orchards. In the distance, the ridge still known poetically as the Pilgrims' Way is backlit.

Momentarily I notice the beauty of the countryside, and my mind remembers dawn walks of my youth, the ground wet from dew, and the musty smells of nature. My reverie is interrupted by juggernauts pounding south towards the coast.

Golden rule number one. No one lives down here for the pastoral beauty. You live here because houses are cheaper and schools are better than in London – but you're still only an hour away from The Money.

The town in which the station is located used to be an important village, on an old coaching road from London to the Coast, with inns and stables and turnpikes to cater for the constantly passing trade. It is now an unimportant town. It has vast, brick, ugly housing estates housing vast, ugly people, and Audi and Mercedes-Benz dealerships to cater for the rich bastards who live (sensibly) out of town. There are DIY superstores, supermarkets, and charity shops as well as every conceivable fast-food franchise known to Wall Street, the wrappers of which are blown along the High Street like tumbleweed in a frontier town.

I park my car, ignore the man who parks beside me nearly every day but with whom I never exchange a word, and walk on to the station. I buy my paper – *The Guardian*, not because I enjoy it particularly but because it is not *The Times* or *The Telegraph*, the *Moseley Mail* or *Practical White Supremacist* that the folk I am about to be surrounded by will be reading.

I flash the first-class season at the ticket inspector and take my place at my designated spot on the platform.

Oh fuck, it's Edward from the village, and he's seen me. It's just not done to talk to people at this time of the morning, but I can tell Edward, en route to his crowded second-class carriage, is going to stop and drone, and there'll be fuck all I can do about it. I pretend to read the front-page article about the effect of global warming on Norfolk (surely it can only improve on that chilly sea breeze?) and hope that he'll realise now is not a good time.

'James,' he says in his upper-class, dull accent, jerking me away from the thought of the Cromer rain forests

'Edward,' I say limply. He's looking old – well, he must be mid-fifties – but as dapper as ever. Handmade Savile Row and Churches, I guess, and the usual old school tie; he looks like a pre-war bank manager. I know him vaguely as Helen golfs with his priggish little wife – Daphne or something.

'Haven't seen you around much,' he continues.

'Because mixing with indescribably dull people like you makes me want to consider taking my own life, Edward,' I think – whilst my vocal chords produce, 'Oh, you know: busy busy busy.'

Edward is something quite big in re-insurance I believe. He owns a larger house than we do just on the outskirts of the village – a mock Tudor pile with a large lawned garden. He drives a large Volvo, went to Cambridge and he and Daphne are childless. I don't know why, never having delved in depth into either of their reproductive organs.

'So how's the creative world of publishing going?' he asks, failing to pick up from my body language that I am currently Cromer-obsessed.

'Mind your own fucking business,' I think but actually reply, rather wittily, 'Oh you know.'

Thankfully, my train comes. He's off to the City and so has another five minutes to wait. I say goodbye, vowing to join him and Daphne for a glass of wine shortly – a vow I have obviously absolutely no intention of honouring.

So, into the moderately plush first class carriage I ascend. Six other men are already in, as they always are, and I take my seat and open my newspaper without so much as a glance at or from any of them. 'Tis ever thus – for the last God-knows-how-many years, I've been getting on this train sitting with the same people, any of whom could suffer a major heart seizure and probably not elicit any kind of response from the others.

Not of course that I want to talk to any of them – God forbid. I mean, just look at them. City bores to a man, striped suits and cufflinks, silk socks, true blue Tory bastards with guaranteed pensions, with their big houses and dull marriages and children at expensive schools.

'Just like you, fuckwit,' the voice in my head says.

And it's right, I know. How can I be sure that underneath these dull city suits does not stir the hearts of a poet, or revolutionary, trapped as I am in someone else's life? This guy opposite, for example – looks like a retired Guards officer, strong chin, pale cold blue eyes, sandy-coloured hair cut short and military. Now, my assessment of him is: major public school, Sandhurst, million and a half pound house, a pretty,hearty wife 10 years his junior called Lizzie and two fresh-faced kids at his alma mater. Oh, and £300K a year plus bonus from an investment bank. But how do I know his heart does not beat to an avant-garde symphony he's composing, or that he's not having an affair with a hairy-arsed Humberside truck driver called Derek?

Appearances, and the assumptions made from them, are dangerous things. I glance at myself in the mirror and see a fat bloke who in no way stands out from others in the carriage.

I glance over the newsprint, read the sports pages, and the journey through the London suburbs passes dully. I think I used to have more fun in second class. At least I could enjoy the dullness of overheard conversations,.

# 2

# No More Heroes

While pretending to read the newspaper, I think about the day, the week, ahead in the office of Intellectual Property Corporation, as we are now proudly known. I am somehow the European VP of Marketing and Sales – I know, it is unlikely, but there you go – and have been for the last three years since my friend, protector and mentor Charles W. Daniels of bottomless pockets and misguided loyalty bought the small company I used to work for, and installed me in charge of the whole shooting match.

Which was awfully flattering, but I wasn't sure I wanted it at the time. I knew it would be a hassle and figures and meetings, and I – poor old-fashioned sod that I was – went into publishing because I Like Books, not spreadsheets.

Then he told me what the salary would be.

Then, stupid bastard that I am, I told Helen what the salary would be.

I'd struggled along in the past, accepting that the industry was never going to make me rich, but that money was not the chief motivational force for going to work. Of course Helen, being Helen, hankered for bigger biggest best, but as long as she was aware of my limited earning potential, she kept a lid on her consumerist desires.

So, when she heard that my salary would double overnight, and that I'd have stock options, which could in the fullness of time keep us in vintage champagne and asses' milk for the rest of our lives, she went into overdrive.

'What do you mean, you're thinking about it?' she asked incredulously.

'I mean I'm thinking about it,' I replied with ready wit.

'What is there to think about? At last, we'll not have to worry about money again. I've scrimped and saved since we've been married, and here's an opportunity not to have to do that again. And you're thinking about it?'

I tried to conjure an image of Helen, shopping in charity shops, knitting swaddling clothes for our emaciated infants and making soup out of potato peelings – but I confess I struggled.

I put the arguments to her passionately – money didn't motivate me, I did not want to sell my soul to a company that was principally interested in value for the investor, that there were other things in life that I'd like to do.

She looked at me like I was mad. 'Take it,' she said.

I'd asked Charles for a couple of days to think about it. On the evening before I was due to make my mind up, he called me at home, laughing.

'You clever Brit bastard – OK, how much more do you want?'

He thought I was involved in a sophisticated negotiation ploy.

'Another 25 per cent on your salary, plus top range car allowance?'

Helen nearly had her head glued to mine like some craniopagal twin in order to overhear what was being offered. Her look said it all.

I accepted the revised terms there and then, basking in the glory of Charles's admiration – and pretended that I'd just taught Helen a lesson in brinkmanship.

Charles is a total Anglophile. He'd traced his family back, and apparently they had been on the second wave of ships from Plymouth to leave for the New World, although I have my doubts. Every American you meet claims to come from stock who were on the first or second wave. According to my reckoning, there must have been about twelve thousand ships in each flotilla, and the Old Country must have been emptied.

Anyway, Charles loves me as the archetypal Brit – sardonic, ironic, sarcastic, irreverent and usually pissed. He is virtually teetotal when in the US but when out with me he's off his face on our warm British Bittah within an hour.

There is no one to touch me in Charles's eyes. I am the Brit he wished he'd been. Stupid bastard.

Once I'd accepted the job, and been granted the celebratory shag that evening, it all started. The orgy of spending, the haemorrhaging of the money that I'd not yet earned.

First of all it was schools. Cameron was in with a bad crowd at the state secondary (which I suspect would have taught him consummate life skills but we'll let that go) and all our (well, her) friends were going private, so we just went to have a little look at the fee-paying heap on the hill and next thing I know I'm signing a direct debit mandate for thousands per annum.

And then Ailsa. She'd been doing really well at the village primary, had lots of friends, but Helen wore the social discomfort of mixing with the riffraff at the school gate like a facial deformity. 'What you do for one you have to do for the other,' she told me. 'And it's not nearly as expensive for girls as it is for boys,' she added, proud of that fact, the sexist irony escaping her.

Of course by this time I was knee-deep in the new job, attempting to bluff my way through spreadsheets and budgets in the hope that the folk reporting to me had some faith that I knew what the fuck I was meant to be doing; so I just signed off on the direct debit to shut the voracious and loquacious cow up.

Then the house wasn't big enough.

When one mixes with public-school parents in the South East one does perceive domestic life rather differently to the average state school parent. You realise that every other silly former beautician married to some chinless no-brain investment banker lives in a moated manor house – each and every fucking one of them. And has a pool, the changing set-up for which a working class family plus their relatives could happily live in. I envisage in 10 years' time a housing crisis where there are no more moated manor houses to live in – what then? A major funding appeal from Shelter will ensue.

Anyway, our smallish but perfectly acceptable detached house, albeit on a middle-class estate, was not good enough. Helen knew she couldn't have a moat of her own – if only she'd married old money I told her, and she involuntarily nodded in agreement – but she wanted a bigger house, far away from neighbours, with some land and privacy.

But most of all, she wanted a house with a name, not a street number. Common people live in numbered houses. I suggested buying a plaque for our current place and, as when the children were born, tried to engage her in a democratic naming discussion (I favoured 'Ocean Sprays' as we were thirty five miles from the nearest beach, but she wouldn't have it).

So fuck me, we moved.

I think I would like on my gravestone the words: 'Anything for a quiet life'.

We moved to this new development of luxury executive houses, six bedrooms, all mod cons, up a private cul-de-sac with an electronically operated security gate, a fifteen-foot crenellated brick wall encircling the whole damn place, machine gun turrets every 100 yards, Doberman Pinchers roaming free, spotlights and a minefield to keep away possible intrusions from members of the working classes except when they're there to valet the cars.

Each house is squeaky clean and characterless, with manicured gardens – most front gardens have shitty Grecian statues (I may have mentioned this before, apologies if I have) or ornamental metalwork statues depicting, well, ornamental metalwork, as far as I can tell. Helen seems to have lost all sense of individual taste since moving in here, and if the neighbours suddenly started pressing their bare arses at the upstairs windows at eleven o'clock every morning I suspect she'd want us to do the same. Not, of course, that you can see the neighbours or even their arses (thankfully), as each house is tastefully positioned behind hedges and trees.

But best of all, apparently, we have no number. We are in 'Honeysuckle House'. Well, cottage would sound so like a holiday home ...

And it costs a fucking fortune every month. Believe me, South American countries have smaller national debts than the amount I am in to the building society for.

And then she showed me just last week, a house in the paper. 'Oh that's us, love,' she said, simpering, pointing out a small manor house in the country with, fuck-me-sideways, a moat. 'We've made so much on this place we could afford to move.'

I pointed out, rationally and coolly, that yes, we'd made money on this place. But the small manor house, bargain that it obviously was, would put an extra £300K on our mortgage and that the only way we could afford that would be for me to stop gardening at the weekends and take up armed robbery of sub-post offices in the local environs whilst she's out selling the children's internal organs. A withering look was all I got for that. I then, rather graciously I thought, offered to dig a moat myself around our current house, which I considered an eminently sensible compromise. I was even reaching for my car keys to go and buy a new shovel.

I resolutely read the same article in my newspaper as we head through the grey London suburbs. I try to banish negative thoughts from my brain as I head closer to The Office.

Only fifteen minutes late – incident on the line we are told: some poor bastard probably jumped on to it when he saw how much his season ticket was costing – and I stride out of Charing Cross railway station towards Headquarters and yet another week of wheeling and dealing and dollars and books.

It is a grey morning and the pavements en route to Covent Garden have that dirty sheen to them, a mixture I suspect of vomit and dribble from last night's pissed revellers. Not that last night was in any way a special night – it's just that any evening in London nowadays seems to see half the population staggering around pissed or drugged or mad.

And often I'm one of them.

London stinks. It always does. Black bags have been dumped outside restaurants in the early hours of the morning and the local cats have split them open to save the rats the trouble. I step past discarded pizza and bits of garlic bread, and guys sleeping in filthy rags in doorways, and conclude that the city is going to the dogs, if not the cats, rats and pigeons.

When I first came to London, it seemed full of interest and fun, sophisticated and buzzing; certainly to a guy who'd come via a Midlands university, a grimy industrial Northern town and prior to that, from Scotland. The women on the tube in the morning were dangerous and sexy, the shops were full of food from far-flung places, the bars were sophisticated – it was like being on holiday in my first few years. I'd be out every night, drinking, listening to bands and doing drugs, trying and invariably failing to pick up women, and walking through exotic streets at four in the morning trying to get back to my flat to wash and shave and get in to work for 9 am. Then we'd be back down the pub at lunchtime topping up the alcohol levels.

It was bliss.

And now look at me. I glimpse my reflection in the window of some cloned Irish bar, and see a fat middle-aged guy heading for work and a photo finish between a heart attack and a stomach ulcer

# 3

# Clown Time is Over

I step into the coffee shop beside the office for industrial-strength espresso and a Danish.

I could kill for a cigarette. I keep giving up, then starting again. Stupid, I know, to pay good money for the privilege of being poisoned by a multinational tobacco company, but hey, the slow death is still a tad glamorous in a 'I won't be told what to do by health fascists' kind of way.

It's 8.10 when I push through the front door of the Intellectual Property Corporation and I am confronted by Janice.

Janice, ah Janice, as radiant as ever – her perfect breasts pushing out from a perfectly non-provocative red jumper. Little make-up, and slightly masculine features with a strong thrusting lower jaw, eyes a little too close together giving the impression that she is slightly startled and looking at a spot somewhere just behind you. She must be 23 or 24, and therefore, shockingly, somehow young enough to be my daughter, and she dresses sensibly and old-fashionably – twinsets and jumpers and skirts that come just over her knees, and her whole slightly middle-aged aura is a terrible turn-on every morning when I can see her strong thighs and firm, firm body through clothes my mother might have worn some 40 years ago.

She's my girl, is Janice.

'Morning Mr. Gallagher,' says Janice.

'Jamie, Janice, please. Good morning, Janice,' I say.

We go through this every morning, and every morning I'm Mr Gallagher. I can't work out whether it is genuine respect she is showing me, or getting off on some master–servant fantasy. Obviously in my lonely hours where I mull this one over I list to the latter option. But still. It's good to get respect somewhere.

'And what's in the post today?' I say, standing beside her, smelling her odour of sensible soap and supermarket shampoo.

I couldn't care less what is in the post today, really, but I try to generate this image of fast-moving publishing entrepreneur with his finger on the pulse of every publishing innovation, combined with a caring eye for detail – an old-fashioned boss.

And also it gets me close to Janice. One day, I swear I'll touch her just to see what the response is. But probably not today.

'See you later Janice,' I say, I think, seductively.

'Have a good day,' Janice replies, smiling at a spot three yards behind me.

I call the lift and enter it; preferring, I reflect, to be entering Janice should I be offered the option, but the lift is definitely more accessible. And as repetitive as Janice. 'Doors closing,' it intones as it does incessantly, in a throaty sexy mechanical voice. For whom? I mean, is it likely that Yanomami tribespeople (about whom, incidentally, we publish the definitive anthropological guide), or any other group unused to mechanical appliances, are going to suddenly storm the building and dive into the lift and be slaughtered en masse by the closing door were it not for this kindly warning?

And presumably, somewhere, someone has been paid to record this message. Are they on a royalty? Do they get 10p for every time their voice is heard? Would they earn more for a full lift than a solus traveller?

Sorry: a little rant.

I press the button for the fourth floor, and inspect myself in the mirror. Not bad for 46 I think.

'Fat bastard,' the voice in my head says.

'Doors opening,' says the sexiest, and presumably richest, mechanical woman in the world.

I know that I must be beyond redemption if I start to have fantasies about the lift woman.

Ah, my empire beckons. The open-plan office is spread out in front of me in its glorious untidiness. Computers vie for desktop space with books and journals, and stationery, and it is a sight I love; to feel that all of this is there for one reason only: to propagate learning. Or if you are an accountant or shareholder, to make a pile of cash and bugger the learning. There are 88 members of my staff in the UK, and a happy team we are, I like to think. They are beginning to appreciate, if not love, my maverick ways and strange motivational tactics, I believe ... hang on, who the hell's that?

In the corner, a desk lamp is on, and I see someone huddled over the computer. This is not on – I'm the boss, I lead by example, I am European VP of Marketing and Sales and always the first in. I march over and see it is my new product manager, been there a week, name escapes me. Young guy, early-thirties, very earnest; I have him down for deeply held Christian views, a timid wife and small child, and a semi in Beckenham.

I cough gently, three feet away from him – he's so engrossed in the screen that I can only assume he's looking at pornographic images of Beckenham lovelies, but when he hears me and glances up, he is not embarrassed or ashamed, quite the opposite.

'James,' he says, 'didn't hear you come in.'

I rack my brains but cannot remember the bastard's name. I want to express my concern, make him feel like the class creep, but realise in time that this level of dedication should be admired and welcomed by me as head honcho.

'What you up to? Couldn't you sleep?' I ask him, feigning interest and concern, and he begins enthusiastically to explain how he has discovered a new ancient history website, which has not just heads of departments and professors on it in universities around the globe, but also key staff members from research assistants up.

'It will transform our database,' he breathes excitedly. 'I stumbled upon it over the weekend, and just wanted to get in early to make a start. It really could revolutionise our history marketing.'

'Fantastic,' I breathe excitedly back and make a note to remember his poor wife in my prayers. 'Keep up the good work – and let me know how it goes,' I say, and head for the sanctuary of my office where I can avoid, temporarily at least, people who take their jobs too seriously.

Publishing. 'How interesting that must be,' people say – usually women married to investment bankers. And it used to be, I guess, when I first went in to it. You'd work on the weird, the clever, the eclectic, and though it was never a well-paid industry it was fun and funky and there were good people about. Then all the good people were sacked by accountants and the interesting, creative publishing houses were hoovered up by large organisations that could be

31

producing drugs or socks (and rock and roll) as long as they kept the shareholders happy.

Publishing. Every two books that made money paid for eight others that didn't, but which probably were worthy and clever and deserved to be published. And that's why I loved the industry in the early days – yes, we were there to make a profit through successfully publishing books, but each book was individual and the product in the main of enormous intellectual effort on some poor bastard's part and for that effort just to be published was often enough in itself. So, I willingly came in to this poorly paid business as it appealed to my then intellectual left-wing sentiments.

Christ, I sound as if I cared. Well, I guess I did in the early days. Not now. Couldn't give a flying fart to be honest. The fun has gone, and I'm surrounded by people too stupid to find gainful employment in investment banking.

And believe me, that is pretty stupid.

Ah, the sanctuary of my office. I close the door – open-door policies are fine but the last thing I want is this bunch disturbing my waking slumbers. I remove my jacket and sit down behind the big walnut desk that defines my status as Boss, and switch on my PC.

Oh joy, my little toy, my bundle of wires and silica and bytes (none of which I profess to having a fucking clue about) – my connection with the outside world without actually having ever to talk to anyone.

I open my emails. Most are cc'd to me from spineless wankers covering their own arses in the organisation, and I skim read them before deleting them. What did folk do before emails? Perhaps they had to talk to other people, interact properly, engage in conversation, argue, discuss, enjoy the nuance of body language. Not now – don't send a gunboat, send a fucking email.

Nothing of importance in this lot, anyway.

I fire off a quick email to my snivelling marketing manager who has taken sycophancy to the point of it nearly being permitted as an Olympic sport. She will go far that girl, she will sweep past me soon on the global slippery corporate pole, but I vow in the interim to make life as hard for her as possible.

'Jean,' I write, direct and forcefully I feel, but also personal. 'We need to be targeting our database compilation activity so that it represents the revenue streams of the organisation, not just the personal interests of our staff members.' Finger on the pulse stuff, I congratulate myself. 'I came into the office to find a member of staff, who shall remain nameless, working on our ancient history list. Such dedication is wonderful to behold, but might I suggest that such effort is hardly worth expending on a part of our list worth less than two per cent of our turnover? Kind regards, James.'

Sometimes, I just love being a work-based shit. You can do what you like – it is the ultimate in legitimised bullying. As a kid, I don't think I did enough bullying – I was too insecure – and I think that now I am making up for lost time. Well, with certain people in the building anyway. With others I smooth and smooch and charm and emotionally stroke them – if they had any classical education they'd nickname me Janus. This I find immensely personally satisfying as no one can ever know how I am going to behave or react, and by cultivating camps of favourites and the despised, I don't half keep the bastards on their toes.

They teach you nothing about real management on training courses or in books. Divide and rule, I say; take shittiness and charm to new heights.

And do I enjoy the power!

I sit and fiddle at my desk for half an hour or so, pretending to be doing high-powered executivey type things, but in reality playing a couple of games of solitaire. I find time in this busy schedule to check the Heart of Midlothian (laughingly defined by those in the know as a 'football team') website. I then fire off a couple of emails to colleagues in the States just to point out that I am still around.

In truth I am passing time until Charles – my saviour, my muse, my protector – arrives and we will spend a pleasant day together as we usually do, beginning with the pub at eleven o'clock.

He's late. The office fills up gradually as the clock moves towards 9am. I don't know half of the people who work here. The pretty new girl from editorial smiles at me, which is always encouraging. I'm not stupid or vain enough to think she is doing this for any reason other than career enhancement but hey, any port in a storm is what I say.

It's ten past nine and still no Charles. Strange. He's normally straight off the red-eye from New York raring to go. Perhaps I should ring his hotel to see if he's OK, but I might disturb him – he has something of a penchant for high-class London call girls, which his Catholic upbringing tries to control. Perhaps he couldn't wait until the evening, so a call from me in flagrante delicto, might not be appropriate.

I open my office door – I can take the distant, man-of-iron act too far, I guess – and I can see some of my young disciples looking towards me. I'm now in messianic mood and I want to welcome my people.

The door stays open for 10 minutes before anyone bothers to cross its threshold to seek my advice. And then it is only the anally retentive Chris. He's three years older than me and has been in the company throughout its various transformations all of his working life and yet still seeks permission from management before allowing himself to even break wind.

'Er … James,' he nervously stammers on the threshold of the great man's (that's me!) office. 'This invoice needs to be paid today, and accounts need a manager to sign off on it. Would you mind …?'

I take the paper manfully and see it is for the princely sum of £72.60 due to a local printer. I sign off as he starts to justify the bill.

'Thanks Chris,' I say dismissively, and turn my back on him as he continues to explain what the £72.60 expenditure entailed and how VAT can be reclaimed. I sit down, pick up the phone and pretend to dial. At last he fucks off.

Business – it confuses me. I am not cut out to be a businessman, of that I am sure and I am not talking about my intellectual abilities here so much as my colossal inclination towards laziness. Ultimately, none of it matters. It's not like being a peace envoy charged with staving off nuclear war between Israel and some rogue Arab state, or a researcher three months and twenty million dollars away from the discovery of a cancer vaccine. I mean, we publish book, books which help students or academics understand certain aspects of the environment in which they find themselves, but if we didn't the world would not be any worse a place.

Christ, I've changed my tune from my early starry-eyed idealism.

But it's not just books. If I worked in shoes or

shirts or cardboard boxes, it would be exactly the bloody same. It is commercial activity for the sake of commercial activity, namely profit, and I'm not going to kid myself that because I work in publishing, I'm any better than if I worked in burgers.

I should have done it differently. I should have been a poet, or played bass in a punk band wearing shades and writing insightful revolutionary lyrics that a spitting lead singer could cascade upon the heaving, hating, sweating masses. I should have travelled the dangerous highways and byways of the world, with photographs of myself in native garb on some rocky outcrop, retracing epic journeys, finding murderous tribesmen and their dangerous treasure, appearing in *National Geographic*.

But somehow it never seemed appropriate. My mum wanted me to do a real job – doctor, lawyer, accountant, banker, that kind of thing (a Profession, I believe was the term) – and I knew that wasn't for me and that I liked to read, so I compromised: a life of rebellion and excitement for the creative poetic world of British publishing. And 25 or so fucking years later, here I am: bored in my job, bored in my life.

I mean, none of it bloody matters – it all ends in anonymity, in anachronism. The book that is the must-read this year ends up out of print and uncommercial to reprint next. And I will be remembered perhaps by my children, and perhaps their children too, and then that will be it. I will have left no mark on the world whatsoever except to have passed on a few middling genes to some future related drones.

I'm sorry, dear reader, but I did warn you – I'm becoming maudlin. Such is the folly of middle age, as I now am statistically meant to refer to myself. It's the hangover, the fag-craving and my age combining to make me like this. I'd perfectly understand it if you put the book down and got out your Nick Hornby for a little light relief.

The morning is failing to ignite. I don't want to start on any serious work yet as Charles is bound to arrive and drag me off to The Pub, as he says so reverentially, then for a deliciously expensive lunch, then perhaps one of his seedy clubs that he seems to know so much about. So I shuffle a few bits of paper around the desk, empty my email inbox, visit the bog a couple of times with *The Guardian* supplement and kill time.

I am temporarily engrossed once again in the official website of Heart of Midlothian FC, trying to memorise the key names lest I should have to have manly banter at some stage about football, when there is a discreet cough, and gentle knock, at my door. I look up and see the Death Head.

Or rather Wayne Simpkins from the US office. In my mind, the Death Head. His skin is white and stretched tightly around his cheekbones, chin and forehead, as if the skull itself has been the result of a poor spray paint job. His eyes are sunk deep and sallow, yolk yellow; and this whole ghastly, ghostly visage is topped off by a blanket of greased hair lying horizontal on top of his head. He has a small weedy frame that is reminiscent of some stage Nazi, bedecked in a shin-length black leather coat. What the fuck is he doing here?

'Wayne!' I bound forward, as if of all the people on God's planet, the man I most want to see here and now is Wayne Simpkins. I grab his hand and shake it enthusiastically. 'How are you?'

Christ, I do sincerity well these days. This is a guy who I've met only twice before in the US office, who was drafted into the company as something of a surprise a year ago, and who my antennae tell me is a dangerous man; but I go into overdrive on my charm offensive. He's here for a reason, something's up somewhere, and I need to establish myself quickly as one of the good guys.

He smiles coldly at me. 'Jet-lagged,' he drawls. 'On the red-eye – should be asleep now.'

'Let me take your coat, get you some coffee,' I fuss, guiding him to the low slung sofa at the front of my office which I use for my intimate discussions. He sits, carefully pulling at his expensive suit trousers to stop them creasing, and I ask Susie, a marketing assistant who reluctantly doubles as my PA, for a pot of coffee, which she sulkily goes off to make, her entire body language telling me 'five years at bloody Oxford to make your fucking coffee, you male fascist bastard ...'

I digress. Simpkins. He sits in front of me, his eyes taking in the slightly untidy office, the large expensive desk and the tasteful print I bought in Covent Garden on the company credit card, and I see him registering complaints and unnecessary expenditure. Distract him, I tell myself.

'So Wayne,' I say enthusiastically, 'what brings you here? I was expecting Charles.' A thought: is Charles dead, or terminally ill? 'Charles is all right, isn't he?' I ask with genuine concern.

'Charles is fine, James, just fine,' he drawls like he's chewing on tar. 'It's just that he's, eh ... having to take something of a back seat now in the, eh ... restructured business.'

Restructured? Shit. Certain words cause fear in the very soul of a company employee and 'restructured' is one. As is 'expenses audit'.

'As Chairman, he will be keeping a paternal eye on us all in future but his hands-on involvement in the business will be diminished.'

And with that he smiles as much as the tautness of his skin will allow.

'Good for him – golf and relaxation will do him good,' I say in a jolly, 'I've-obviously-nothing-to-fear-

and-indeed-have-loyalty-to-nobody-or-nothing-except-the-company' kind of way. 'Erm, who is taking over? Who will I be reporting to Stateside in future?'

'A new man. Someone with a, shall we say, broader view of the publishing business.' He smiles cadaverously and I know he is waiting for me to ask who that could be – which I don't, as I will not give him the satisfaction of being handed the opportunity to say imperiously, dramatically,

''Tis I – I, Wayne Simpkins.'

# 4

# I Can't Stand Up
# (for Falling Down)

Oh woe is me, dear reader. I am sitting in a pub on Villiard Street. It is 8pm and I have consumed my fourth pint of strong lager since making my escape from the Simpkins clutches just under an hour ago. The first thing I did was buy cigarettes – what the hell, I thought, poisoning myself slowly through tar and nicotine must be preferable to death by boredom that close association with Simpkins is guaranteed to bring – and I am halfway through the packet already. And fuck me, whatever people tell you, cigarettes taste good, certainly in my current beleaguered circumstances.

I phone my lovely wife to explain my absence from the joy of the family home. My son picks up and in the background I hear the clash between his kraang heavy metal music and the television blaring out the Simpsons.

'I'm late – will you tell your mother? I'll be back at ten-ish.'

He replies fulsomely, grunting what I think is, 'Yeah,' and then he puts the phone down.

Another beer and I let my mind assess the horror, the sheer knob-numbing, awful, shocking, horrific, tedious horror of the day.

Simpkins had wanted to look at the finances.

'Sure,' I had responded quickly. 'I'll get finance to run you a set of management reports.'

'No,' he had said. 'I want to spend time with you now, looking specifically at your department's expenditure. And indeed your own expenditure.'

And that's what we did. All fucking afternoon. Virtually every expense claim I had made. Why this hotel in Paris? Why this meal in Frankfurt? How much was my car costing the business? The staff party ... you bloody name it, the bastard went through everything. After an hour I was exhausted. After two hours I was seriously pissed off, and without wishing to upset my new boss, felt that my seniority in the global business was being scrutinised a little too closely. I decided to challenge him, somewhat meekly.

'Erm, isn't this what we have a finance department for?' I said, with what I thought was a light touch. 'We have to justify our expenditure to the revenue, and we are well within budget, so forgive me for asking, Wayne' – an old trick there, judicious sprinkling of the Christian name in difficult conversations usually works like a treat –

'but what is it we' (nota-fucking-bene: not 'you') 'are looking for here?'

He stopped looking at his printout and turned to me, his cold eyes meeting mine.

'Shareholder value,' he stated, as if it was the most blindingly obvious response possible.

And with that, his head returned to the printout. 'This trip to Prague last April. What was it for?'

And so on. No breaks, nothing to eat, the man was an automaton, needing no sustenance but the devouring of figures and then defecating questions.


I drink my beer, contemplate another one but decide against it as I have to drive from the station back to the house. And anyway, my darling wife and delightful children await.

I board the train and find a seat in a compartment by the window. I take out the newspaper that I have not glanced at since this morning and halfway through my second paragraph I feel my eyes droop.

Gentle, floating, half-conscious, shallow sleep fills my mind. Images: Wayne's deathly face and dry hands; figures float in the ether, and images of a half-visited book fair in Prague; it all blends, all gels into one. I feel the train's gentle motion and I am dreaming of Janice and her tight sweater when suddenly up pops that little voice in my head that has been absent for the whole of the day:

'He's going to sack you, you know that, don't you? And a sacked forty-five-year-old European VP of Marketing and Sales is going to struggle to find a job unless you fancy stacking shelves at the local DIY superstore?'

I wake suddenly. This is not on, being awakened from nightmares by voices in my head. What happened to the semi-drunken Janice lech-fest? How dare my subconscious ruin that for me.

The Voice continues. 'You're going to get found out, pal. They don't care about a few quid here or there, or first class to Australia last year when company policy states business at best. They don't give a flying (forgive the pun) fuck about extra days over in luxury hotels for fun and sightseeing. Everyone does that. What Simpkins recognises is what's in your soul, my old son. You don't belong. You're anarchic, disruptive, an unbeliever. And your time has come. Simpkins has just read (or is in the process perhaps of writing) *The Stalin Guide to International Management*, and what he's learned in Chapter 7 'Purges and Motivation', he's about to apply to you …'

A cold shiver hits me. The Voice knows, the Voice is indeed right: I am going to be ceremoniously chucked out for one false postage stamp claim or something equally petty. The Voice leaps in – scarily, it has taken on the W. Simpkins timbre:

'It doesn't have to be so petty does it? I mean, there's Sofia last year and what you blew your cash on then ...'

A memory. Drunk in a nightclub, a beautiful Slavic hostess telling me she wants to fuck. I resist – believe it or not, I always do – telling her I am happily married, I have children and she kisses me and I buy her champagne and she strokes my thigh and tells me she thinks I might have 'Somethink for me in your trousers, yes?' and she touches me delicately. She tries to lead me by the hand and the prick to a back room, but I resist, telling her I want to talk. She perseveres until her patience is exhausted. 'Go talk to your mother, asshole!' she shouts, a traditional Bulgarian farewell I believe, that loses a little in translation; and with that she leaves me and the bottle of champagne for another middle-aged businessman who's just come in the door. I finish my drink, and stagger out of the club into the cold night.

I awoke in an alleyway, my head resting on cardboard which I think had been kindly placed there in lieu of a duck-feather pillow by whoever it was who had stolen my wallet, mobile phone, air ticket and passport. The wallet containing £500 of company money and all my credit cards.

The police were very kind. I explained how I had been drinking, how someone must have slipped something into my drink … how I left to go to my hotel and was grabbed from behind.

'Which sex club sir?' said the sergeant impatiently, and I knew I was one in a big fat file of sad, robbed middle-aged fucks to whom this happened. He told me gruffly that the appropriate forms needed to be filled in for insurance claims to be made, and that there was an administration charge of £500 paid in sterling to him now in order for this to happen. On being reminded that my money had been stolen I was asked to leave.

Back at the hotel, a short granite-faced man dressed in black from head to toe and wearing Ray Bans despite the dull morning and being indoors, stopped me. He opened his coat and showed me a bulge which I assume was a gun, and my wallet, passport and air tickets, and told me in a low whisper that I could get everything back for two thousand pounds. We walked together to the Amex office where I withdrew the money in sterling, paid him off, then spent the rest of the trip trying to find a way to justify the loss to the company when I returned. No police report – no insurance claim. I'd had a choice – either to swallow the loss myself and, given the fairly perilous state of my personal finances, attempt to claw it back over the next few months through creative use of the expense form, or come clean to the business. Explain, how I'd been pissed out of my brain in a dodgy part of a city that all business sense dictated I should never even have visited, robbed and drugged. Oh yes, and then the police had tried to blackmail me. Perhaps it was my Scottish Presbyterian upbringing, but I realised if I took the honesty route, my sin would out.

So, I exaggerated some already lavish lunches, doctored some receipts and invented long car journeys over the next few months. And carefully, secretly and I have to say, cleverly, the loss was hidden.

Until that bloody accountancy Nazi Wayne (from Stalinist to Nazi in just a couple of pages ...) started to get involved.

I drift back to lightly drunken sleep, my inner voice silenced momentarily. Except when it wakes me saying, 'The money's neither here nor there, pal. He wants you out. There's been a coup, a purge, and you, my friend, will be hung out on the metaphorical lamp post as a warning to all about loyalty.'

The lights are on in the house as I pull up outside. Oh joy. As I step out of the car I can hear the booming bass line of what passes for music coming from my sixteen-year-old son's bedroom. The poor neighbours, I consider, having to put up with that day in, day out; before remembering that they are all a bunch of twats and my pity is wasted on them.

I open the front door. Ailsa, my thirteen-year-old daughter is in the process of slamming the lounge door and swearing fluently and with some ability, I assume at her mother.

'Evening darling – kiss for Daddy?' I say, as she glances at me as if I am dog dirt and flounces upstairs.

'I'm taking a fucking overdose,' I hear her say.

I head to the kitchen, find a tumbler, some ice and pour myself an industrial-strength whisky which even four years ago would have felled me for the evening but which right now will dull the senses for all of 10 minutes until the next one is needed.

Taking a deep slurp and a deeper breath I prepare, as if on the first day of the Battle of the Somme, to go over the parapet and face the emotional terror that is the lounge and my wife.

I open the door, and she is sitting, vodka and tonic in hand, watching some fucking awful reality TV programme. I think, to continue the Stalinist theme, it's 'Celebratory Gulag Archipelago' tonight, where P-list celebs are deported to inhospitable climes (Kilmarnock, I suspect) by the voting public. Or some such shit. I take a mouthful of Scotch and say, 'Evening darling,' which elicits a sideways turn of the head, her eyes still enraptured by the plotting of one contestant to steal the buff but stupid boyfriend from her bestest of mates. (I may be making this up but you get the drift), and grunts, 'Oh, it's you.'

'It is indeed,' I reply, the booze making me feel a tad brave. Oh fuck it – after the day I've had I'm spoiling for a fight and a night in that well-appointed guest bedroom. 'Busy day hon?' I ask in my best simpatico manner.

'The usual,' she replies.

'Who did you see?' I'm never usually interested and she knows this is a game I'm playing, and it is starting to get to her.

'Margaret – we went to the gym and had lunch.'

'Where?'

'Where what?' she tetchily replies.

'Where did you have lunch?'

'Chez Nikki's,' and at last she looks at me, angry that she has lost this particular skirmish that is the ongoing battleground of our marriage.

'What did you have, darling?'

'YOU'VE BEEN DRINKING,' she bellows to distract me.

'In one, Miss Marple,' I flash wittily. 'But I don't need to have been drinking to be interested in you, my angel. I'm just intrigued to know if you had a good time piling debt on to my credit card when the fucking house is full of food.'

'Don't swear at me, you drunk pig.'

I don't mind being accused of drunkenness, and often am, but I think this is the first time I've been called a pig. That hurts a tad. I take up the gauntlet and reply calmly,

'Well, show some fucking interest in me then,

rather than that mindless prole crap you seem to find so fucking fascinating.'

I am pleased with that.

'If you were in the least bit interesting and less self-absorbed,' she says, calmly, 'then perhaps I would. Until then, I'll watch my prole crap. OK?'

A good, if not great, response I think, and I consider tactical withdrawal. Immediately, I decide on one last small-arm volley.

'I have had the worst day of my professional life, I may not have a fucking job at the end of this week and you obviously don't give a flying fuck. So I'd be obliged if you switch on the news please, darling. There's a poppet.'

She looks at me, pure unadulterated venom and disgust and there is just something, through the make-up and the slight ageing of her face, which reminds me of the young funky girl I married, the girl who cared about apartheid and left-wing politics and the shame of unregulated arms deals and loved great sex ... but then the shadow passes, and I see a woman heading towards middle age with a husband who is just a meal ticket, nothing more, a fuck of a sight less.

'You are such a selfish, self-pitying bastard, James. You bring everyone down.'

And with that she flounces out of the room, slamming the door.

'So I take it there's no chance of a shag tonight then, darling?' I call after her.

She was 24 when I met her, I was 26. She came in for a job as a temp when I worked in North London in my first office-based management job. She was obviously a bright woman who, although not university-educated, was clever and shrewd. And very, very sexy. A sensuous mouth was her best feature, with lips that you just wanted to join with your own, and a jaw bone that suggested unbridled pleasure. She was tall and slim, and wore ethnic clothes and her hair short, which suggested a hybrid post-punk post-hippy style all of her own. I think it safe to say that from the moment she walked into the office I felt trouserly stirrings – and that said stirrings did not abate even after we'd first consummated what turned out to be our mutual lust.

Sorry, I get ahead of myself, and indeed I am surprised to find faint trouserly stirrings still at the thought of the events described in that last sentence ...

At first she was cool towards me, polite but fairly formal. I pursued her with all my silvery, slippery charms, and she kept her distance until one night we both got very drunk on Guinness and champagne at an Irish bar in Islington and I walked her home, my arm around her so that we staggered in unison. She lived over in Camden and we got lost and we talked and walked, and I kissed her in the doorway of a dry-cleaners somewhere at the back of Euston and with that kiss stars exploded in my drunken head and her soft lips and warm tongue tasted like the nectar of the gods. I told her this, and expounded my theory that the nectar of the gods must have been created from Guinness and champagne, and she called me a wanker and we kissed again.

She would not let me into her flat that night. 'You are my boss,' she said, accurately. 'I like my job – I don't want it to be compromised,' and with that she kissed me goodnight and I floated away from her.

It was another two weeks before she agreed to have dinner.

It was another three weeks before she agreed to have sex. But what sex it was – wild, passionate, endless, probing and touching, stroking, kissing and coming.

And it was like that until her father died.

Daddy was something in the City, a profession she condemned on account of her dislike for international capitalism. But Daddy had always been very generous in doling out his ill-gotten gains to his honey-bunny daughter, and consequently she could afford to survive upon the meagre wage of a marketing assistant in publishing. So when the dear old man died, and it transpired he'd lost his shirt in a stock market and currency crash, and Mummy had to sell the house and grounds and stables (ie two-thirds of Surrey, by all accounts) to cover the debts, dear wee Helen was slightly stuffed.

Of course I went to the funeral with her, although the affair was still clandestine around the office. Human Resources (Personnel as we knew them in those days) folk considered it (rather churlishly, in my humble opinion) to be bad form for employees to be concentrating upon trying to shag each other senseless in the lunch break rather than on profitable publishing. I was respectful and told her mother how sorry I was. But in truth I was beginning to tire. The sex had continued to be wonderful but it was becoming a bit of an effort and part of me longed for a casual shag where it was acceptable to fuck off once both sides had achieved orgasm rather than the endless touching and probing (etc etc) and conjuring up of yet more desire later on.

So I was thinking of cooling it when she told me six weeks later, through sobs and with her cheeks awash with tears, that she was pregnant.

It is every guy's worse nightmare to be presented with such news by someone who they do not love. And I had realised of late that passion and infatuation, however spectacular, do not a true love affair make. But what was I to do?

I didn't suggest marriage straight away. I hinted at abortion and was told that, although lapsed, she had been brought up in a convent school and her remnant Catholicism would not allow that course of action. Shame that hadn't applied to pre-marital rumpy-pumpy, I thought, but sagely decided against saying so. I asked her if she was sure she was pregnant, then if she was sure it was mine, which very nearly (quite properly) resulted in her kicking me in my fecund bollocks.

I backtracked. The compassionate new-chap *Guardian*-reader in me took over. 'I'm sorry darling,' I said, eyes bright on hers, holding her hand, mopping a tear, silently cursing the headstrong spermatozoa that had broken through her seemingly impregnable defences. 'I'm just a little shocked, that's all. I mean, I thought you were on the pill.'

'I was,' she said, 'but I forgot to take it a couple of times when Daddy died ...' and here her face crumpled and her cheeks became waterfalls again, and I knew I was trapped and I knew that she had done this deliberately in order to be looked after again.

'I will do whatever you want,' I said big-heartedly.

'A child needs a father,' she pronounced like the first female Pope, 'and parents should be married.'

Me and my big gob, I thought.

Reader, I married her. Three weeks later we sealed our blissful nuptial agreement in a red-brick registry office in south London with a couple of friends witnessing the joyous event. Six months later I was presented with an ugly baby whose head was distorted like some Hollywood alien by his forceps birth and told I was a father and this was my son.

Ah, Romance!

And 16 years later it has come to this. Where has that time gone? Where does that highway lead to? How did I get here?

Should have been a bloody pop star rather than a crappy publisher.


I pour another large whisky and briefly surf the mindess that festoons the satellite channels at this time of evening. I awake at 1.30, whisky intact in its glass – Glen Gyroscope is a wondrous brand. I finish it off and head for the wonderful solitary guest bedroom. Would every night were so happy

# 5

# London Calling

Dear reader, I apologise heartily for leaving you in limbo, obviously concerned for your narrator's well-being, but I have been a little busy.

It is Friday fucking night and I am in a theme Irish pub in Covent Garden getting rapidly, dramatically, fantastically and ecstatically pissed. On my own, only the lite Mr Marlboro to keep me company. I am on my sixth Guinness and it is only eight o'clock.

Look around. What do you see? Boys and girls in their early twenties, excited at life, at the prospect of meeting someone tonight and waking in love in the morning. Excited at the clandestine discussion with their bosses about possible promotion, about climbing the career ladder. Or planning to resign and travel around the world for a year.

Pretty girls smoking and drinking in tight short skirts, eyeing up handsome boys in loud suits, laughter and happiness dripping from the air as the weekend is here and they can have fun fun fun. And me at the bar like some vacuum of misery, spectating through the bar-room mirror on joy, drinking steadily and seriously and, might I say it, bloody well, to erase the week that has just been and the weekend coming up.

My phone chirrups in my pocket and I can barely hear over the shrieked estuary vowels the voice of my beloved.

'You're pissed,' I make out.

'I'm in a meeting,' I reply convincingly, and cut her off.

What a bloody week. Day after day of sitting with Morpheus looking at all aspects of our business. Answering questions about campaigns and launches and mailings and costs – truly the man started his training with the Stasi but transferred to the Chilean Secret Police as he was not being challenged enough.

And then, joy of joys, at 4pm this afternoon he announced that he was off, back to the States.

We shook hands, and I thanked him for his input. 'It's good to get someone else's perspective on the business,' I said, with as much sincerity as I could muster.

'I'll be in touch,' he said. 'Remember, we are here for our shareholders. That's all that matters.' And then the punchline. 'Tough decisions may have to made to get us back on course in Europe.'

Tough decisions. When I first came into the Bobby Sands Snug of the Gerry Adams Irish Funbar or wherever the fuck I am, I took this to mean that I was definitely for the high jump. My sins had found me out, my incompetence had bubbled to the surface and that was it. I wondered if they'd just sack me there and then for gross negligence and avoid paying me any compensation.

Middle of the second pint, I'm having a rethink. What have I done wrong? We've delivered in the two years since I took over, this is the first time that I've had any warning that the US had any issue with me.

By the sixth pint I'm spoiling for a fight. They're fucking lucky to have me, I'm much sought after in the little world of academic books and I'll pick up another job tomorrow and sue their arses for wrongful dismissal. I am going to be all right.

'One more pint please. And a large Jamieson.'

Saturday morning, 6.30am. I am awake as usual – this time the invasion forces having already arrived – with a colossal hangover, tongue stuck to the roof of my mouth, which resembles now, not one nun's gusset but all the gussets combined (sadly I don't know the collective noun) of one of your larger nunneries. My bowels feel as if they are about to explode, my breath is cloacal from beer and fags and Scotch. Hunger makes my stomach explode periodically like distant thunder, because of course I didn't eat anything last night, as to dilute the alcohol in such a way would have been a sin against the Lord himself.

Bits of last night flood back. Being asked to leave the Irish pub as I was so pissed I could hardly stand. Waking up on a train – miraculously, the right one – as it pulled into my station. Slumped in a cab, fumbling for my keys outside the house, then tripping over the threshold and collapsing in a heap on the hall floor. Helen standing in the kitchen doorway looking at me, with such contempt.

'You total pisshead,' she said, and walked upstairs.

I awake, ablute, return to bed and await that awful post-alcoholic, sweaty paranoia which I know will kick in any time now. I drink some water to try to reconstitute my body but I know nothing can save me. It is only a matter of time when it happens.

Oh, and here it comes now. A tidal wave of fear and pity and disappointment and self-loathing, a heady cocktail of every destructive emotion a man can feel. All here now in my own diminutive little brain, the whole fucking set.

I'm 46 (I know, we've done this but I have no control here at all) and I am in a loveless marriage that has produced loveless selfish kids and a massive overdraft. I work in an industry that bores me and will probably be fired shortly from a well-paid job thus compounding my financial misery. I drink my own not insubstantial body weight in alcohol on a daily basis; I am again smoking like Dickens's London; I look 10 years older than I actually am.

And am three stone overweight.

That about sums the situation up.

I get up – what's the point in lying here with such thoughts rattling through my brain? – and go downstairs to make myself a reviving coffee and drink a gallon and a half of orange juice. The house is silent and that pisses me off too. It's the house and its inhabitants that have reduced me to this state and yet it and they slumber contentedly while I am tortured by my mind and my guts.

The paper is shredded through the front door and I go to take it. Shit. The *Mail*. I remember now that one of my recent pathetic finger-in-the-wall-of-the-Hoover-Dam economy drive rants had been about how we have two papers at the weekend delivered and how nobody ever reads them. So taking me at my word and with an unsurpassed obedience the cow has cancelled my *Guardian* whilst keeping her middlebrow Tory – but cheaper – rag.

I snatch it from the letterbox and head to the toilet – an appropriate reading location.

Yet again, dear sensitive reader, I spare you the details of what happens next. I can only hint at the toiletry mayhem caused by buckets full of Guinness and half a bottle of Scotch the previous evening and the subsequent imbibing of strong coffee and orange juice.

The paper is its usual balanced, well-written, modern self. The Queen is a wonderful lady, immigrants are flooding our towns and cities, a twice-divorced Hollywood actress has found true love at last, gays and lesbians are taking over our town halls, someone dies/gets raped/has a drugs overdose in next week's soaps round-up, flowers look nice in gardens, Mrs Thatcher is being nominated for sainthood, Mr Churchill is not very well and India wants independence.

Or some such. How on earth can I be in a household that reads this undiluted shit? I swear this has crept up on me over the last few years when I wasn't paying attention. We used to be a bright family, taking only broadsheets, encouraging the kids to read, turning the TV off occasionally, going to the theatre or museums. But now we are the marketer's dream, consuming crap at a fantastic speed.

I should be writing in a cottage in Yorkshire overlooking a post-industrial mining landscape 10 minutes from the wild moors, with talented children practising the violin in our outhouse and writing poems and plays which have caused the school (state-run of course) to deem both of them 'very talented'. We wouldn't have much money and struggle to keep a twenty-year-old Beetle on the road, but we'd be happy, and I would have a couple of novels in print, and have had interest from some television executives but I don't want the pressure or the compromise, so I choose austerity and art over popularity and wealth. I'd have a lovely corduroy jacket – sandy brown, I think – with leather patches at the elbow and I may wear an earring and have a ponytail. I can see it now.

Or travelling. Or working for a charity, or mourned for my premature drug-fuelled death whilst working on my definitive new album – anything but this soft-shite, South of England, middle-class, ever-consuming, always-spending, never-ending, money-haemorrhaging workwheel that is my life.

I stare out of the kitchen window and think of my day ahead. What I'd really like is to head to the pub at 11, buying a *Guardian* en route and return some time tomorrow sozzled but more attuned to a left-wing view of the world. But I'd better not – would probably be the end of the marriage, a tempting prospect in itself right now but one I sadly cannot afford. No, I shall do some chores.

It is too early, cold and damp for the garden, and anyway I am doing my best to resist strange creeping desires that I have been experiencing of late to start (whisper this) enjoying gardening. I mean, come on, gardening in my world has always been for old bastards, not dynamic bright clever folk like me. And yet of late, I've found myself devouring Sunday supplement articles on dead-heading dahlias. But I shall and will resist for to do otherwise is to say to the Grim Reaper: 'I have had my time – come and get me.'

That being said, I refused to sanction the employment of a gardener that Helen had been nagging on about, as part of my attempt to stem the endless flow of cash from the household. And staring out at the sculpted beds and the soft-flowing lawn, the bloody thing does need a tidy up, so I will do it later – I won't risk the wrath of the Neighbourhood Watch by mowing at 7.30 in the morning.

But what I will do and will do with some relish, nay abandon, is tidy this fucking kitchen which is an absolute fucking disgrace. I mean, I sweat my balls off every week to keep these folk in some degree of luxury and they cannot even be bothered to put their plates and glasses in the dishwasher.

Actually, on opening said dishwasher, I find the bastards cannot even be bothered to empty the dishwasher of the plates and glasses which have already been washed.

I feel one of my cold furies coming on. They come on frequently these days. They never used to. A few years back I'd have just said with a happy sigh, 'what the hell,' sat down and read the paper with a cigarette. But not now.

I stomp around the kitchen, the door wide open for the benefit of my sleeping family who will, by

God, be dragged from their unjust slumbers by my stomping. To say nothing of my crashing. I shall be avenged. I bash saucepans together and clink cups, pull open drawers and doors and slam them shut. Once emptied, I load the dishwasher at peak volume, and when that is finished I hunt down dissident groups of cups, glasses and plates lingering in the hall and the living room – and the bloody toilet, for God's sake – and continue loading the dishwasher until I am certain there are no more offending dirty items of crockery or cutlery anywhere in the house.

I slam the dishwasher door shut, switch it on, satisfied, pick what masquerades as a newspaper up, scraping the stool across the Rustic Flagstone floor for maximum jarring effect and start to study the sports section – which is fairly safe from right-wing rantings, even if a little short on news of my wondrous team, Heart of Midlothian.

More of my exile from God's own country later.

Two pint mugs of tea later, it is 8.30 and I am feeling a little better, hangover-wise. The house is silent – the bastards must be feigning death or something. Sod it, I'm showering and getting into the garden regardless of potential ostracism from the neighbours. I can take it.

At 4.30 she reminds me, as I'm just taking a seat to watch the football results, that, 'Mike and Christine are coming over tonight.'

'Who they?' I ask, anxious to rile, knowing full well that Christine is some brain-dead, skinny blonde that Helen met at the gym or on a shopping odyssey and that Mike will be a whiz in the city, a pin-striped, chinless no-hoper, earning more in a month than my old man earned in a decade – cue one more socialist rant.

'I have had a busy day – I washed the cars, I have done the garden. I want to chill,' I say, a tad petulantly.

'Get a gardener and get the cars valeted,' she says, as if talking to a simpleton.

I want to say, 'Do you think money grows on trees? I'm in enough debt already. I want – no, need to – save some money, so I do it myself. I cut the grass, tidy and potter in the garden not, God forbid, because I enjoy it, not to prove the point that a garden can be maintained without the exploitation of the working classes or the old.' (Though that doesn't strictly follow, as the hourly rate a gardener in these parts commands elevates him immediately from working to upper-middle class status and would make an old-age pensioner rich beyond his wildest dreams indeed.) Instead I say limply, 'I do it to try to save money, and to stay out of your way,' one eye on the TV.

She says nothing. I, sweaty, tired and aching, feeling like some Soviet statue depicting the dignity of labour (OK, albeit a fat one on a leather sofa) have to accept the inevitability of guests for dinner who will be indescribably dull.

'We've no food in the house,' I retort, desperately.

'Chez toi,' she says in an accent part Dijonais, mainly Dagenham.

'Homemade food at its very best – you are spoiling them, my darling. Watch you don't overdo it.' God, I do irony well, heading for the wine rack where a fruity Burgundy beckons. Me Burton, you Taylor, this 'Who's Afraid ...'

'Listen – people like us do not have time to cook these days. And what's the point? Chez Toi's food is better than anything you make at home,' she says huffily.

I open the bottle, pour a large glassful of the finest elixir known to man, and ignore her.

By the time the door bell chimes at 8pm (sorry at 8.20pm; the English middle classes – may I abbreviate that to EMCs for the sake of my typing fingers in future? – always deem it fashionable to arrive 20 minutes later than the time specified) I am halfway through my second bottle, showered, shaved, fragrant, feeling groovy and frankly angling – positively busting – for a fight.

Christine enters. She's unquestionably attractive, blonde, slim, (she obviously works out) dressed, expensively in a way that shows off her (to my sloshed mind) body well.

I smile my best sickly smile, kiss her on the cheek as if I like her, and try to get a peek down her blouse as I do so.

And then Mike. 'Good to see you Mike!' I say, hale-fellow-well-met-like, shaking his hand vigorously, staring into his eyes. I have to look up a tad, as Mike is well over six foot. And wiry. With a perfect complexion and striking blue eyes unblemished by burst blood vessels.

As he tightens his grip on my hand I know he works out. Strong bastard – he's won.

'Drinks,' I say, hoping they'll want something that is open – you try opening a bottle of wine with one crushed hand. They go for the half-decent Chablis, damn them.

We chat. Schools. Kids. Cars. Houses. More kids. More houses. Holidays – winter and summer.

Fuck me, I am trapped in someone else's life here.

Some kind of alarm goes off in the kitchen. 'Supper's up,' says Helen – and she and Christine disappear together, leaving me and Mike to dazzle each other. Well, I'm fucked if I'll start the small talk, I think, quaffing another half gob full.

'So you're a publisher,' he says.

'Yes,' I reply. 'You?'

'Oh, the City now,' he says, languidly.

Thank Christ I didn't put that tenner on him being a social worker, I think.

'Yes, lure of the mighty dollar,' he smiles. 'Was tempted to stay in academia after Harvard – in fact was offered a book deal from you guys in the States but I thought: what the hell? Take the money and pack up at 45.'

The fucking bastard. I'm already past that age and but still a lifetime away from retirement – he looks 10 years my junior and he's already nearly loaded enough to pack up.

We prattle on. If I try to score a point he bats it back. He's been to every city I've ever been to, he has stayed in better hotels than the ones I stayed at, he flies First to my Business, he was in Berlin when the wall came down, he played junior country cricket and rugby, is a scratch golfer – 'and all from a midlands comp'.

And a nice guy, too. Because the only reason he's offered this information in, I have to admit, a self-effacing manner, is because I stupidly bloody asked him. There is no vaingloriousness to him at all.

I am in the presence of a God who in turn is in the presence of a half- pissed malcontent.

Thankfully Helen summons us to the dining table. 'More wine darling,' she instructs with a beautiful smile on her face which tells our guests just how fucking happy we are, but which tells me subliminally not to drink any more as I am on the cusp of causing a scene.

I drink more.

The food is surprisingly good, and Christine and Mike are very complimentary.

'Helen will give you the recipes if you like,' I say, helpfully, hoping to embarrass her.

'No problem,' she retorts. 'I'll copy them out for you.'

Schools, holidays, cars, houses. I try to steer the conversation in some interesting direction whenever possible – if a woman friend of theirs is mentioned I ask, 'Isn't that the one who was having it off with her gardener/postman/undertaker?' and after the first couple of occasions I am ignored. Like some retarded child. Or bad smell that everyone is too embarrassed to mention.

To coffee. 'Brandy or Malt, Mike?' I ask, longing for the killer alcoholic effect of spirits.

'No thanks, James. Playing squash tomorrow at 8.30. Bloody league game.' Christine recklessly has a Baileys or Tia Maria or some such concocted syrup that we keep in the cupboard – we don't have her first choice of Armagnac. A social faux pas – will we ever recover?

Coffee and hand-crafted petit fours at two quid a pop and tasteful classical music (Kennedy knocks out Vivaldi) and the scotch bottle at my side, and I'm slugging it back and the room and the people are distanced by scotch and tiredness and words flicker into my consciousness – Val D'Isère ... scholarship ... yacht club ... wake up you selfish miserable bastard.

She's pulling at my arm and trying to slap me in the face as she punctuates: 'Wake up you selfish bastard.'

I've fallen asleep. Our guests have gone. 'Where'd they go?' I ask, and she torrents: 'They left because you were snoring and they felt that they'd outstayed their welcome. I have never been so fucking' – smack – 'angry' – smack – 'you' – smack – 'are' – smack – 'such' – smack – 'a' – smack – 'bastard' – smack. 'I hate you.' Smack smack smack.

And with that, in tears, she flees the room. I hear her running up the stairs, her bedroom door slamming shut.

I finish my whisky and pour myself another.

# 6

# Milk and Alcohol

It is Monday morning, dear reader, and I am in my car heading for the station once more. And I have the mother, grandmother and great aunt of all hangovers.

Yesterday was not my finest, I confess

I awoke, cold and sweaty at 6.30 as is my wont, in the armchair downstairs. I abluted as noisily as possible on my dearly held 'If I'm awake then so should the rest of you' principal, then staggered to the guest bedroom which I noted had not been touched since I used it Friday night. The bed was unmade and there was a pair of my pants lying festering in the middle of the floor like some peculiarly unpleasant piece of installation art.

Under the duvet, trying to get warm, trying to remember what life was like before continuous hangovers, I undertook an audit of my life. On the plus side:

I have a well-paid job.

I am married and have non-deformed children.

I am not divorced.

I have my health.

Now to the negatives:

I hate my job.

I do not love my wife.

I am indifferent to my children.

I have not known joy or happiness for some time.

I have no real friends.

Those friends I do have are fuckwits.

I am definitely overweight.

I am probably an alcoholic.

I am utterly, totally, unarguably bored by my life and suspect actually that I am living in someone else's.

I cannot remember when last I smiled without irony, bitterness or sarcasm.


I stopped at 10 as I was running out of paper.

A mildly depressing activity, I concluded.

I lay in bed and tried to sleep. I failed. I tried to imagine having sex with Janice in the foyer of IPC – and failed. I couldn't even imagine a sweet young thing like her coming near enough to me to kiss her, such would be her revulsion.

You are right, dear reader – the depression was kicking in. And I recognised it and I decided to counteract it.

I willed myself to accept the unthinkable. 'This is

my problem, it is me against my world and it's me that's to blame, it is me that must change, adapt, play the game and not be so unspeakably ghastly to all I come into contact with. Perhaps I should try to find God, or do yoga, dedicate some of my time to good deeds, charities and the like.' I resolved, on my own duvet-clad road to Damascus, to change.

And I resolved to start with Helen.

I abluted again, and seeing my fat body in the mirror resolved to shift weight. I cleaned my teeth, squirted some deodorant on my chest and between my legs, and decided to start at the source – Helen.

I knocked on her bedroom door deferentially and, not hearing her reply, took this as tacit welcome to enter. I crept in and slipped under the duvet. Nothing. I couldn't tell if she was asleep or awake (no change there then, the old me would have noted – but I push that thought aside).

'I am so sorry, darling,' I said in my most penitent voice. 'I am such a pig.'

Nothing.

'I will make it up to you, I promise. I will change – we will sort this out and be good together.' And with that I put my arm around her and cuddled in.

Faint trouserly stirring – encouraging, after so long. Surprising, indeed, that marital trouserly stirrings and my good self are even on nodding terms these days. Through the hangover – if indeed I was not actually still pissed – I chanced my arm just a little. My fingers felt her left breast through the silky sheen of her night gown, I smelled her perfume and she's the girl I first met and I moved my groin sensually against her bottom and reached to stroke her nipple.

'Fuck off,' she said, deadpan. 'Don't you dare touch me, you revolting creep.'

I won't bore you with the verbatim Hansard version of the next five minutes. She said did I really think I could expect her to just open her legs and shag me and it would be all OK and I said, no not really, that she was obviously frigid, she said she was only frigid with me because I was so crap at sex and I said that if she was less frigid I'd be better in bed with her and she said I'd always been crap and so on and so on. You get the drift. Pleasant, it wasn't. Dignified and satisfying – well it wasn't that either.

I made my excuses and left. By eleven I was down the pub and by twelve had bumped into Edward. I bought him a gin and slimline and we spent an amiable hour discussing his new patio doors and his wife's Volvo, during which time I drank four pints of strong lager and equivalent whisky chasers – proud of my athleticism. Edward left for his Sunday lunch just as I started to tell him about the state of our marriage.

Elegantly, I staggered back home, avoided Helen

who was in the living room. I opened a bottle of wine, drank half of it and fell asleep. I woke up, went to the toilet, finished the wine, went to the study, broke wind, yawned and watched telly. I went downstairs, opened a bottle of wine, read the paper, fell asleep in the chair, woke up – it really was my own personal decathlon and I was Daly fucking Thomson. Finally, when even I knew I had had enough – oh, sorry, I had a couple of scotches as well – I went to my solitary bed, awoke before the alarm and found myself here in my car heading for another fun day at the office, probably over the alcohol limit for driving legally, and definitely, definitely, not at my best.

I even used the inside lane at the lights, truly a lightweight heavyweight.

After the weekend I've just had, I'm even somewhat perversely looking forward to work – it will be sweet release to be out of the house away from the cause of misery that is my domestic circumstances.

The train journey passes in a blur. I hold the paper in front of my face but the words on it fail to register. I feel tired and sick at heart – even my internal voice is silent this morning, disgusted I suspect with the weekend's performance.

Automaton-like, I leave the train and at the café I decide on double Danish and a colossal espresso, hoping that caffeine and sugar will boost my day. As

I approach the building I prepare my best jaunty walk and beaming smile for the lovely Janice.

Who, I realise with horror, is not there. Sitting behind the desk instead is some middle-aged Harridan who insists on seeing my security badge, which I haven't seen myself for weeks. Finally I dig it out from the bottom of my backpack and, somewhat reluctantly, she allows me in.

Christ, lovely start to a fantastic day. Thank goodness I'm feeling so robust.

I enter the lift – strangely silent today, perhaps the sexy voice is striking for better money or better lines – and as it glides upwards I feel in the pit of my stomach a sense of encroaching doom. Today, I know, is going to be a very very Bad Day.

# 7

# I Feel Free

It is three o'clock, and I am on my seventh pint in the bar of the Lamb and Flag. And my second packet of fags.

Oh, the Lamb and Flag. When first I came to London, this was the place I'd always meet up with old buddies. It was the pub to come to, just on the outskirts of Covent Garden, but slightly off the beaten track. You had to know of it to find it, so it was not awash with tourists. And in the days when taste mattered more to me than alcoholic content, it had a good supply of real ales. Dryden was stabbed in the adjacent alleyway, which to my then literary sensitivities made something of a difference.

I haven't been here for about 10 years, preferring big modern theme pubs with noisy youngsters and happy hours.

And why, I hear you ask, dear reader, only friend, am I here on a Monday, pissed in the afternoon when I should be working, making money from inspirational leadership and cutting edge marketing strategies?

I think you may have guessed it.

I have lost my job.

I am unemployed, I am on the fucking scrap heap. I have been severed brutally from gainful employment. No more the discount soap fragrance of the fair, sweet, virginal Janice. No more the sexy lift. The acres of adoring reverential staff will soon be fawning to a new master.

Worst of all, though – farewell the means to pay the mortgage and just about keep on top of the overdraft.

And before you start with the 'Oh Christ, more-maudlin-self-pity-is-coming-my-way-bit,' dear reader, I am drunk in this pub, not through self-pity, actually, but because I bloody well can be and fucking well want to be.

The truth is – I FEEL LIBERATED!

Fuck 'em all. Fuck those brain-dead half-wits that worked for me that spent their time waiting for my mistakes so that they could undermine my position for some possible coup at a later stage when they would take my job. Fuck my bosses, American and British, who have no fun in their lives apart from masturbating over a balance sheet.

I, to quote Cream and Jack Bruce (one of the finest male vocalists of the rock genre in my not so very humble opinion) Feel Free.

I'd gone into the office and it was indeed deathly silent. Somehow, word had got around that today was going to be a day of bloodshed and torment and consequently folk seemed to have disappeared. Days off, or ill. Ravens circled, blood red poppies bloomed, tumbleweed blew down the corridor from the editorial department, in the distance a solitary mournful bell tolled.

I sat at my desk, switched on the PC, cursorily glanced at the screen for new emails, interfered where I felt I was meant to, or could be bothered to, and was just about to demolish a sales report I'd been copied in on from our East European rep who, I swear to God, was taking the piss, when the phone rang.

'James,' a voice said seductively.

'Blimey,' I thought. 'Sultry voices at this time of the morning. Verily the augurs have fucked it up.'

'It's Caroline.' Pause as I failed to realise who was talking. 'Caroline O'Reilly – head of HR.'

The penny dropped. New head of Personnel. Hadn't met her yet – she'd only started a week or so ago. She's in corporate HR, looking after the magazines and journals we publish as well as my humble books division, and so had been appointed by and reported direct to the US.

'You got a minute?' she breathed, more seductively than any HR director before her (though admittedly that is a low bar to fly over).

'Up to my eyes a bit,' I said, closing Solitaire. 'I could do ten for 20 minutes if that suits?' I said jauntily, not a care in the world, barely able to breathe.

The next 40 minutes I cleared as much paperwork as possible, answered all my correspondence, asked for reports to be on my desk within the week, anything to give the allusion that should the impossible happen, I was not expecting it, and that I certainly did not deserve it.

Ten o'clock came, and fashionably at five past (EMC approved), I stood up, put on my jacket and said to an assistant, nonchalantly, 'Off upstairs – I'll be 10 minutes max.'

I took the lift three flights up, looking at myself in the mirror, trying to adapt my gaze so that the fear left my eyes.

I sat outside her office, kept waiting fashionably for five minutes (HR branch of EMC, sans doute), until the door was opened by the most attractive woman I had ever seen at work before, Janice excepted. She was 27 or 28 years of age, tall, with a shock of brown-red hair, intelligent eyes, lips that promised unearthly delights. Make-up – enough to show she cared about herself but not so much that you could doubt she knew her innate beauty and felt any need to disguise it. She was dressed in an obviously expensive dark blue trouser suit that looked to me like it was Chanel. She shook my hand firmly, smiled, looking me in the eye and beckoned me into her office.

I glided in, enraptured.

I stumbled out, sacked.

In the nicest, gentlest, possible way – she almost made me feel grateful that she'd taken the time out to spend with me – she told me that there was a lot of pressure from the US. Shareholder value, new blood, fresh start, career counselling, golden parachute – I heard the words, but they held no meaning for me. I just kept looking at this woman, as if she was the first person I ever truly loved.

Now, don't get me wrong, I hadn't fallen in love with the HR director in some weird example of Stockhausen syndrome. What I meant to say is that she was the absolute spitting image of the first woman I ever truly loved, Carolyn Adams. She had the same way of glancing at you while she spoke, part seductively, part as if she were checking she had your full attention. She flicked any stray hair from out of eyes distractedly in the same way Carolyn had done all those years ago. She was Carolyn as I imagined Carolyn would have been, approaching 30.

I last clapped eyes on Carolyn Adams well over twenty years ago, vowing I would call her, after a night of such passion, such need and such love.

Carolyn Adams – Christ, I was besotted, which is precisely why I never called her. I was too young for love. Me, I was up only for casual relationships, a love 'em and leave 'em approach. I was twenty, at university, and had a world of experience in front of me.

Ironically, this late '70s Lotharial philosophy was not founded as a result of a surfeit of conquests – quite the opposite. I had a few drunken exchanges of bodily fluid as a student (occasionally not with a packet of Handy Andies) but I was hardly up for a place in the British Olympic Synchronised Shagging Team.

Carolyn Adams. For the first few years after I'd left her, I'd think of her often. She grew up in Nottingham, and during that time if I was there on business I'd look for her face in the crowd. And gradually her image faded, her features merged into a homogenous mass, and only when feeling maudlin, or looking at old photos did I think of Carolyn Adams and the love that could have been.

Until now. Sitting in this pub pissed, I can see her perfectly – and I remember some of things we did together in bed. Don't worry, dear reader, I am not about to bore you with graphic details from twenty years back, but you will forgive me my own internal reminiscence which is, you may be horrified to hear, causing trouserly stirrings even after all of this time.

Which after the amount I have consumed thus far does remarkably suggest that there may be some life in the geriatric canine after all.

We'd met when I was working in the summer. My parents had moved from Edinburgh to Teesside and for those of you who know the latter area you will understand why I tried to avoid spending any time there at all. I found through a friend, a job for a month in a factory in Nottingham. The friend's parents owned a colossal house and spent most of the summer away, so I stayed in an annexe and worked with a view to earning enough to see me round Europe.

Then Carolyn exploded into my life. She appeared in the staff canteen, and our eyes met and she smiled at me as she took my 50 pence for sausage, egg and chips. 'That's healthy,' she said and I smiled back at her and that night she was in the pub opposite that we'd frequent on the way home, and we chatted. She was doing fine arts in Manchester, and we kissed and the universe exploded.

The next night, after an impromptu party at my friend's house, we went to bed together, and we spent every night together for the rest of our time at the factory. We parted; she was off to Italy with her parents on an arts fest, I was travelling around France.

We toyed with trying to meet, but the logistics didn't stack up. We swore undying love, swapped addresses in the brief window between bodily fluids and I planned to join her for a weekend at the end of the summer as soon as I could.

Europe was fun. Drugs, wine, sunshine and women. Well, if the truth be told, drugs, wine and sunshine, and lusting after women. I had every intention once the Kerouac experience was over of contacting her. When I returned to my parents there were letters and pictures from her, and I intended to write back to say hi, but my course started again and I met a girl, and her letters dried up, and I forgot about my magical summer as the horrors of finals kicked in, and then it was all too late and too much in the past to resurrect.

But, I realise now, sitting in this pub pissed, she has stayed inside me like some virus. I realise, too, that this is potentially like some great Medieval Romantic tale. Think of the signs – a woman explodes into my life who is the spitting image of my long-lost love, and this woman, as if by magic, gives me the freedom to go on my quest. You couldn't make it up!

I decide, there and then, I will find the fair Carolyn.

My phone chirrups. It is Jean, my favourite marketing manager.

'Where are you?' she asks. 'You OK?'

'Fine,' I reply, trying to sound jaunty, 'enjoying the liberation of unemployment.'

'What pub?' she asks and I tell her.

'I'll be there in five.' Which she is, and this in itself surprises me. She shows up, her face strained and looking as if she has been crying, buys me a pint and herself a gin, sits down, hugs me and bursts into tears.

'Had no idea you cared,' I say, not a little shaken by this outpouring of emotion.

'We are all in shock,' she says, swigging a mouthful of gin. 'I mean, we've all been so worried about you over the last few months – you've obviously been under a lot of strain. I've been wanting to say something, but you've been so distant. But I never thought they'd get rid of you.'

'It's been coming for a long time,' I say, nonchalantly.

'But why? I mean, I don't think you've been well for some time, but surely they just can't sack you?'

'I've been fine,' I say, a little defensively.

'You've been hellish,' she says argumentatively. 'You've hardly spoken to anyone for months – we all assumed you were having trouble at home.'

'I had no idea,' I say. 'I've just been tired and low of late. Midlife crisis, probably.'

'Well,' she says, 'what are you going to do? Fight them, I hope?'

'Nope – it's a good package. I'll just go quietly. Truth is'– I say this conspiratorially, 'I was out of my depth in that position.'

'Bollocks!' she says. 'You were brilliant – only reason I joined the company was to work with you. Same with most of the others.'

'Bugger me,' I say, and sup long and hard. Finally, the milk of human kindness.

We chat and drink more. She thinks it unlikely that anyone internally will be offered my job, which makes her fear my successor.

'God help us if it's an American number cruncher,' she says with feeling. The spectre of Wayne arises, but I do not share it with her.

'What are you going to do, James?' she asks quietly.

'I am going to find Carolyn Adams.'

I tell her of the strange scenario this morning with Caroline. 'Jean – that woman, Carolyn I mean not Caroline – is the love of my life. I have to find her. I don't know how, but I have to find her.'

'It's easy,' she says, and we have another drink.


I arrive home by taxi at 10 o'clock, feeling strangely sober despite a belly full of beer and a few whiskies on an empty stomach. Helen glances up at me as I enter the dining room. She barely acknowledges me over the prole TV she's watching.

'I've lost my job,' I say jauntily, as if informing her that the train was late by five minutes.

'Oh my God!' she says. 'How? Why?'

I feel, despite the nascent draw of My Quest, that I do owe it to her to sit down and tell her what is going on. She even turns the television off. I explain patiently that the company has been very generous and has given me six month's pay. I am explicit – this money has to be used wisely as I may not get another job at this level at my age.

She nods sympathetically. Fleetingly, she looks as if she's about to touch my hand supportively, but she pulls out of the action at the very last moment, rather like a Red Arrows pilot who fears his wing is about to touch a team mate's.

'You'll be fine, James, you'll have a job in no time.' I am touched by her confidence.

I go upstairs and switch on the computer. I resist the temptation to pour myself a large whisky. I am a changed man. I am at the start of a new life. Alcohol dulls and rots. The. Brain.

I want to be fresh and bright.

# 8

# Slippery People

Bloody computers. I use them reluctantly at work, but rarely at home. Normally I can't get near it anyway for Cameron. He can spend hours up here playing stupid games, chatting on Messenger and doubtless surfing adult porn. But at least when he's doing that he's not giving me attitude.

It takes me half a fucking hour to remember my sodding password to get logged on. Christ, I could do with a bucket of Scotch already, and the new me is only 20 minutes old. Still – at least I'm calm about it.

I hate the internet. I mean, it has its uses, obviously. It can be a marvellous research tool and helps to build the global village (I think that's what *The Guardian* expects me to think) but in reality it is used by folk to access porn, chat to people they'd be too scared to talk with face to face and to find locations of places without having to go to the bother of buying an A–Z atlas.

But I am different. I have a Quest. Jean has written it down on my fag packet – www.old-pals.net.

I've heard of these sites. The papers were full of

stories about them. Hoards of sad middle-aged folk sit in their studies and make contact with equally sad people from their past, childhood sweethearts, and best friends from way back

They meet and fall in love all over again, or are reminded why they lost touch in the first place. The past is big business, the present dull and stressful, so all over the country people are contacting each other, getting low-down and dirty or wistful and nostalgic.

Christ, how I've despised it all. I have a few friends from my past who I see occasionally, but I've certainly never felt the inclination to look for anyone, as I've never lost touch with anyone I cared for.

Except Carolyn Adams. And that Titanic blow job she performed on me in 1980 ... sorry, dear reader, more detail than needed, I know.

OK, so I find the site eventually, and start to fiddle. Bugger me, my old primary school is there – a quick scan down the names brings back images of small Scots kids, the smell of stale vomit, and Miss McFaddion who, in truth, I think I had a crush on when I was seven.

My secondary school, fuck me – there's Dougie and Laurence and Chris and Graham – and twats and prats who smelled or who were despised for being uncool.

I scroll. Fucking hell, my life is here. I randomly click on a name – Rob Hughes – who I remember as being a good rugby player, hard-working and very dull. His personal message reads:

'Studied law at Edinburgh. Married Josie in '85 – have two kids, a dog, a house in Morningside and my own lawyer's practice. Buying or selling? Contact me for great rates!'

Mr Bloody Normal. Where have I gone wrong?

I scan names with dimly remembered memories attached, of fights and slights, of insults and friendship, of laughter and hurt. My teenage years here.

But I am not here for these random people. I am here to find Carolyn Adams. I'm not sure where to start and something is holding me back – kind of like the moment before you might step off a precipice, which is a shit analogy, dear reader, as I have never experienced the moment before stepping off a precipice, as I've never stepped off a fucking precipice, and I suspect the same is true of you unless someone is reading this to you while you're in a coma. Anyhow, forgive that outburst, but I'm tense and nervous and I can't relax.

I decide to procrastinate. I delve into the listings for my year at university. Fewer names ring bells because of sheer numbers but there's Maggie from Classics who I once snogged, and Jenny from English who I would have given anything to snog.

And, oh Christ, the memories pour over me.

There's Lizzie, darling, upper-class Lizzie, the poshest person I had ever come across. How her home-county tones had set my small town Northern heart a-racing. I went out with her for two whole terms in my second year, and we were in love and we spent every available moment curled up on single beds in our student flat shagging until she left me, me with my nascent poetry and love of art and Dylan and Brahms – what a cultural sophisticate I was! – for rugger bugger Phil who was thick but whose family owned half of Wiltshire.

In fact, thinking back, it was being hurt by Lizzie that made me mean and moody towards women; because of her, I realise with increasing indignation, that I dumped Carolyn.

So it's her fucking fault that I'm unhappy, I conclude, not unreasonably.

I click on the personal info button by her name. It reads starkly: 'Married. Two teenage kids. Living in Cheshire.'

It cannot be possible – she was but a teenager when I knew her. To think of her with kids herself of nearly the same age as she was when I knew her is against the laws of nature, against the natural order of things.

Ha! I think. If you hadn't dumped me so spectacularly – I actually caught her in bed with that bastard and was on the point of hitting him until I realised that landowner's sons may be thick but in his case were built like brick country houses. Instead, for the first and last time in my life, I flounced indignantly. And then spent the next two weeks drunk.

Which, whilst we come to mention it Ms Lizzie-fucking-Borden, was the state I found myself in for the rest of my university career, thus causing a promising academic start to collapse into a very jammy and frankly undeserved 2:2 at the end.

I'm getting into this. My blood is starting boil. I hit the 'Contact Lizzie' button on screen and whilst it whirrs and clicks – well, OK, computers don't really whirr or click unless you have an iBabbage, but let me express myself for fuck's sake – I compose a message, which will explode into her life like a supernova. How her past will come full circle to haunt her ...

I'm not registered. It appears one can look at the data, but to be able to send emails and make contact one has to pay the good webmasters some dosh. A tenner to be precise.

Without hesitating I send the credit card details and within five minutes I am sitting with Lizzie's contact details in front of me.

But I'm nervous. I break my earlier vow and go downstairs and pour myself a moderate Scotch, which I knock back when I'm down there and immediately replace with a not-so-moderate Scotch which I bring back upstairs.

Ridiculous man. At this rate you'll be stalking every person who's ever given you the least offence. Ridiculous. Forget her, concentrate on Carolyn. She was the great unknown, she was the one I hurt, she was the one who I thought about today when being beautifully humiliated by her doppelgänger in some lovely circular act of godly vengeance.

Carolyn. Carolyn Adams. I search for her first through Manchester University and the year which I guess she graduated in (assuming she did graduate and didn't tragically die of a broken heart). Nothing. Perhaps she took a year off to get over me? I check the next year graduates and the year after. Nothing.

Christ. Just my luck. Every bastard I've ever been insulted by or hurt is on this stupid fucking website except the one person I really need to contact. Typical technology – controlled by God himself, the ultimate Webmaster – and he sticks his fucking ginormous spanner in to frustrate and to depress.

I go back to the home page. I'm distracted by the message board, which I access.

Messages from sad lonely people the world over leap out as I scroll down. A woman who hasn't seen her father for 34 years has finally tracked him down. Why, I wonder? For backdated Christmas presents? Sisters and brothers, neighbours and best friends gush their enthusiasm for the joys of the old-pals.net community.

Pete and Katie, childhood lovers in junior school who lost touch when Pete's parents moved to Aberdeen and they'd both spent the last 30 years with other partners wondering what happened to the other – and they made contact and met and are now in love after a FANTASTIC weekend in Rome and are planning their life together ...

Endless stories of love and friendship re-found, all told against a background of adverts for dating agencies and credit cards and flash cars. A knocking shop for those too sensitive to go to a real knocking shop – an electronic emporium of dissatisfied love and hurt pride and disappointed lives.

And here I am – as bad as the rest of these sad losers.

But no, I'm doing this for pure motives. I want to find this woman, tell her I was wrong, tell her that I need her in my life.

But hang on, it's nearly 25 years since last I saw her. She'll be married, she'll be happy with kids and dogs and a career – I imagine her as a social worker, a carer, sympathetic and loving to the suppressed and depressed, her massive kindly smile the sole ray of light in their otherwise bleak world. She'll have consigned me to the dustbin of her memory, perhaps sometimes vaguely remembering a beautiful boy she once fucked senseless some years back, but pushing the image from her mind.

A theory kicks in here. If she's happy, content, at one with those around her, then it's unlikely – very unlikely – that she will have registered on this site anyway, and if she hasn't then that is it. I will give up this crazy quest before it has properly begun. I mean, the site is obviously for the unhappy, folk who regret their past, not for people ecstatic about their present.

So, it's in the lap of the Gods.

I fiddle some more on the site, read a few more testimonies from previously devastated but now ecstatic users, and then notice the 'name search' feature.

This is it, once and for all. If she's there, this will find her. If she's not, sod it.

I neck the scotch and type 'Carolyn Adams' and, my heart beating faster, I wait for the machine to do its thing. It whirrs and splutters (oh don't be so fucking literal), and then flashes up the results.

Forty three bloody people called Carolyn Adams! Can't be!

But there are. The Oracle has spoken.

I plough through the first page and note that one of these women considers the fact that she worked on the angel cakes section of Master Baker 1989-2001 worthy of inclusion in her personal details. Fuck me, I hope that has not been a lifetime high.

Second and third pages bring nothing except amazement that some people are so young who are registered. I mean, there are folks who only lost touch two years back! Bloody ridiculous.

My head explodes. There she is. Must be. Carolyn Adams. 1965-1971: St Augustine's RC Primary School, Barston, Nottingham. 1971-1978: Sherwood Hills Comprehensive Schools, Notts. Then nothing. No personal details, just those bare facts.

It must be her, but I scroll through the remaining names and sad lives to check there is no one of similar age or background. There isn't.

What to do? Write, and scare the crap out of some stranger who is either totally the wrong person, or worse still, is the right person but who has totally forgotten my existence?

I shall tell you what I will do, dear reader – have another whisky and think about it.

I go downstairs, note the house is quiet as all are in bed, empty the bottle into my glass and head purposefully up the stairs.

I click on the 'Contact Carolyn' button and a screen appears.

'Remember me, Carolyn?' I gush. 'Nottingham, 1980, in Pete's parents' house … ' No, no, no – a woman approaching middle age does not want to be reminded out of the blue of her teenage sexual activities. How about: 'Carolyn – this is James Gallagher. I often have thought of you over the years and wondered …' No, bollocks. More demure.

What about: 'Dear Carolyn, forgive this electronic intrusion but I wonder if you are the same Carolyn Adams who worked in Harpers in Nottingham in the summer holiday of 1980? You were studying fine arts at Manchester. If so, it would be great to hear from you. If not, apologies for disturbing you. Kind regards, James.'

Seems perfect to me, I think. Right mixture of detail and concern, enthusiasm and reticence.

I hit the send button, and the site acknowledges that the message has gone and cheerily wishes me 'Good luck' with finding my old friend.

Now what? My heart thumps still, and I decide to leave my sad past behind momentarily. I surf, not something I do often, look at the Heart of Midlothian website, and to stop getting depressed update myself on the news at the dear old BBC.

I keep pathetically checking my emails every five minutes or so to see if anyone has replied. I feel like some guilty teenager.

At 2.30am, I reluctantly accept that

1) Carolyn has either no interest in, or recollection of, me;

2) This is the wrong Carolyn Adams;

or

3) She sleeps during the evening.

I log off disheartened and stumble to bed. I forget the of late embargo of the marital boudoir and climb in. My mistake realised, I anticipate being told to fuck off, and try to lie as far away from her as possible to avoid disturbing her.

Well bugger me, she turns around and puts her arms around me. I feel her breasts through the nightie and I stir trouserly.

I decide not to push my luck and accept this gratefully, my first piece of physical human contact for some months.

Christ, I've slept in. I look at the clock at the bedside and see it is 8.30 and realise that I don't have to get up for anything today because I DO NOT HAVE A JOB! I'm free, liberated – and not a little hung over.

I drift back to sleep, and my mind takes me to a seedy pub in Nottingham with the Clash constantly playing on a juke box and a group of us students and some real working men, and smoke and Formica tables – and if you stayed there late enough Mad Georgie would come in and bash his head on the base of a beer glass without breaking either and then he'd walk round the unimpressed clientele collecting money for his efforts which immediately found its way back behind the bar. And you were there, Carolyn Adams, standing with a pint and a fag looking at me the first time I walked in and I smiled shyly and you had blonde punky hair and attitude and a man's suit jacket with a badge on the label which said 'Rien' – a kind of Sartre-meets-the-Pistols-statement, and I thought you were the most sophisticated person that I'd ever seen, and we started talking and ended up in bed.

No one else seemed to matter. You were seeing mad Billy the railway worker from Moss Side in Manchester – how you liked your men before me to be mad, bad and dangerous – and you lived for the moment and drank too much and took far too many drugs and talked of art as being essential to the human soul and would recite Keats while we made love – although in retrospect my knowledge of Keats was such that I only took your word for it that it was indeed Keats – and you were exotic and fragrant and we dreamt of travelling and writing and painting and sculpture and then made love again. And again.

Helen breaks the reverie. 'Morning love,' she says and as I stir I realise that I have the biggest erection in my living memory. I hide it – it is something private and special and not of the present.

'Why are you being so nice to me?' I ask her cautiously.

'Because you have lost your job, and because you have to stop drinking and smoking and you have to lose weight and return to the man I married, the man I loved,' she said, as if stating the bleeding obvious. 'And because of late, Jamie, you frankly have not been well. Everyone, the kids, our friends, everyone has noticed it. They all think you are on the verge of a breakdown.'

Christ I think, that's what they think. Truth is, if it wasn't for the kids or our friends or even Helen I'd be fine and dandy. I consider for about one nano-second expressing this thought at exactly the same time as discretion beats the shit out of valour.

'So, you are going to take a couple of months out to get better and then find a job where they appreciate you. OK?'

It's like a classroom assistant talking to a special needs child.

'To hell with that,' I bluster, climbing out of bed, my tumescence thankfully dissipated. 'I can't afford to stay off work for a couple of months, not the way this household consumes money. I have to get out, find work – and quickly. I'm putting together a CV this morning,' I say, a man of action as I slip on my dressing gown.

And I head for the office and the PC, hungrily convinced that Carolyn will have awoken, logged on and swooned.

Bugger all, the screen reveals.

I spend the morning half-heartedly constructing a CV (did I get D or E in my Physics O level?) and every 10 minutes logging on to check my emails – by 11am I am downhearted, convinced that my one chance of happiness has evaded me. I go downstairs for coffee and a sandwich. Helen is reading *Hello!* Or *OK!* Or *Shiteceleb!* or whatever, and looks up at me as I walk in.

She smiles and asks me how it's going.

'Fine,' I reply. 'CV two-thirds of the way there. Just checking out some recruitment websites, then I'll phone for appointments.' Christ I lie so well – was it an A or A Star at Mendacity O level? 'Coffee?' I ask her, loading up the sparkling machine.

I make her a cappuccino, make myself a double espresso and head back upstairs, still in dressing gown and slippers, to the office.

Fuck. I have an email through from old-pals.net! Carolyn!

Actually, I realise as I scan I, it isn't. It's from George Burroughs, a sweaty ginger kid from Edinburgh who smelled of piss. I used to have to sit beside him in French, and he always wanted to be my friend, and kept asking me round to his house and I never went because, quite frankly, even in that 1970s private school, which was packed to the late Victorian turrets with uncool kids, George Burroughs was the uncoolest kid of all. Ever. And he smelled of piss.

'James,' he wrote. 'My school day recollections are scarred by the thoughts of your cruelty.' (I can just hear the pompous Morningside lowland Scots drawl as I read.) 'You really were not a very nice child. I hope that you have grown to be a better man. All I ever asked for in my childhood was some friendship ...'

I'm afraid it went on thus, for two pages. He informed me that he is an Elder in the Kirk and head of Edinburgh's biggest law firm, with a mansion in Morningside and a villa in the Dordogne.

'George,' I write back. 'Lovely to hear from you. I have obviously made you the man you are. All contributions to my pension fund gratefully accepted.'

Blimey, that kid's got problems. I mean, I ask you ... the Dordogne! Surrey empties July and August – shut your eyes and Sarlat becomes downtown Godalming.

This twilight world, of the past, of *temps perdu* that I am beginning to inhabit, is not healthy, I am certain. Still, neither is sitting on a train every morning with a bunch of wannabe panzer commanders, I guess.

# 9

# Teenage Kicks


Well bugger me, dear reader. A week has passed since George 'Wee Wee' Burroughs dumped his psychological problems on me, and what a week that has been.

I put the CV together and emailed it to the agencies with a sinking heart. They replied, I spoke to various consultants, some of whom sounded as if they'd only just left their teenage years behind them, who purred over my experience and qualifications, then told me how tough the market was. Last year? No problem! Companies were offering private helicopters, Samsonites full of Krugerands and the sexual services of East European princesses just to get the chance to interview candidates like me. But right now, James, it's a tad tricky, I'm afraid ...

It's fucking obvious – I am too old and too expensive.

But dear reader, do I despair?

No, I jolly well don't! Why am I not in the slough, nay Uxbridge, of despond, contemplating a life on the streets, tap dancing for cinema queues?

You, with your incisive intellect, and might I say, rather charming smile, dear reader, have guessed it!

Carolyn Adams.

Carolyn Gorgeous Nubile Sexy Dirty Clever Funny (c.1980) Adams, has been in touch.

Yes, two days after the urinally challenged George used me to delouse himself of every psychological hang-up he ever had, I had still heard nothing. I was convinced she was happily married to a conceptual artist and living in Hamburg or some such. Or, as life usually turns out, working in 'administration' for a private healthcare company.

I'd bundled around the house for the day, had poured my first G&T (my resolution is now only to drink diluted alcohol, and do you know something? I feel better for it already) and at the sound of the regular soap theme music, I headed up to the computer telling Helen that I was hopeful of some news on a job from the US. Actually I was going to check my emails and then play Solitaire.

So I logged on in some desperation and there it was. 'You have email from old-pals.net.'

My little old heart a-fluttered. Images of every stinking vomiting child I had ever encountered at school flew through my brain — bound to be one of them blaming me for the fact that they are in Broadmoor for slaughtering their family after I refused to lend them a crayon in junior school in

1967. Or: 'You stole my position of milk monitor in '65 and as a result my father left my mother for a trawlerman named Sven.'

Sod it. I clicked and – as angels sang in my ears, licked my nipples and gently stroked my testicles with peacock feathers – I saw the words 'Carolyn Adams'.

The message was unconventional – but I have had my fill of convention. Not for her details of her life and loves, her kids, her career. No. All Carolyn said was,

'You are 22 years late, you arsehole.'

And I knew what she meant both chronologically and anatomically.

Carolyn had written to me at home at the end of those long holidays. She'd asked me to visit, she invited herself down, she planned meetings on equidistant moors where she promised we would fuck each other's brains out. And I had done nothing. I meant to reply, but thought it cooler to break hearts, play fast and loose, a Keatsian Byronic figure into art and nature and free sex.

I knew I was wrong. Not for not answering the letters, but for having held that girl in my arms and sworn love and devotion and promising that we'd see each other again. That was what was wrong: the trickery, the lies.

Especially as she herself had told me that she lived for the moment, that fidelity, monogamy were not for her, that free love and great sex and huge amounts of drugs and not a little rock and roll were all her brain and body needed.

So, I sat and stared at the message and, for the first time for months, genuinely did not know what to do. Seven simple words. Start with arsehole – granted, a little harsh, but how well she knows me even after all this time. But the rest of it?

I think she wants me to try to win her back.

Why? I hear you ask. How can I possibly surmise that from those seven little words? Simply because there aren't eight. If she'd said, 'You are 22 years *too* late, you arsehole,' then that would have been somehow final, but she has left space for further discussion. Remember, words are my tools. I understand the subtle nuances of additions or omissions having spent a lifetime in publishing (though granted, from the narrative style of this tome, you'd be forgiven for forgetting ...)

I am about to fire off a witty, passionate response, a torrent of memories, intimate though not dirty references, when I stop short. Twenty five plus years. I am fat and grey and a million miles away from the young slim Jamie who would never work in an office and wear a suit and tie and understand business. Who'd write for a living, travel, live life on the edge, compose symphonies, be a punk poet ...

So, what's she going to be like? If I've changed from John Cooper-Clarke to Kenneth Clarke in just 22 years, what might have happened to her? She's mid-forties, obviously. I remember when I was young, looking at my mother's friends who were forty-something and they seemed to me like museum pieces, mothers themselves, nothing else. Even when the pre-adolescent hormones kicked in and a small erection would appear when within two hundred metres of a bra advert in *Woman's Own*, no such response would appear around mothers' friends.

She might be fat. She might be lined and creased, and wearing sensible dresses bought from catalogues. And her breasts might have sagged and she might be drying out pre-menopausally. She might be mad, diseased. Murderous. She may have been married to an accountant for 20 years who left her for his secretary and now she's living on an estate outside Halifax with hanging baskets and teenage kids and she's boring and bored and wants someone to take her to the nearest shopping superstore designer outlets and buy her a crap lunch in an overpriced French restaurant on a mall served by spotty kids. (Jamie Gallagher, Gold Medallist, Olympic Free Rant Competition.)

But instinctively, I know she's not. Why? Two reasons. 1) The slightly hip off-the-wall response and

2) This is the sexiest freest woman I have come across ever and even 22 years will not have softened her funkiness, her artiness or her ability to think about things in a completely different way from anyone else I have ever met.

And if the years have dulled her, I have the ability to rejuvenate her. That is My Quest.

People may grow up, but the core of them, their essence, their very soul, remains the same as when they were young – of that I am utterly convinced.

'So what happened to you?' that Goddamn fucking voice in my head interjects.

'I still have the mind, the soul of an eighteen-year-old poet,' I reply internally. 'It's just that you'd need industrial diamond-head cutting equipment to find them beneath the layers of middle class, middle age flab.'

I sit and think how to reply to the fair Carolyn. Should I be angst-ridden, honest and open, or witty, cool and collected? Should I pretend that I have forgotten all about the explosive sex we enjoyed (I assume she enjoyed it, too) all those years ago? Or should I stun her with my pinpoint memory of acts and tastes and tongues, and orgasms?

I decide honesty is best.

I begin to write. I tell her that hardly a day has gone by when I didn't think of her (which is kind of true – at least of the last week). That I have tried to track her down since the internet gave the means and the method. That I would see a woman in a crowd with flowing hair and my heart would skip at the thought that it might be her. That whenever I was in Nottingham I would look for her on the streets and in bars.

That on returning to university after that summer, I had contracted glandular fever and had become very ill, and had to work incredibly hard to catch up with missing work as a result of the illness, and once my exams were over I resolved to contact her, but then found I had lost her address in the move from my student house.

And I'd tried, I'd even phoned the Art Department at Manchester University, to be told that they couldn't give out students' details over the phone but that there was an alumni service and that if she were on that then I would be able to contact her. But she never was.

Some of which – OK, a very little of which – was true, but it sounded urgent and heartfelt, and frankly read beautifully. I'd have wept if I hadn't written it myself.

I then give her the potted history of my life since university. How I'd tried to spend two years writing my novel (I'd always talked of writing way back then), but couldn't get published, so decided that I would have a better chance of literary success if I worked in the book industry. How I'd travelled and, this faux coyly, somehow I had been a great success despite my abhorrence of all things to do with industry and business. I tell her I married a beautiful woman who gave me two beautiful children who I adored, but that she had run off with a brilliantly talented writer three years ago leaving me distraught and lonely and with the children to bring up. And how she had snatched these children away from me despite her cruelty by way of a sharp divorce lawyer, and now I was living in a bachelor flat again, having rejected the corporate world, with a novel to write.

Bloody convincing and startlingly truthful, I felt as I spellchecked it and refined it – apart from the bits where I lied.

And off it goes, into the ether, to explode on to the screen of this woman from my past.

I check my other emails – there are a couple of possible sniffs from job agencies, but nothing to get excited about. I play the only game in town for a couple of wasteful minutes when bang! My server tells me I have email.

It is she.

'You lying bastard,' she responds. 'You are probably holed up in a leafy Surrey suburb in a dull marriage and sending emails to every woman you ever shagged in the past, pretending to your loyal and loving wife that you have to sort out a report for the board meeting tomorrow. I guess you are overweight, drive an expensive car, do sailing holidays and vote Tory longing for the return of Mrs Thatcher.'

Bugger. Rumbled (apart, dear reader, for the Thatcher bit. And the sailing). And not every woman – she is the first.

And she's not going to be easy.

I confess a little. I tell her I am still – unhappily – married. And it's Kent, not Surrey. But I did think of her, and tall women with chestnut hair always made me think of – and long for – her.

She's not taken in any. 'What do you want James?' she emails back quickly.

'To see you,' I tell her.

'No chance – not after 22 years and you still being an obvious colossal bastard.'

'I am intrigued to find out what happened to you,' I tell her.

'Disappointment and old age,' she replies and the somewhat frantic correspondence stops with that.

I go to bed, remembering. Remembering her in bed with me on long summer afternoons talking poetry and art and dreams. Oh, and taking cartloads of, mainly soft, drugs as well. I hope to dream of her – a dirty flashback erotic dream which would result in a tumescence the like of which this part of Kent rarely sees, but instead dream that Hearts won the

European Cup and that I was in goal for them and saved a last minute penalty. With no trousers on.

# 10

# Present Arms

I have heard nothing from Carolyn for three days. I resisted the temptation to email her again – well, I resisted it until 10 o'clock the next day, when I sent her a slightly bemused message – 'Why the silence?' – and heard nothing back. Resolute as ever, I then sent her a follow-up at 11.30 the same day, then something similar on the hour every hour until 5pm.

I think I may have become a little infatuated. It's not just a question of wanting to communicate with her – I need to communicate with her. I have to find out what she's been doing, how she is, what she looks like and most importantly of all if she was the one – the woman who could have made me happy. Really happy. Who would have saved me from this life of boredom and superficiality.

In the meantime, I have had an offer of a job interview. Same job as I was doing before only for an even bigger company, again American, still academic books but more technical and medical. Based in sunny Royal Berkshire.

And I know the CEO.

Phil and I worked in the same company for about two weeks way back in the mid-eighties, before he went on to a life of corporate stardom. Somehow the ginger-haired twat has risen to quite dizzy heights with seemingly no ability and even less intellect. Amazing. But he's heard of my demise and has emailed me to say that there is a position coming up that may well be of interest. Would I send my CV?

I stop to think. I assess my situation – and know that I have to go and see him. Frankly I would rather lose both my testicles in a freak combine harvester accident than work for him or his crummy company. But needs must when the building society drives. And anyway, it keeps me away from the PC and my current infatuation.

So, having forlornly checked my emails again just before departing to see if Carolyn is offering to shag me senseless, and finding that she isn't, I am now stuck in a traffic jam masquerading as the London orbital route, running late for my interview with Mr Pond Life himself. Ever the consummate professional I phone to inform his secretary that I am running late and will be there as soon as possible.

I arrive half an hour late and, having been smoking for most of the way, am aware that I smell less than fragrant. I haven't even got any mints to freshen my breath, but what the hell, they should be interested in me for my talent, not for resembling a

Provençal meadow in the summer whenever I open my mouth.

The building is a four-storey sixties brutalist disaster. As I approach it I note that the directors each have their own car parking spaces allocated – how quaint. I park, look in my mirror and cursorily sweep my silvered locks back over my forehead and check my tie. A large sign with the company's logo is attached at the top of the building with the corporate slogan 'A lot of learning is a wonderful thing' – which they probably paid some wanky design consultants thousands to come up with – scrawled in jaunty letters beside it.

With a sinking heart and a desire to apply for a job as a shelf-stacker in my local supermarket, I head for the front door. I sign the form that the vacant receptionist offers me, pick up my visitor's badge and sit in the be-fronded reception area.

There is a copy of the *Daily Telegraph* on the glass coffee table. I scan the rabid right-wing rant of a headline and decline to pick it up. Various product catalogues and leaflets extolling the great virtues of this wondrous company lie beside it, and I pick up a couple to flick through.

A young woman walks across the reception area and glances at me in a bored manner. Then a couple of middle-aged men carrying laptops walk past in a bored manner. Then a man who looks like a warehouse operative walks past in a bored manner.

Ten minutes later a woman approaches, sticks out her hand and says, 'Hi, I'm Clare. Phil's PA. We're so sorry to keep you.' I rise to my feet and take her hand and say, 'No problem. I'm James Gallagher.'

We walk up the stairs one flight talking about the rigours of travelling by car and the delights of living in Royal Berkshire (it probably is delightful if you are royalty but it's a shithole for the rest of us) and I am shown in to Phil's office.

Phil is sitting behind a desk the size of the *Ark Royal*, grinning inanely. He's aged a bit since I saw him last at a trade show, and his ridiculous moustache is now matched by an equally ridiculous goatee beard. And he's awfully red-headed. He's wearing a regulation designer suit and tie, and looks a little flustered. He shakes my hand sloppily, grins inanely once more and introduces me to the woman sitting in the corner.

'This is Rachel Morgan, our senior marketing manager,' he says, a little shamefaced; his too-small eyes dart between the two of us. I smile sweetly and shake her hand.

She's a pretty woman – late twenties I'd say, with big blue eyes and a rather sensuous mouth. She's wearing a long patterned skirt and florally cropped blouse and this together with her jewellery – big round earrings and gold bracelets – suggest some silent-movie gypsy. And I ask myself: why is she in on this interview?

It soon becomes apparent. Dear reader, my only friend in the world, I shall not recount the humiliation of what followed. I shall not tell of the vacuous questions this silly little red-topped man put to me (as vacuous I suppose as those I had put to many many candidates in the past – but at least I would have performed with panache and charm).

To cut a long story short, I answer his questions to the best of my ability – which is pretty high – and he nods, looks at Rachel, who then trots out 'What our current strategy is ...' then proceeds to contradict me.

And at the end of each recital from her, Phil looks at me with something approaching pity, and at her with something approaching worship.

The interview grinds on. I find myself disinterested, bored, and increasingly angry as I realise there is a game being played here, and I am not sure of the rules. But it is pretty bloody obvious that nothing I say is going to result in gainful employment.

As Phil goes on to describe the company's international strategy, I switch off and glance around this stupid bastard's office. He has all the trappings of the successful executive: a perfectly tidy desk, ethnic artwork procured one assumes from his trips around the world. An unopened bottle of thirty-year-old malt. Awards from the company for various marketing campaigns. A photograph of Phil, grinning inanely and looking for all the world as if he's just been dropped off at a funfair by a Sunshine coach, outside the US office shaking hands with the global CEO. And best of all, a photograph bathed in the golden light of his wife and kids, squeaky clean and well-dressed, posing casually against some studio backdrop of clouds, grinning happily for the best father in the world.

Little do they know that the silly bastard is probably entertaining the lovely Rachel in the stationery cupboard.

I'm aware that I've been asked a question, and I don't know what it is. In a split second I decide against bluffing through the answer – which I am afraid I could do easily – and reply,

'Quite honestly, Phil, you can take your job and stick it up your arse.'

'I beg your pardon?' he asks, looking a little less smug than previously. I stare him in the eyes, and repeat my response.

'I think this interview is now over,' he says, glancing somewhat startled towards the lovely Rachel.

I remain seated. 'Two more minutes, Phil, while I explain.' He's caught, half out of his chair, while I proceed. 'I wouldn't work for you, pal, if my life depended on it. You are probably the stupidest man in British publishing, and that frankly takes some doing. You have dragged me along here for a job that you have no intention of giving to anyone but the woman of your dreams.' Here I nod dismissively at Rachel, who flinches. 'Who has probably resisted your flaccid attempts to penetrate her on the grounds that you are married with kids, and she doesn't want to hurt anyone, but will give in if absolutely necessary (if she hasn't already), hiding her revulsion at your ginger body, for the chance of a mighty leg up the corporate ladder.' And then the proud climax. 'I always thought of you, Phil, as an idiot savant, and you are – except you're missing the savant bit.'

God, that felt wonderful.

He stammers a reply and sits down. Rachel has gone bright red.

And with that, I stand, say, 'Thank you for your time,' shake his hand, nod at Rachel, and leave.

I get into my car, feeling as good as I have felt in months.


I arrive home at four o'clock, and to my surprise see Helen's coupé (she's stopped of late hassling for a Porsche) parked in the drive. I'm surprised, because the shops are still open.

She's in the kitchen as I go in, and she turns to

smile at me.

'How did it go?' she asks.

'Wonderfully well,' I reply with my best winning smile.

'Do you think you've got it?' she asks, genuinely pleased.

'I wouldn't be surprised,' I say.

'You are clever,' she says.

'Thank you darling.' I make a cup of tea and go up to the study.

I'm now feeling angry. Did I overreact? Of course I did. Was my behaviour acceptable? Yes, on a human level. But professionally, it was pretty hard to justify. Everyone plays games in business, and I even begin to feel a little sorry for Rachel. Perhaps I misread the situation, perhaps she's just a bright young thing (I used to be one of those, too), wanting to get on, and is as able and a lot cheaper than an old fart like myself. More practically, it's a small world in British publishing and it wouldn't be beyond the bounds of reason for people to get to hear about dear old Jamie's breakdown. I wouldn't put it past dull Phil to tell his equally dull corporate mates of what had passed.

Still. Deep inside, I am actually pleased with myself – I have behaved as my twenty-year-old self would feel it was right to behave. Take shit from no one, speak your mind and don't compromise.

I bask a little in newly-gained self-respect.

I switch on the PC and glance at my emails. I have 43 new ones, most of which appear to offer me the chance to extend my penis through herbal tablets (if only) and find a lovely wife in Thailand. Two job agencies are confirming receipt of my CV and inform me that I am being kept on file, which means, 'You sad old bastard we can fill any job you are qualified for with someone cheaper and equally able,' and there, the last item in my in-box, is a message from Carolyn.

I open it not a little excitedly.

She writes: 'I am replying despite myself. I vowed two years ago to have nothing further to do with men. After that summer, I returned to Manchester, and met a boy, a year younger than me, who I knew from school. He was studying philosophy, and was serious and deep, very handsome, and full of dreams of his future. He moved in with me within a week.

'He wanted to travel when he left university – travel and write. I knew that I needed to provide for him so his obvious genius could thrive, so I packed in my art and trained as a nurse on the thinking that I could work anywhere in the world. While I trained he went to the Middle East. When I qualified, I joined him.

'We stayed for three years, and then moved on to Thailand and Vietnam. All the time, I shovelled shit to allow him to write. And write and travel he did, and literary agents kept saying he was good, but the market needed something more commercial.

'And we grew apart, without frankly my realising it. He treated me like I was a handmaiden to his genius. He'd disappear off to some remote place for months on end, leaving me alone and lonely. I don't think he had other women – he was too self-obsessed.

'Eventually in Penang, I had something of a breakdown. I spent a weekend never leaving the apartment during a massive thunderstorm, singing Charles Wesley hymns. He returned eventually. I told him I had to go home.

'He let me. I stayed with my parents, but then his father was diagnosed with cancer and he returned, too.

'More of the same followed. I worked in psychiatric hospitals to keep us going. And at the same time I started to long for a baby. He told me he would be a hopeless father – he was probably right – that travellers and writers can't be tied down.

'Six months later, he got the book deal. Big money, a US publisher as well, we were made.

'Two years ago, he tells me he is in love with his researcher and is leaving me for her. She's young and pretty and dazzled by him I'm sure, and though I hate her, I pity her, too.

'Last month she delivered him twins. They live in

a big house in Highgate, and he is a rising star of the literary media circus.

'We're divorced and to be fair he was generous with the money. I now live near the Yorkshire coast, feel old and bewildered and am trying to resurrect my art.

'So, James Gallagher, you can see why I am reluctant to start communicating with you. I am hurt and I think you could hurt me further.'

She signed off 'with love' and for the first time in ages I felt genuinely moved by another human being. Tears came to my eyes as I reread her message.

The bastard, I thought. Treating a goddess like that. The poor woman, allowing herself to be trodden on and disposed of.

Blimey, I know how to sum up a complex situation well.

And I feel not a little responsible, too. Perhaps if I'd stayed in touch we would have been happy together and lived a life of rural idyll. Which of course I recognise to be abject nonsense as soon as I've thought it. I glance out of the window and see the manicured gardens of my suburban neighbours and think, no. She would have shrivelled in my life and I, though I talk the talk, would never have shown her the things she had seen.

For once in my life I resist the temptation to act impulsively. I close down the computer and go and mix myself a very large whisky. I go through into our spacious and immaculate living room, where the kids are eating oven pizza and chips and watching, as if their life depended upon it, some crap cartoon programme.

'Hi guys,' I say cheerily and am greeted with nothing but a grunt from my eldest.

'Homework tonight?' I ask tentatively.

'Done it,' he grunts. My daughter ignores me, entranced.

'That can't have taken long,' I reply to myself. Honest to God, twenty grand a year on private education per child and they have all the cultural acumen of some kid in the bottom stream of the local sink comprehensive.

Helen comes in. 'How are you getting on, love? Any more job interviews?' she asks sweetly.

'A couple of leads,' I say. And then impulsively, 'I may have to go away for a few days. Some people to see about work. Long shot, but hey, better try it.'

I have become convinced in the last few minutes that I am going to have to see Carolyn. Every emotional sinew in my body is pushing me to meet her again for – for I don't know what. The fact is, I don't really do adultery. Never have. Of course, I do my Jimmy Carter bit – committing mental adultery with nearly every fully-limbed, non-hideous woman under the age of about 63 that I see in the course of the day – but never have I strayed in the swapping of bodily fluids department. Had a few opportunities in my younger days, but resisted mainly because it's such a bloody cliché – house, school fees, big car, mistress.

But right now I feel that this is probably what I am planning, given half a chance.

'OK, darling,' she responds pleasantly. 'But not Monday or Tuesday – Cameron and Ailsa have parents' evenings then – I did tell you about it.'

Bugger, I think, for two reasons. I lose the ability to act impulsively for one – I can't just head north on a whim. Secondly, everything about that bloody fucking school puts me in a very bad mood – to the point where I consider mass murder through poisoning of the water supply there, or a well-positioned sub-machine gun on the lush green sports field.

'No problem,' I reply sweetly through a grimace, aware that she is now engrossed in her celebrity magazine and not listening to me.

I look at her as she sits there and try to imagine what it would be like to meet her now if I had not seen her for 20 years. Actually, she is still an attractive woman – she's kept her figure and uses enough make-up to hide the signs of ageing. Indeed, if it had been 20 years, I would not be disappointed. I think I could see in her the girl I once knew and, to use the teenage vernacular of the time, fancy her.

'I'll just go and do some more work,' I say, emptying my glass. I stop in the kitchen for a refresher and go back up to the office.

I log back on and reread Carolyn's email. Again, a wave of sadness for the emptiness of someone else's life washes over me.

I have to see her, but how do I avoid scaring her off?

I reply.

'Carolyn, your email is very sad. I don't understand how he could treat you so awfully. Men are bastards.'

I then go on to give some background to my own circumstances. That I am trapped by economic circumstances, that I have no relationship with my family, and that I long to be somewhere – anywhere – else than in this executive box in leafy Kent surrounded by people who think about nothing but houses and investments and cars.

'I want to see you again,' I say. 'To catch up. To see who you have become. I am a little convinced that if I can sort my past out, I may be able to sort out my present.

'I will drive anywhere to meet with you for just an hour. I am not trying to resurrect the passion of the past – I am twice the weight I was when you knew me, drink and smoke too much, and I have no doubt at all that when you meet me I will shatter any fond memories you may still have of me forever.

'Suggest somewhere for lunch next week and I will be there.

'With love, James.'

My best shot. Not too heavy, not too plaintive – enough I think to get her interested.

Five minutes later she replies.

'I am not prepared to sort out your obvious psychological problems when I have so many myself.'

Bugger bugger bugger, I think, and leave it at that. A fairly final piss-off-you-total-wanker-type reply, I think you will agree.

Indeed, bugger bugger bugger.

# 11

# Burning Down the House

It is parents' evening for my son and monosyllabic Neanderthal heir. I have spent the weekend busying myself in the garden, down the pub, at the supermarket – anything to avoid thinking about my future.

I've spent a fair amount of time, too, on old-pals.net, too. Thinking about my past.

I realise with some horror that of, say, 30 people that I consider significant in my life, who have to a lesser or greater extent influence on what and who I am today, 22 of them are contactable.

From Stewart, with whom, when growing up in Edinburgh, I watched every single Heart of Midlothian home game from 1972–74, when Donald Ford was the man I wanted to marry; to Stephanie in Teesside, the sight of whose cleavage displayed before me in French lessons at my sixth-form college caused me, I swear, to only achieve a D pass when I was expected to get an A. (And would the exam board listen? Not a bit of it.) And Malcy, the funniest guy I ever knew, with whom I swore eternal brotherhood at Blackbush aerodrome when Bob Dylan was headlining in the summer before I fluked my way into my second-rate university (soon to revert to polytechnic status, so I believe) – they are nearly all there.

And Barbara, who I undressed in a broom cupboard at some adolescent party, who had the greatest nubile body I have ever come across (or possibly over), but who had the intellectual acumen of a carrot.

My past before me.

And I feel the need to meet them and talk to them and find out what they are doing, and to see how my dull life compares to theirs.

And to find out what precisely happened to Barbara's nubility.

But at present my big expensive car is purring its way up the drive, through the woods, to the big expensive school. I park beside other big expensive cars, and Helen and I walk across the gravelled entrance into the school hall.

The school sits on a hill, surrounded by acres of woodland. It was a large, privately-owned manor house, build originally in the sixteenth century, and fell into a dilapidated state in the 1960s. It was converted into a school about 20 years ago and because it is a Grade A-listed building, most of the original features remain. Including the feudal robber baron mentality of most of the rich bastards whose children are there.

Helen takes my arm – oh, the wonderful pretence of the happy marriage – and we greet the headmaster, who frankly has always had something of a disdainful attitude to me principally, I suspect, because I never respond to any of his fundraising letters asking for cash donations to help build the sports hall or the swimming pool or whatever. I can tell, just by the way he looks at me, that he knows I am skint and keep my children here by the skin of my yellowing teeth. He respects real money, so sidles up to the brokers and dealers and estate agents whose children frequent this place.

And they are all here tonight. The sharply dressed makers and shakers of the City, fresh off the Cannon Street train, cross that they've been dragged away from their desks to discuss their kids when there are more deals to be done, more money to be made. They are a mixture – old public-school boys with crisp, almost military accents, with their county wives. And the new and the brash, the Essex lads with one O level who joined the bank as a tea boy and now trade millions in currency options. Estuary accents abound, as do skinny women married to these guys, who were shop girls or secretaries or dental nurses until they struck it lucky with their marriages.

Don't get me wrong, I don't resent other people's

good fortune and consider the ability to become wealthy through the capitalist system a truly democratic leveller. It's just that they are all thick bastards, aggressive and self-confident, and their wives are stupid and soon to be disposed of when their husbands swap them for a younger version, as inevitably they will.

(Oh, and by the way, I was lying. I do resent them and come the Marxist revolution, I will advocate that these people are first up against the wall – but you knew that, didn't you?)

Helen chats to some of the women, and I stand and look bored and moody, while the other husbands ignore me and discuss the Hang Seng Index or some such bollocks. Coffee is served – Christ, at the prices we pay for the place it should be vintage Armagnac – and we are then led into the old library to meet with the teachers.

Oh, the tedium. I really don't know why I bother. Cameron, we are told by every teacher, is clever but idle, cheeky and surly, rude and talented. 'He needs to work,' they chorus – and it's all true, and if the kid were in the local school then there would indeed be a problem, but assuming he stays at this school he'll get good enough A levels to win a place at just as crap a university as I did. That's what we're paying for, to shortcut the system and it's wrong, but hey – that's the world we live in.

We finish, and I want to go, but no, Helen stops to talk to yet more ponytailed bimbettes and their fascist husbands, but thankfully there is some wine on offer, so I quaff speedily three glasses and decide that I have to sort my life out.

We eventually leave, after Helen has talked of our skiing trip at Christmas, and our plans to move and the villa we are hoping to rent in Tuscany in the summer – all, incidentally, news to me. I feel weary and discontented, and long for freedom.

It is the end of the week, and I am in the study with half the annual liquor production of the Spey valley in my glass and feeling good. Ailsa's parents' evening had been more of the same, except ponies and ballet were discussed, and I drank yet again despite the school's apparent reluctance to feed my alcohol habit (I swear they were trying to restrict me). Different parents in the main, but exactly the same bloody sort.

But now, I am staring at the screen and feeling excited for the first time all week.

She has agreed to see me. Tuesday lunchtime. At a restaurant on the Yorkshire moors.

The weekend passes lumberingly slowly. The kids are nowhere to be seen, Helen suggests a shopping trip to some out-of-town mall which I decline on the grounds that I have work to do. In truth, I busy myself in the garden, visit the pub, tidy the garage, watch some sport and drink yet more alcohol. She suggests we go out for a meal on Saturday – I decline on grounds of expense.

I have to hand it to Helen. She obviously realises, I think, that I am feeling depressed and unhappy with my lot, and she's trying to jolly me along. But she has no idea about the real source of this overwhelming ennui.

Monday passes as I pack my bag. I have decided to stay at the hotel adjacent to the restaurant as it is too far to do the return trip in a day. Reality is kicking in – this is going to be disastrous, I am certain. She'll look like the side of a house and have wrinkles and grey hair, and we'll have nothing to talk about. But if that is the case, I can at least have a good night out on my own, a fine meal and lashings of wine, and find some space on the moors to work out what I am going to do with my life.

I even pack my walking boots.

I leave at 5.30 on Tuesday, way too early, but I cannot sleep. I feel like a teenager on a first date. I'm now excited and scared and guilty at the deception – I've told Helen that I have to go to Leeds to meet with a man to discuss setting up our own distribution network for US imports.

I'm dressed in smart casuals – chinos and loafers and a light summer jacket (I decline the blazer as that makes me look like some Henley outcast), and my best casual dark blue shirt. Not affluent, just respectable. I have even created a playlist on the iPod from the time I knew Carolyn – Elvis, The Clash, The Teardrop Explodes and the like, as well as some statutory Dylan, and I head off North listening to fine songs from my past at maximum volume.

I know I should stop for breakfast, but I don't – I just want to get there, to get this craziness sorted once and for all. I drive fast, stop just once for a pee, and find myself on the York–Scarborough road at 11.30 in the morning.

It is a beautiful day. The sun is shining through the remnants of mist, and as I head off from the main road across the moors, I wonder why anyone should wish to live anywhere else. Solitude. I drive through stone hamlets with just a local pub and a post office, and old men in agricultural garb stare at me as if I am some kind of alien.

The world has changed little here. It is a different country to the hassle of the South East. The nearest out-of-town shopping experience is probably 40 miles away. I bet these people have never tasted pesto, or sun-dried tomatoes.

My grandfather came from round these parts, some hamlet whose name escapes me, and there is a romantic part of me, which makes me feel as if I am home. I see old men, and wonder if their fathers had known my grandfather. Perhaps they'd played together as kids. Perhaps my grandfather had climbed that hill over there or gone to that church.

And I realise with a sudden shock that I don't belong anywhere. OK, I live in Kent, but I don't feel affection for it, or pride in it. It's just somewhere I sleep and somewhere from which I can get to work. And I don't belong anywhere I've ever lived – the Midlands, the North East, Edinburgh – because I've always had to move on.

And perhaps that's why people are unhappy – they have no ownership of their local culture (if such a thing exists), no time to enjoy their environment.

Whereas here, on the moors, I presume people can trace back their families for generations.

I muse thus, homespun philosophy oozing from every orifice, and nearly miss the entrance to my hotel. I screech to a halt, realise I am an hour early, but decide to go in.

It is beautiful. Cottagey gardens, ivy-clad, ancient flag stones, real beer. A friendly, bosomy, local lady greets me at reception, and my room is ready she tells me, so I check in. Not a trouser press or shower cap in sight, just a functional, comfortable, spacious room with fine views.

I think mischievously – I wonder if Carolyn will cavort naked with me here this afternoon. I make sure that the room is tidy, just in case, and go down to the bar.

Where, despite the temptation to drown out my increasing nervousness, I resist a beer, and settle for coffee. I choose a table with a view of the main entrance, light a cigarette, pick up *The Guardian* and pretend to read.

Every time a car pulls in, I glance up, despite myself. I want her to find me cool and calm, not panting, but every movement – even a bird flying across the garden – causes me to look up. I swing in moods, from excited and aroused to fear and dread. This could be without doubt the stupidest bloody thing I ever have done.

It could be the finest.

I order more coffee, and halfway through this, my third cup, I start to get the caffeine sweat. Bugger, why didn't I just have mineral water? Now she's going to find me, a perspiring, fat, middle-aged bloke with grey hair and I'll be her worst nightmare, and she'll regret coming immediately, and the day will have been a waste.

I look at my watch – 10 minutes before her ETA, and guess what, I now need a pee. And I regret suddenly the choice of trousers as I always manage to splash myself, and how embarrassing is that after 20 years? And if I go to the toilet, and she turns up when I am in there, she could turn on her heel and disappear forever.

I am in what my dear old mother, God bless her,

would call a 'tizz'. I am taken back to my first date, not 40 miles from here, in 1975 with Madeleine the Geordie, who had big eyes and a warm heart, and who I managed to say nothing to during the entire course of the one evening out we had together and who chucked me next day.

I was in a bit of a tizz before that date, too.

I decide on action. The blousy lady is back at reception, so I tell her that if a tall lady with brown hair comes in and looks puzzled, she is to use all legal resources to restrain her from leaving before I come back.

I sprint to the loo, use a cubicle so that I can pee into the lav, not the splashing urinal, wash my hands, and then my face in cold water and am back in my seat seemingly within seconds. The blousy one assures me that no one has arrived or departed.

I pick up my paper, and turn to the sports pages in the desperate hope that there will be some distracting reference to Hearts, and just as I start to internally bemoan the Anglo-centricity of all national daily newspapers, I glance up at a motion by the front door and see a middle-aged woman with long dark hair, dressed in a long straight summer frock, with bare arms and flat shoes look around her quizzically before holding my gaze and walking towards me with what can only be described as grim resolve.

She is a stranger.

Who suddenly, mystically, mysteriously before my very eyes transports me back twenty years and it is, I realise with glee, Carolyn. Like some Hollywood special effect, she changes in front of my eyes from another slightly sad, deserted, dissatisfied, middle-aged woman into the girl I knew and loved.

I gape. My mouth opens like some landed carp, but words fail me as she comes close, pecks me on the cheek, sits down and says, 'Aren't you grown up?'

I pull myself together and manage to say, 'You look great,' and we swap small talk about where she lives, and why she came here, and the hotel.

Five minutes pass, and we pause, small talk seemingly over. 'Pleased you came?' she asks, and I say, 'Of course,' while my head is telling me that I want to get the fuck out of here. 'Shall we have some lunch?'

We go through to the restaurant, and I decide that I have never ever needed alcohol as much as I do right now. I order a strong lager, Carolyn has tonic water. I light a cigarette without asking if she minds.

She stopped smoking two years after we'd last met, she tells me. 'Saw too many people die of it,' she says. And she hardly drinks now, either. 'Makes me depressed,' she adds.

Verily a soul mate.

Oh God, I have made a mistake here, big time. This next two hours are going to be excruciating.

We order food, and I ask her about her travels, about her marriage, about her life post-divorce, and she answers at length. She's still bitter (and rightly so, I tell her) about her husband's spectacular dumping of her for the younger model.

'I wanted to die,' she says dispassionately.

'Do you hate him?' I ask.

'No,' she replies, 'I hate her. But if you wait long enough on the river bank, the bodies of your enemies will eventually float by.'

And I believe her. We discuss the nature of love, how you never stop loving someone in some small, perverse, almost corrosive way, despite what you've been put through. 'Odi et amo,' I quote pretentiously, and she picks up the Catullus reference immediately.

'Still something of an intellectual snob, eh, James?' she smirks and I squirm – she has rumbled me.

I order another beer and the food. I'm having a steak, and so I order some wine with it, knowing that it will help.

'So what about you, Jamie. Why are you here?' she asks.

I tell her bits. I tell her I am bored with work, I am bored with the South East of England, how I seem to have lost great chunks of my life and have nothing to show for them.

And how I never forget her.

'Mid life crisis,' she says observationally.

'Maybe,' I say.

'When you contacted me, I dug out from the loft my box of old records. The Clash, Magazine, Heads – and one night I stayed up listening to them and closed my eyes and I was 20 again. It was lovely. But I woke the next morning and looked and felt middle-aged.'

Oh God, I think. Am I lunching with a mad woman?

'Well you look great,' I say again, trying to sound convincing.

She asks me about my publishing career, and I tell her, deliberately underplaying my successes, putting them down to luck.

'I would never have imagined you in the world of business,' she says. 'Me neither,' I reply, looking at her and holding her gaze just a little bit too long.

It must be the wine, but she is becoming increasingly attractive as I gaze into her eyes, and glance suggestively at her lips which are slightly pouting and covered in just this side of tasteful red lipstick. I remember how well they had been put to use all of those years ago and feel strong trouserly stirrings. And she is looking at me and the sadness has gone from her eyes.

She starts to reminisce. Drinking and drug taking, gigs we'd been to together. She never overtly mentions any act of congress, but in a veiled way refers to 'Your friend's big house we lived in that week,' and gives me a knowing glance.

I am beginning to feel a little like a barking village dog that chases after every car that passes, but when one stops, wanders off embarrassed, not actually knowing what to do next.

She even has a glass of wine.

She asks about Helen. She asks about the children. I try not to trot out the corny 'My wife doesn't understand me ...' bit. I tell her there are faults on both sides, that we have both changed.

'Would you leave her?' she asks.

'Can't afford to,' I say.

'A dreadful reason if you are both unhappy,' she pronounces, and takes another sip of her glass of wine.

'I'm not sure we are,' I reply. 'I sometimes think that this is just how it is.'

There is a pause whilst we both take in this profundity, and then I ask,

'And you? Are you seeing anyone?'

'When he left I vowed I'd give up sex. I like my own space. And the only way I'd meet anyone is through a dating agency, and I am not going down that route of true humiliation.'

She takes another mouthful of wine and says, 'But I may have changed my mind about sex.'

And with that she fixes me with a coquettish look. I smile back. Embarrassed.

We finish the meal. 'I have to go,' she says. 'I have work to do.'

'Not even coffee?' I ask. I am now feeling horny, confused, scared and slightly pissed. This is like watching myself in a film – I have no control over this situation at all.

'No,' she says, business-like. 'I have to work.'

I stand up to see her out of the restaurant, my hand on her elbow. As we reach the entrance, she gently kisses my cheek and says, 'Come round for dinner tonight. Eight o'clock,' and slips a card with her address into my hand.

I go back to the bar, have two more pints and go slightly blearily to my room for a sleep.

I wake up at five o'clock. I dreamed of a river full of bodies.

I lie on the bed and try to order my thoughts. It seems fairly obvious, even to me, that Carolyn is, to use vulgar parlance, up for it. The question is, am I? Which seems a strange question to ask, given my self-confessed obsession with this bloody woman over the last few weeks. But maybe obsession is healthy up until the point of reality when it ceases to be so?

And would I be up to it, anyway? I mean, she's slim and well-preserved, and probably has lost none of her appetite from her youth for vigorous lovemaking. I've settled down now to the functional view of lovemaking – couple of minutes bonking followed by 20 minutes of smoking and introspection, and am not sure I have the mindset let alone the blood corpuscles to take it up again recreationally. I suppose what I'd be worried about is: would she be disappointed?

The answer, I am pretty certain, is yes.

So what am I doing here? I ask myself.

I go to the bar and have a pint to answer this question.

Two pints more, and I know that I have to go to see Carolyn. This is what I wanted, she has supposedly haunted me down the years, and for me to walk away now would surely trigger off another round of 'If only/what if?' a few years later.

I finish my drink and return to my bedroom to try to freshen myself up.

I am walking along a narrow country road towards an ever fading light which is, the obviously malicious and misleading cow behind reception assures me, Carolyn's house. I was going to order a taxi, but the font of all local knowledge told me it was only 10 minutes away, I couldn't miss it. Well that was fine, except that after travelling two minutes down the road the haar came in off the sea, and it is bloody freezing and damp, and every so often some bloody pissed farmer in a 4x4 drives too damn quickly along the lane forcing me to take refuge on the verge which on two occasions has meant me slipping into a shit-filled ditch. There should, in my view, be a law introduced banning 4x4s from the countryside – they're a bloody nuisance.

Eventually I arrive at the house. It is an old stone cottage on its own in a field. I can hear the sea and assume we are only a couple of hundred yards from the cliff edge. It has pots of flowers everywhere, seashell mobiles and pieces of drift wood littered randomly.

I knock at the door. I am now numbed to my fate as I am cold and tired and my feet are steeped in effluence. A voice from inside calls, 'Come on in,' and I open the slightly warped door with a little effort, and enter.

Everywhere is candlelit, and there is a strong odour of joss sticks. 'Go into the living room on the left,' the voice calls from upstairs. 'Get yourself a drink.'

I do as I am told. The room is kind of as anticipated. Wooden floors, painted walls featuring various works of art. Conceptual paintings jostle for space with drift wood sculptures, ethnic rugs, and masks from around the world. It has a good feel to it, the room of someone who has created it for themselves because it pleases them, not because it's the way rooms should look. At the far end is an old wooden dining table with two candles and flowers.

This feels good. I find an open bottle of Côtes du Rhône on the table and pour myself a large glass. My nerves are subdued by the first alcoholic top-up. I am doing nothing wrong, I reason, I am simply visiting an old friend, and I am perfectly entitled to do so. I sit down on the sofa, a slight tingling of anticipation in my heart, and my prick, and I resist the bowl of olives as they appear to be immersed in garlic and I suspect that I may need to keep my mouth fresh for later on.

I look around the room and notice books piled everywhere, spilling out of the recessed bookshelves. I can't resist it – I get up to look at them through professional interest. They are not your usual selection. Books on artists I have never heart of, European philosophers beside Eastern mystics, and books on spiritualism and indigenous peoples. There are travel guides to places I have only ever flown over.

Truly, this is an interesting woman.

I hear her footsteps coming down the stairs, and I stand in the middle of the room waiting for her to enter and for my heart to surge. I feel old and foolish in my muddied chinos and loafers in the middle of this room of bohemia.

And in she walks, and I gasp.

She is wearing a tight black dress, which stops mid-thigh. Her hair is swept back off her face and she is wearing Siouxsie Sioux make-up. She has nothing on her feet. A small badge on her left breast that says 'Rien'. And I remember a gig we went to all of those years ago, a tour of post-punk newcomers, and I swear she was wearing that dress and was made up thus.

She looks at me and does a quick twirl. 'Well?' she asks and I say 'Beautiful,' and she laughs, kissing me gently on the cheek. She takes my wine glass in her hand and takes an almighty swig.

I have to try to sit down lest she notices the hard-on which is rapidly swelling my trousers.

She sits opposite and looks at me quizzically. She laughs as I tell her of the journey here and laughs again at the state of my trousers and shoes. All of the time fixing me with a look which says so much, none of which I understand.

'More wine?' she says, going to the table, and I notice her body – firm and hard underneath the tight little dress. She catches me looking and smiles. 'You do look fantastic,' I say, by way of explanation.

'Some music?' she says. 'I made this especially.'

She picks up a remote control and points it at the far corner of the room.

The room explodes to 'Spellbound', and for a moment I am transported.

She sits down beside me and we kiss, gently.

I am tumescent. We sit together and she takes my

hand, and we sit listening to Siouxsie scream.

Next is Elvis Costello. 'There ain't no such thing as an original sin', according to the specky bard.

'You've been busy,' I say. 'How long is the playlist?'

'It goes on for days, full of songs from that time,' she smiles, and kisses me again, her tongue gently probing.

'We'd better eat,' she says.

The starter, some hummus concoction with salad and olives and a lot of garlic see us through 'Mirror in the Bathroom', the Ramones and 'Take Five' (that pub juke box had an eclectic mix). Another bottle of wine is opened to 'Down in the Tube Station at Midnight', and the main course, simple herbed chicken on a bed of wild rice, is brought in as Mr Byrne starts 'Once in a Lifetime'.

Then Sinatra, then 'Hey Jude', followed by a Stiff Little Fingers number I had forgotten I'd ever heard.

And a thought arises – I thought I was obsessed, but this woman has even better recollection of those times.

By the time she brings out the cheese and yet more wine, we're on to the next CD and we've hardly been able to say a word for the volume of music. I ask her the history of the house and where various objects around the room came from and she shouts answers, only part of which I hear depending on the raucousness of the song she's competing against. It would seem horribly middle-aged to ask her to turn it down.

I need a cigarette and as I can see no evidence of her smoking I suggest that I should partake outside. As I get up she stands and kisses me very, very gently on the mouth.

'Have one of these,' she says, walking to a shelf and taking down an ornate mother of pearl box. She passes it to me and I open it. It contains about twenty spliffs. The odour is overpowering.

Bob Marley starts singing 'Buffalo Soldier'.

I am a little pissed by now and hesitate. I actually haven't smoked a joint for nearly 15 years, alcohol as well you know being my first drug of choice and I'm not sure I'm ready to be unfaithful twice. But to refuse would seem terribly middle-class and safe and somehow not in keeping with this bohemian evening.

We sit down beside each other. I light the joint, inhale deeply and pass it to her.

Little happens, so I take it back and inhale again. And again. And pass it back, and we sit in silence looking at the billowing smoke. 'Alison' by Elvis, and the joint is finished and we kiss again and I slide my hand on to her breasts and stroke them gently through the ethnic cotton. She groans. I want to rip her clothes off and take her there and then, I realise, but I am aware that this is a special evening and that what is inevitably going to happen must happen slowly and beautifully as it will change the course of the rest of my life.

The dope is kicking in gently and pleasantly and I reach down for the box to light another spliff. I miss it and nearly fall off the sofa in the effort, then I manage to drop the box and its contents on the floor and we both start to giggle stupidly, then uncontrollably. I fumble again on the floor and produce the joint with a flourish and say, 'Là voila,' and we both start to giggle again. I find my lighter and I light the spliff, and we are giggling and Joe Jackson is wailing about it being 'Different for Girls', and she's rubbing my crotch and I have a colossal hard on but I cannot stop giggling.

'I have to go to the loo,' she says, uncontrollable with laughter. She gets up, strokes my groin lovingly and whispers, 'but I'll be back.'

It's the last thing I remember about the evening.


I wake up and do not have a fucking clue where I am. My head feels as if it has been mauled by lions. My throat is dry and I feel sick. I glance at my watch and see that it is 6.30. I look around the room – the remains of the meal, the wine glasses and the ashtray filled with spliff stubs help to add to the feeling of nausea.

I have to find the toilet. I get up, stagger a little, and crash upstairs. Three doors. Which one? I open the first urgently and Carolyn wakes up as I do so.

'Bit late, lover boy,' she says, and pulls back the covers to reveal her naked body.

I throw up all over the carpet.

Two hours later. I've tried to sleep on the sofa again, but the room is spinning and my head hurting and I feel humiliated and miserable. I want to leave but I cannot. I have to explain, to apologise to Carolyn and offer to pay for her beautiful bedroom rug to be restored. I doubt the vomit stain will ever come out. So I am lying here waiting for her to get up.

I have to go to the bog again and I try to sneak upstairs. Clad only in my boxers, I find the loo, realise that I'd been sick there too and that I need to tidy this up as well.

I find a cloth and some bathroom cleaner and start scrubbing the bowl and the surrounding area, down on my hands and knees.

Carolyn says from behind me, 'Lovely that romance isn't dead,' and I hear her going downstairs.

I finish the cleaning as best I can, wash my hands my face, my rancid armpits and my bollocks and prepare to face her.

There's a steaming cup of tea on the table. I pick it up and join Carolyn who is sitting on the sofa.

We sit in silence for a couple of minutes, before I take a deep breath and say, 'I am so sorry.' I look at her properly for the first time that morning.

Her make-up has run and her hair is falling lankly. There are wrinkles round her eyes and I notice her neck looks old. She looks sadly at me and smiles wistfully.

'Let this be a lesson to us, Jamie Gallagher. You can't recapture the past. Never ever forget that. OK?'

I drink my tea. My stomach half rumbles, half farts and she laughs. 'Jesus,' I say, 'I am so sorry.'

'Don't be,' she says. 'Learn from it. Go back home, forget about all of this and make a go of it with your life – get on with it. It's what you chose so make it work.'

I was actually apologising for the fartlette, but think it inappropriate to say so.

'I think my life chose me,' I say and she responds forcefully, 'Bollocks! It's what happens. We were stupid to think that we could press a button, play some music and be twenty again.'

'I so wanted it to happen,' I say. 'It was the dope. I'm not used to it.'

'Superskunk,' she said. 'That combined with three bottles of wine was not a brilliant idea.'

I put my arm round her and hold her to me without the least impulse of desire. I kiss her gently on the forehead and say, 'I must go.'

# 12

# Road to Nowhere

Six hours later, after an hour's nap at the hotel and a further one in a lay-by off the A1, I reach the M25 which has ceased once more to be operating as a road. I am dreading my return, defeated and humiliated. Two hours later I have completed the final 70 miles and am heading up the drive towards the Grecian statue and my darling wife and children.

I open the front door and go straight to the kitchen for my recuperative glass of whisky. I can hear my loved ones are in the front room watching their favourite soap, and I join them. The kids do not even bother looking up. Helen glances at me and says, 'God, you look awful.'

'Thank you,' I reply.

'What have you been doing?'

I take a slug of scotch and say, 'Food poisoning.'

'How did it go?' she asks me.

'What?' I reply.

'The job interview?'

Shit I think, remembering my reason for the overnight stop.

'Crap,' I say. 'Waste of time. Not nearly enough money and I'd have to relocate to Cambridge.'

'Well, you have had some correspondence,' she says. 'Maybe something here,' and she stands up and goes to the table, returning with some envelopes which she passes to me.

There are three letters from recruitment companies. The sound of east Londoners fighting each other on the TV is too much for me in my delicate state so I say I'm going to check my emails – I'll look at the letters upstairs and go to the office via the kitchen for yet more calming libation.

I open the letters – two promising but immensely dull jobs have come up and they are wondering if I'd like my name put forward for them, one from a large company that I would rather take my own life than consider joining. I can't get my head around any of this right now so I put them to one side.

And fall into a light sleep where I dream of Carolyn as a corpse.

It's a week later, and I've been trying to behave myself, taking gardening leave literally and laying off the booze at least until nine o'clock at night. The letters from the recruitment companies are lying there unanswered and I resolve to do something about them now.

I switch on the PC which I've left untouched for three days and see there are 82 emails awaiting my attention.

Seventy two of them are wondering if I'd like help with premature ejaculation, an extra three inches or an answer to my cesspool problems. Two are from Nigerian émigrés kindly asking me to help dispose of thirty three million dollars that their tragically deceased fathers had salted away. Three are chasers from the recruitment companies.

I answer the latter. I tell them how passionately I'd like to work for these people and would love to pursue the matter.

But my heart is sinking ever lower. I've emailed Carolyn to tell her how sorry I am, what a prick I feel, and she's not replied and I know that in her own mind her humiliation is probably as great as mine. I also know that she isn't going to reply.

And in truth I am sorry, and am trying to appease my own guilt towards her by offering an explanation. I realise I'd built my memory of her up into a grand affair, when in fact all it probably had been was a post-teenage romp. If it was more I wouldn't have dumped her. And to see her in the regalia of her twenty-year-old glory ... well, Miss Faversham springs to mind.

I know now what I should do. I should accept my lot, accept my modicum of talent for the business that has put me where I am, and make the best of it. I need to grow up. My head resolves that I shall snap out of what is probably a minor and temporary depression, and get on with my life which, let's face it, is not that bad. I mean, I'm not ecstatically happy in my life or with myself but who the hell is?

I've even tried talking to Helen – of course I haven't confessed to her about my recent attempt to become 20 again. I know how she'd react – it would be that withering look of pity all over again, and I don't think I could stand that.

I've also tried to talk to the kids but it is apparent from their response that I am from another planet.

No, I resolve to get on with the life that I have chosen for myself, put behind me my longings to be 20 again and, if not exactly try to be a good husband, at least try to avoid further debt through divorce proceedings.

Two weeks and three interviews have passed. I am on the shortlist for two of the jobs, the other I have turned down as it was too lowly and poorly paid for me. Carolyn has not been in touch, and thankfully the memory of that night and the accompanying toe-curling embarrassment are beginning, just slightly, to diminish. But of course, being a recovering addict, I still sneak the occasional glance at old-pals.net out of idle curiosity, and names and images do flood back, chiefly from my Edinburgh youth. It seems from the number of new people signing on virtually daily that I am not alone in my desire to recapture my former years.

I open an email and see that the best job on offer, a senior vice president of marketing for a huge US company, want to see me at the end of the following week – and because the president is a golf freak, he wants to meet at St Andrews. To play a round of golf and talk through a deal. The thought fills me with something approaching horror. As a youth in Edinburgh I played a lot of golf but badly. And subsequent to that I've played a little golf, badly. Don't get me wrong, I can hit the bloody thing, and hit it long, but it is a question of where it ends up and how I stop myself breaking the fucking club over someone's neck through a fit of anger and frustration at my own inability to even slightly master the most irritating game ever invented.

I do not have the temperament for the game. But I think that if I say 'No' then the job, with a fat-ish salary and much travelling, will be snatched away from me.

I email back and arrange to meet him on the first tee of the Old Course at 11am next week.

Which leaves me with a week to kill.

And then it occurs to me. By leaving on Tuesday, I can drive to Teesside, stay for a day in the seat of my adolescent misery for a night, drive to Edinburgh, stay there for two days, get to St Andrews, humiliate myself at golf, drive south and break the journey at my alma mater in the Midlands before heading south for the restart to my life of hopefully wage slavery.

I present the plan to Helen who decides she wants to come with me. 'It'll do us good, a week away.'

I unconvincingly talk her out of it on the grounds of expense (she won't like the kind of economy hotels I'm planning to stay in and would swoon at every opportunity to stay in some country mansion at three hundred quid a night). I tell her I hope to bump into a couple of old friends and visit some pubs I used to frequent in my youth. She'll be bored. She looks at me suspiciously but decides thankfully not to argue.

It is Tuesday afternoon and I am entering Southorpe on Teesside. Twinned with Bhopal, the welcome sign should probably say.

This is a place I have resolutely avoided visiting since I left it to go to university at the age of 18. Just driving up there, passing the delights of York and Ripon and Richmond, and the rolling moorlands, makes me question my sanity.

Teesside gives itself away about 10 miles before you can see it – there is a vulcan haze of smog and chemical fog hanging over it and you wonder why anyone should want to risk their health by visiting it, let alone by living there. And then it gradually unfolds in all its glory, the Transporter bridge and the black river and the shitty council estates, the chemical plants and the old steel refineries. And in-between, endless estates and high-rise flats. Apart from retail parks and faster roads, and of course the multi-million pound new football stadium, little has changed at first sight. Middlesborough was never somewhere we'd go as kids as it was perceived then as too dangerous and depressing. So, I head along the bypass towards the east, with the moors to my right and shite to the left and wonder what I am doing here.

Southorpe looms. It's endless, featureless, low-rise council estates with scraps of recreation land in between; and memories do flood back, of parties and girls and the few friends I had in those days.

I decide first on something approaching a grand tour. I am feeling in the need of a bit of suffering and this is it.

Firstly, I drive into the estate where we lived and sit outside the house I shared with my parents and remember. It's middle-class, middle-income stuff – privet hedge, four-year-old saloon territory. I remember rows with my father, and every weekend trying to get through the hallway at midnight, pissed, without waking my parents upstairs. Fumblings in the dining room with my first girlfriend, with my parents next door watching the 'Black and White Minstrel Show'. The first time I touched bare female breast.

Even now the sound of a banjo and a faux-negro voice can cause trouserly stirrings.

The Saturday jobs and the paper rounds and the bike rides and the walk to school – all of the time trying to fit in, changing my Scottish accent to fit in with the flat, heavy, half-Yorkshire and half-Tyneside gutturals of the other kids. Not to do so was to have the pissed ripped mercilessly from you every time you opened your mouth, from the moment you walked into school to the moment you left.

Christ, the culture shock from Edinburgh, moving to this strange seaside town where I could read in my bedroom from the lights of the oil refinery three miles away. I hated it, I hated everything about it and I hated my parents for taking me there.

I feel the anger building just thinking about it.

I drive off.

Off towards the sea, the Stray where we'd gather on the few summer nights when the North Sea winds weren't freezing your nuts off. Because at 16 I did begin to adapt, and have a social life, and find girls who would go out with the strange, lanky, quiet Scottish kid. I began to do OK, adapted a little and began to tolerate the set-up.

But the place was a cultural time warp. In '76–77, when the rest of the country's youth were rebelling with the rise of punk, we'd still be listening to Deep Purple, Yes, and God forbid, Van der Graaf Generator. This punk nonsense was something generated from down south by a bunch of wankers who wouldn't recognise the delirium of a 20-minute drum solo if it bit them on the arse.

A night out involved visiting one of the trashy night clubs where the girls were brazen and older and I couldn't dance to the disco classics of the time – Donna Summers, or KC and the Sunshine band. Occasionally they'd play 'All Right Now' and I'd join the other saddos who had failed to pull a girl and shake my head and play air guitar like I was the happiest kid on Teesside. I'd get wrecked and walk home, stopping only for chips and scraps and curry sauce.

Up to the High Street, along the sea front with the amusement arcades and ice-cream parlours and stunted pier and shitty cinema. It's as grey as I remember it always being and large container ships are out at sea approaching the Tees for unloading.

I wonder what I am doing here.

I drive to the first school I attended before college, a sixties four-story grammar of some academic repute, where I was dumped on day one and left to get on with it, reduced to following people

I recognised between classrooms because no one had bothered to show me where I was supposed to go. The school is now some community college, the playing fields half-covered in box-like housing, A few kids kick a football around.

This is too fucking depressing. I decide to leave my evening in the lap of the Gods. I will go to what used to be a half-decent hotel all those years back and if the place still has a roof, I will book a room and stay the night. I will get the bitterness of this place out of my system by confronting it head on.

En route I see that a mammoth new supermarket has been built and I decide to stop there to buy some scotch for my room.

As I walk through the brightly lit entrance I am smiled at by some twat in a uniform handing out baskets who should be working in a real industry if they hadn't shut most of them down, and head for the booze aisle.

Where a guy I vaguely recognise is buying beer.

Fuck me, it's Desser. And, apart from a drastically receding hairline and two extra stone, he's not changed at all.

In some ways, Desser was the author of my misery, not through (I think) malice, but simply because he was the class clown, always pulled the most attractive women and was a brilliant mimic. So from day one he captured my Edinburgh accent and used it mercilessly, to the delight of the other kids, to take the piss out of me.

I pretend not to notice him and walk to the spirits section.

He turns round, sees me, and says, 'Fucking 'ell, it's Nelly!'

Now Nelly was my nickname there, due mainly to the fact that my dad had insisted on me turning up for day one at school with a brutal haircut that accentuated my rather large ears – Nelly the fucking elephant. And it stuck, and to be truthful I didn't mind as to have a nickname meant in some way I'd arrived, or at least been noticed.

I feign incomprehension briefly, then say, 'Christ, Desser!' and he sticks out his arm as if I'm a lost brother and shakes my hand vigorously. 'What you doing here?' he asks and I tell him I'm up on business.

'Come for a pint?' he asks, and seems so genuinely pleased to see me that I don't feel I can refuse. I tell him though that I've travelled up from the south and I need to check in to a hotel. We agree to meet at seven in the Crown, an establishment in town that we used to frequent which I remember only from those distant days as always employing busty barmaids.

We shake hands again and I think, maliciously, that I can always change my mind and fuck off to somewhere civilised like Durham for the night instead.

I pay, and head for the hotel which is still standing in somewhat grubby splendour near the station, and yes, they do have a room. I decide bravely against Durham.

I sit in the bath with a plastic tumbler full of scotch and decide that I shall indeed go to the Crown.

It's ten past seven when I get there and I'm wet from the haar that soaks the town. Desser is in the corner nursing a pint and looks genuinely pleased to see me when I walk in. We shake hands again and he goes to the bar returning with a pint of the local bitter.

I light a cigarette and ask him, 'So what you been up to then?'

And he tells me. Left school at 18, job in the steel works for seven years till they closed it down, married Julie (I assume this was the lovely Julie who he was dating when I last saw him), two kids, several affairs the last of which Julie found out about and slung him out of the house the same week that they closed the steel works. He travelled, went to Russia to work and hated it, worked in South Wales and hated it and came back to be near his kids some eight years ago.

'Why?' I ask, to which he says, 'Because I love 'em,' and I smile and say, 'No – why come back to Southorpe?' and he looks at me and says simply,

'Because it's home. There are worse places than Southorpe, you know.'

I'm tempted to ask him to name one but refrain.

He asks about me and I give the potted history, playing up a little the story of my successful international publishing career to counteract the impression that I suspect still lingers with him that I am still some sad big-eared loser.

'So, do you still see the old lot?' I ask, as conversation lags momentarily.

'Aye,' he says, 'in here every Tuesday night – should be here by now,' and I realise with some horror that they are coming tonight and I am trapped. My humiliations will in some way be repeated, of that I am certain.

I buy another round, and chain smoke.

Gradually they begin to turn up. Each says something along the lines of 'Bloody 'ell, it's Nelly,' as they see me sitting there and buy a pint for me. Fat Dave and Treearm and Den and Tubby and Bif and Spack. They seem genuinely, maybe pleased is too strong a word, but at least intrigued to see me.

They are all recognisable despite extra pounds and hair loss and a hard, aged look to their faces. They banter together, and ask me questions and I find out that most married their childhood sweethearts and most are now divorced with kids and living in flats and trying to hold on to their jobs

165

having experienced unemployment about five times each.

'It's family life in the North East, man,' Fat Dave explains. 'All divorced, all with kids who have to think who their dad is.' He looks impressed and not a little incredulous when I tell him of my many happy years of blissful marriage.

It seems Tuesday night – tonight – is boys' night out, and Friday is totty night when they hit the clubs. They still see many of the girls we knew and when questioned I am told of the various disasters that have befallen each of the young lovelies I remember. Divorce, fattening, drugs habits, sexual voracity, they seem to shag each other at regular intervals in an attempt to replicate teenage parties of old.

Then a cry of 'Brett, man!' and I look up with horror to see the fat, drunk carcass of the class superstar wobble in.

Brett Chadwick was a legend. As thick as shit, he was, however, fabulously good looking with pale blue eyes, a lopsided grin and hair that would fall foppishly over his face. He was a shy, quiet boy, but the girls loved him, and he never failed to cop off with some staggering beauty despite – and this hurt – his total lack of intellect or conversation. They fell for him because he was gorgeous and because without doubt he was going to be a professional sportsman.

At rugby he was in a class of his own. When he got the ball, he'd jink and sidestep then run like a gazelle past the opposition. At football, he'd stay out on the wing, collect the ball, and either trick his way past defenders to deliver the perfect cross into the middle, or go straight for goal himself. At tennis he had a sweeping forehand drive that beat all.

This guy interests me, and although it seemed he didn't recognise me – why should he, as I was conscientious second-team fodder who made it into the firsts only when bubonic plague or some such swept through the team? – I want to find out how he's turned from Adonis to arsehole in 25 years.

'So Brett, what you been doing with yourself?' I ask him.

He tells me that he's been laid off from counter duty at Southorpe Post Office after 15 years due to illness.

'Alcoholic,' Desser mouths to me, miming a shaking hand clutching a pint.

'What happened? I thought you had a trial for the Boro?' I ask and he corrects me.

'Na, Leeds. Couldn't hack it.'

'Pisshead,' mouths Fat Dave.

And Brett knocks back his pint, goes to the bar returning with a pint and a chaser, then sits sullenly, staring into space.

If Gillian or Pearl or Allison could see him now.

The rest ignore him. They start to reminisce. How Fat Dave had a fight with Jacko the class psycho and lost. How Jes shagged Heather and Barbara at the same party one after another (news to me and both the girls, probably), but I laugh along with them to show middle-aged solidarity. The time the chemistry block burnt down. The wonders of Miss Burns from the French department and her beautiful be-jeaned bottom that sent the entire class into masturbatory raptures.

I'm getting pissed now and I ask stupidly, 'So why do you lot stay here?' and they look askance and say, 'Because it's home.' As if it is the most obvious answer in the world to the stupidest question. And they shuffle around a bit, and the warmth has gone, and I realise I have blown it a little with them.

'I lived down south for six months,' says Fat Dave, taking a swig of his pint and lighting a cigarette – another point of solidarity, I note, as eight out of ten of us are smoking. 'Couldn't fucking stand it, man. Busy as hell, people so stuck up their own arses. No,' he takes another swig, 'it's a different country down there. Southorpe may be cold and wet, but at least people talk to each other here.'

They all agree and I resist the urge to say, 'You lot didn't talk to me for two years.'

The conversation moves on to who has left and where they are. Gary apparently did get to medical school and works out of one of the big teaching hospitals in London – no one's heard from him for years. And Andy is something in oil and up in Scotland worth a fortune, and Barge is a pharmaceutical salesman in Surrey and doing very nicely indeed. Just about everyone else we can think of from the class is still local but too deformed to meet up with, or disappeared.

A woman walks up to the bar and all heads turn, and conversation stops. Fat Dave suddenly yells about a foot from my ear, 'All poofs can't tap dance!' and to a man the group, overweight, smoking, balancing their pints, start to tap dance clumsily on the carpet. It is a bizarre sight and a funny one, given the apparent concentration and effort they bestow on this weird movement. I'm not sure the word homophobic has reached this part of the world yet.

The dancing ceases as the woman comes over. She's laughing and shaking her head as if to say, 'You daft buggers.'

She's a little overweight and her skirt is too short, her blouse too tight, revealing as it does a not unattractive expanse of bosom. 'You daft buggers,' she says to the group and takes a drag on her cigarette.

'Remember her?' Jes asks, and a vague memory stirs. He puts me out of my misery. 'Barbara. Barbara Edwards.'

'Fuck me,' I say and am transported back to that broom cupboard and the heaviest petting session of my then young life, and I feel an erection growing just at the thought of it.

And she's being paid a lot of attention by what I have come to think of as 'the lads'. I watch as she totters on high heals and feel a sadness that the beautiful young girl I remember has aged so. Not to say she isn't attractive in a ten-pints-of-lager-end-of-the-evening type of way, it's just that she looks old and tired and let down by life.

But then, don't we all?

She glances at me, then talks to Fat Dave – she's obviously asking who I am, because she then smiles at me and walks around the table, flings her arms around me and says, 'Nelly', and kisses me on the lips. She tastes of sweet, cheap alcohol and cigarettes, but the sensation is not unwelcome, nor is the obvious kudos her attentions towards me have caused.

'So you have grown up, love, haven't you?' – same words from Carolyn – and I feel tongue-tied and shy in front of her. 'You were always a nice lad – this lot,' she points dismissively at them, 'were only ever interested in shagging, but you, you were a bit different.'

She asks me about my life and I tell her a little potted history.

'Clever bugger, aren't you?' she says, smiling.

'Not really,' I say. 'Just lucky. What about you?' I ask. 'What have you been doing?'

She tells, me. Pregnant at 19, married at 20, three kids by 24, divorced by 27. Now living with a guy, but it's not working.

'When the kids are off my hands, I want to travel,' she says, finishing her drink, and I look at her and we both know she'll never have the money or the opportunity to travel.

I get a round in, and look at my watch. It is 10.30 and I'm exhausted and pissed – it has been a tiring night reliving my teenage years and given the chance I'd be back at the hotel, but it is and always has been important to prove one's decency by getting a round in. It'll be my last.

Barbara demolishes her Bacardi and coke quickly, kisses me on the cheek and says, 'Always wanted you to fook me – thought you never fancied me,' and gets up to go. She waves at the lads.

'Think you're on there, Nelly,' says Fat Dave.

'We all have been,' laughs Jez.

The evening dies before me. I'm pissed and tired and have smoked too much and the conversation bores me now, and I want to get away.

'We could go clubbing,' says Jes, and they start to make plans and josh each other over failed liaisons.

'Not for me lads,' I say, finishing my pint. 'I'm off to Edinburgh tomorrow – got an early start.'

We shake hands and part, brothers in middle age.

I walk along the main street, which now has a selection of pissed youths and young girls in clothes inappropriate for the damp mist pouring in off the North Sea. I try to walk steadily, aware that a man of my age, bladdered in a place like this, could be licence for a beating. I stand tall, and walk past the clubs, pubs and shops, few of which have changed in 25 years, and feel old and alone.

I think of the guys in the pub, and my initial instinct is to pity them. But why? What have I got to make me feel superior to them? At least they have a social life based on friendship rather than one-upmanship. And OK, Southorpe is the arsehole of the empire without a doubt, but at least it is their arsehole. They belong. I can pity their shallow little disappointed lives – but what right have I to do so? They are no less shallow or disappointed than me.

It's like one of them said – they are comfortable here, they belong. And that matters more than houses with names not numbers, and convertibles and school fees. They are no worse off than I am – most of them are divorced or separated, and never far from losing their jobs – but hey, I can relate to that.

No, as I walk past the Clarendon and the Pig and Whistle and avoid the exodus of drunks and high spirited revellers, I'm struck only by the fact that this place is like lots of places, with people living here who would no more want to live in the South of England than relocate to the Middle East.

Culturally, the north and south are a million miles apart; this is not one United Kingdom, but a thousand disunited areas, each with suspicion of everywhere else.

I'm tempted by the thought of chips, scraps and curry sauce at the chippy we used to use in the old days, but decide that I've travelled far enough down memory lane this evening.

I get back to the hotel, and have a night cap in the bar. The girl serving is friendly enough and I chat to her. She tells me she's at college and doing this job to earn some money for university.

'Where do you want to go?' I ask her, and she smiles and replies,

'As far away from here as possible.'

'There are worse places,' I tell her, sagely, and she replies,

'I've yet to see anywhere worse than this shit hole.'

With that I make my way to my bedroom, and settle down with a large Scotch and the TV remote control.

When there is a knock at the door.

'Who is it ?' I ask.

'Barbara,' comes the reply.

Shit, I think. What to do? I'm in my underpants, I'm tired, I want to sleep, but I'm not a little intrigued and also feel that it must have taken some nerve to come up here, and not a little ingenuity to find me. And where's the harm in letting her in?

'Hold on,' I say, as I pull on my trousers and shirt quickly.

I let her in.

'How did you know where I was staying?' I ask her, as she stops and takes in the room.

'One of the lads told me. And I know the lass at the bar so she told me your room number.' She seems nervous, shy, a little embarrassed. 'Nice room,' she says, looking around her at the chintzy decoration. She glances at the bed.

Oh shit, I think. What do I do now? What am I expected to do? Leap on her? Ask her to leave?

I pull myself together. I am a sophisticated fellow now and easily able to handle this one, I tell myself.

'Can I get you a drink, Barbara?' I ask. 'Tea coffee, whisky, or there's a mini bar.' I go to it and take out various miniatures.

'Brandy, Nelly,' she says, and we both smile. Two middle-aged folk in a hotel bedroom still using a nickname from 25 years ago. 'Sorry, James,' she corrects herself, and sits on the edge of the bed. I pass her the drink. 'Cheers,' she says and we clink glasses. I have a nearly overwhelming desire to sit beside her and kiss her, but somehow it seems wrong, as if I was taking advantage. I sit on the sofa at the other side of the room, take a swig of Scotch and watch her.

'I meant it earlier,' she says. 'About you being a gentleman. In them days it was rare. I was just thick, blonde Barbara with the big tits, and all the rest of them were out for was a casual fuck. But I remember you one night ...'

'The broom cupboard?' I interrupt and she laughs.

'Yes, the broom cupboard. And you touched me and kissed me and I would have let you do anything you liked, but you didn't. You said we weren't ready. I don't think you knew I'd worked my way through half the year already by then.' She takes a swig of brandy. 'I was such a mess. Thought people would like me if I fucked them. Used to get my heart broken once a fucking fortnight. Look at me now. Forty five, three kids who are nowt but trouble, a shit job and a lazy-arsed partner who couldn't care less about me.'

'It goes with the territory,' I say. 'It's normal to be fucked up and to feel you've fucked it all up. But you haven't – no more than anyone else, anyway. It's called life, Barbara.'

'I know, love,' she says, 'I know,' and she finishes her drink, and I finish mine. I refill both glasses. She asks me about my wife, my kids, the house I live in and I tell her as honestly as I can.

'So what are you doing here?' she asks and I reply,

'I've been fucked up for the last few months and blamed the past. I though I could sort it by coming back. Revisiting.'

'And have you?' she asks.

'Of course not,' I say, and we both smile.

I'm now feeling very aroused despite my better judgement – oh to have a brain with more willpower than my gonads. Barbara's skirt shows a lot of thigh and her breasts are bulging – I realise she is probably positioning herself deliberately to accentuate her charms, and I, my friend, am falling for it. Ah those breasts, I think, recollecting their firmness all of those years ago. And she's looking at me and I am gliding towards her and I sit on the bed beside her and I kiss her and I taste the brandy and her tongue finds the inside of my mouth and she falls back on the bed and my hand reaches to her breasts and ... she's crying.

'What's wrong?' I ask her. Then, 'Sorry – I thought you'd wanted it, me ... ' Fucking hell, will nothing simple happen to me again, ever?

'I did,' she said. 'God I did.'

'So why the tears?'

'I just had an image of you waking up beside me in the morning and seeing regret all over your face. They all do these days. Oh, and brandy always makes me cry.'

I realise that's exactly how I would have felt.

'Rubbish,' I say.

'I just want to be wanted, that's all. But you are so nice, such a nice lad still – I just wanted to get back at that bastard at home by spending the night away from him. But if we shag it'll be just like all the others.'

I'm now sick of this confusion. I mean I'm more than fucked up for one person, I feel – I don't need every bloody woman I meet using me as some sort of homespun psychiatrist.

'I'm sorry, you're right. I mean, I still think you are very, very attractive and sexy, but we should stop now. It's not right.'

'Jamie, let me stay the night.'

Oh fuck.

'Barbara,' I say, 'I don't think I could do that.'

'I'll sleep on the sofa,' she says. 'Give that bastard something to think about at home.'

I look at the two-seater sofa and look at Barbara and my chivalry precludes allowing her to sleep there.

'You have the bed,' I say. 'I'll have the sofa.'

'You are lovely,' she says, and kisses me on the cheek. 'You always were.'

She gets up and goes to the bathroom. I pull out a T-shirt from my case and say, 'Use this.'

I search the cupboards for extra bedding and

wonder what the fuck I am doing. I have a horrible suspicion that I may be turning into an honourable man after all. I find a pillow and a somewhat moth-eaten blanket and contemplate the sofa which is exactly half the size I need it to be for me to sleep properly.

Barbara comes out and, I hate to admit it, she looks very sexy in my oversize T-shirt.

She smiles and climbs into bed. I go to the bathroom, and when I come out she appears to be asleep already. I switch off the lights and squeeze myself onto the sofa and pull the blanket round me. I feel like I've been stuffed into a dwarf's coffin.

'Oh come here,' Barbara says through the dark. 'You can't sleep there. Just a bed shared by friends, though?'

With relief I walk around the bed and lie on top of the covers so that she knows I'm not going to jump on her.

'Oh, this is nice,' she says. 'Didn't know a man could be so good to me.'

Then she proceeds to talk to me for most of the night. Every detail of every man she's been with and how she'd been dumped more times than having hot dinners. Of how she always picked men who were bastards. How married men lied their way into her pants. How the big love of her life, her first husband and father of her children had been shagging her best friend two weeks into their marriage. On it pours – I try to make the right noises at the right time, but it is such a torrent, such an endless stream of dreadful happenings, such abuse and deceit and pain that I realise I don't need to do anything except lie there. She's not wanting a response, she's not doing this for my benefit, purely for hers.

But I still can't get to sleep.

Daylight begins to break, so she eventually stops.

And cuddles up to me and whispers in my ear, her hand sliding between my legs, 'You could fuck me now if you want.'

I groan and say, 'Barbara, I have to get some sleep,' and with that my eyes close and I grab two hours of disturbed and disturbing slumber.

I wake up, and see it is eight o'clock. I hear noises from the bathroom and assume Barbara is in there. I recognise I have felt better. I'm tired and post-alcoholically sweaty and I need to visit the loo, and last night is like some surreal dream/nightmare. I want my room back, I want my life back, I want to abandon this madness.

She comes out, dressed in her party clothes. She looks embarrassed, tired and, I have to say, old. She smiles at me and says, 'No regrets then?' And I realise that is one of those questions which it is impossible to answer without causing offence.

'My life is one long regret,' I say, movingly and not a little poetically, and she comes up to me and kisses me hard and rather skilfully and says, 'Next time you are up here, you phone me and we will fuck each others brains out. OK?' She writes a number on a magazine at the desk and leaves, blowing me a kiss.

And I regret being the gentleman already and suspect that this experience will be the start of a new obsession that will find me phoning her in 20 years time ...

I ablute, return to bed for an hour's sleep, smelling Barbara on the bedclothes and resolve never ever to come back to this place again.

# 13

# Sunshine on Leith

OK, not the best song to appear on shuffle for a Hearts fan, but it's a great song anyhow.

I leave after a late breakfast and drive north, relaxing a little when I see Teesside's sprawl in my rear view mirror. I start to look forward to the drive and The Proclaimers in a timely manner announce my approach to the homeland.

It reminds me of my father, this part of the world. Driving back and forward between Edinburgh and Teesside in the early days before they'd found a house to buy and my mother was still living in Edinburgh. We never talked much when we were together at the time – it was mainly observational stuff about the state of the roads and the terrible drivers and how busy the Tyne Tunnel was. He never asked me about school, for example, or about whether I was settling in and making friends. We never had that type of relationship when we talked, but teenage kids, I know so well, are hardly verbose with their parents then or now.

Past Durham, and I decide to go through Newcastle

rather than round the Tyne Tunnel as I want to see the city and view the Angel of the North. It towers spectacularly above the skyline and I appreciate it greatly, not just for its aesthetic beauty but because of the furore it cause when it was built. Tabloid headlines screaming about the waste of money and saying how it would be pulled down for scrap within months by local ne'er-do-wells.

Newcastle sprawls to the right of me as I drive over the river and I want to visit, to see for myself how it has been redeveloped into the fun city of the North; when I lived nearby you'd never dream of visiting for fear of having the crap beaten out of you. But all that's changed apparently – as with most old industrial centres, warehouses have been converted to luxury apartments and fashionable wine bars and the problem families have all been shipped out to modern estates in the suburbs where they can be safely ignored.

But I decide against a trip to the centre. I'm feeling exhausted and hung over and decidedly confused about my response to Barbara. And what the fuck I am doing on this nostalgia fest.

And it is strange, but everything about this journey is full of sentiment. My father died eight years ago, and whilst I missed him greatly at first and wept for my loss, I cannot say that I have thought about him much over the last few years – life has just gone on. But on this journey, so many memories flood back. Of stops for lunch or petrol, of my father's knowledge of the roads and the best places to overtake. Of stopping in a pub south of Coldstream and persuading him to buy me a pint despite the fact that I was two months away from drinking legally. Of the time when we broke down when I was driving and I thought it was my fault.

And I think, I never really knew him. You just end up in, not even growing into, a relationship with your father and he's probably as fucked up and disappointed in his life as you are in yours but because he's your father you don't investigate or question, you just get on with it as he just got on with it.

In this car, driving through places that we'd been together, I feel overwhelmingly sad: not just for the relationship I've lost with him – indeed, never really had with him – but also for the danger of repeating the same with my own kids. I resolve to do something about it.

Then with something of a shock I realise that I cannot under any circumstances imagine my father having spent such an evening as I have just experienced – I feel momentarily that his spectre is beside me in the car, shaking its head reproachfully.

It's the hangover that's making me have such dark thoughts. I stop in a lay-by and hope an hour's sleep will clear it.

I wake 20 minutes later, partially refreshed, turn the music up loud – Ian Dury, The Police – and speed towards Edinburgh. The border country is exquisite: gentle undulating hills, dark volcanic soil, patches of pine forest and stone-built villages. Real countryside.

I pass over the bridge at Coldstream, whooping as I cross the border into Scotland as I used to when I was a child. I stop on the High Street – reminiscent of some straggling cowboy town – for a hot pastie and a milky coffee, buy some cigs and continue on towards the metropolis.

Speeding through the bright sunshine, noting that some bastard appears to have positioned speed cameras every half a mile, I decide to go a tad pastoral in my musical tastes and stick some seventies' Dylan on – bit of *New Morning*, the best and worst of the great man's output and a favourite from the old days. I'd quite like to build me a cabin in Utah, right now, though.

I'm feeling good now. Exorcised. Seeing the lads last night was a tad cathartic – it's mad, but the fact that they seemed pleased to see me and didn't rip the piss from me was kind of reassuring that I'm not a total social misfit. Seeing Barbara, however, was utterly surreal, kind of like Kafka and Buñuel combining to write, and indeed film, one evening of my life. But hey, yet again, I am just about morally intact with only a gentle grope of Barbara's middle aged chest to stain my soul. Even my father's spectre can't condemn me for that, surely?

I am now 20 miles or so from Edinburgh. Down Sutra Hill which has been transformed into some kind of 1950s sci-fi movie set by a wind farm. The turbines glint in the early afternoon sunshine – there's a scary beauty to them. I see the landmarks of the city in the distance: Arthur's Seat, the Castle, then Corstorphine Hill.

Ten miles from Edinburgh – it was ever thus – mist gathers and the blue sky disappears. Through Dalkieth and up the hill the mist turns to soaking haar. Not rain as such – just all pervading dampness, like travelling through a dark cloud. I cross the city bypass with the windscreen wipers trying to shift the wet sheen.

The city has changed even out here. There's a brand, spanking new hospital sitting like a space ship near Craigmillar Castle. New continental- looking developments of apartments – coloured panelling and balconies – have sprung up between the red stone mansions of suburban Edinburgh. Towards the centre, it's more familiar. Tenement blocks, grocers and small, dingy-looking local pubs, old guys shuffling along the road, local hooded neds hanging around on street corners. Then right towards the heart of the city, cutting through the University area towards the Old Town, past Greyfriars and Chamber Street Museum, I start to feel at home. Just a little.

I find my hotel – a way-out-of-my-budget chain just off Lothian Road, built for the conference centre and the Usher Hall, where in my memory just wasteland used to be that was always washed over by the smell of the brewery. Very civilised nowadays, though I note that two minutes up the road seems to be Lap Dance Central. I resolve to walk before meeting my old mate David.

Edinburgh must be my favourite city. It has everything: the splendours of the castle, of the sandstone New Town, of the colossal schools and hospitals built to resemble Loire chateaux. And the surround of hills, the Pentlands, and Salisbury Crags and Arthur's Seat and Carlton Hill. Endless beauty (if you ignore the housing schemes on the outskirts).

It is late-ish afternoon and I walk past the lap dancing joints, up Castle Street to the High Street and head for Grassmarket. I'm damp, and feel part-tourist, part-local. I feel I know the city, but it has changed.

Take Grassmarket. In the old days this was an area you'd go only if you were a down-and-out drunk. But now it's full of fashionable media sorts and their associated watering holes – they'll be telling me Leith's fashionable now – and I'm looking for a Tapas bar, El Pasos, where I am to meet with David.

David. My first real buddy, two years younger than me; I have known him from when I was seven. He lived in the same road, and we were instant friends. I last saw him 10 years ago when he was working in London for a merchant bank earning a pile, living in Docklands bliss with his utterly gorgeous, fresh-faced Edinburgh wife. Trust me on this, gorgeous she was – I was at their wedding and can clearly be seen dribbling in all the photos.

Truth was David, from the age of about eight, became a figure both of friendship and hatred. He was so bloody fucking indescribably good – at fucking everything. He'd dance around me at football and reduce me to clumsy attempts to foul him in order to get the ball – and he was usually too nimble for me to succeed. But as I was the eldest my word as referee stood, so his shins when I could catch the bastard were black and blue and he had no recourse, absolutely rightly in my opinion, to the law. He could hit a golf ball long and straight, he was in the firsts for rugby and played tennis for Edinburgh. He was offered places at Oxford *and* Cambridge. He went to St Andrews for the golf (he made it to the Scottish Junior Championship and there was talk about him turning pro) after stunning Highers. He was tall and good looking, his dark complexion and blue eyes an unusual enough combination to attract the attention of most women.

And to cap it all, he was and undoubtedly still is, a thoroughly nice, pleasant and charming fellow.

Makes you fucking puke – he must have a flaw somewhere, surely?

Is it really just me and those I contaminate with friendship that have these relationships based ultimately on testosterone-fuelled rivalry? Seems everyone I know wants to be bigger, better, best – around me, anyhow.

Anyhow, I'm here to meet the saintly David.

I find the tapas joint and take a seat at the bar. I order a large glass of house Rioja and wait. I'm 10 minutes early.

I look around me and realise that this could be London. Hardly a Scottish accent can be heard. It seems full of media people and publishers and vaguely glamorous men and woman. Twenty years back this place would have been a fleapit full of drunks. Now it's all smoked glass tables, cool Latino jazz and not a pint of Heavy in sight. I know which I prefer – for fuck's sake, you even have to stand out on the pavement to smoke these days.

David's now 10 minutes late. As I am ordering another glass of wine the door opens. David comes in, sees me, his whole face a happy smile. He strides across the floor with his hand outstretched.

'Jamie!' he yells. 'Good to see you!'

The hand then drops and he hugs me. I hug back

awkwardly – same-sex hugging never having been a strong point of mine (you just feel so dirty afterwards).

During my participation in this display of human warmth, of friendship of old, all I can think as I smile back at him – what the fuck is wrong with me, for God's sake? – is, 'Thank you, Baby Jesus.'

You see, this perfect guy, so clever and sporty and handsome and charming and successful – this paragon, this Adonis is GOING FUCKING BALD! He's an account holder at Tonsures-R-Us.

This is possibly the best thing that has happened to me for days – even better than the brief grope of Barbara's breasts.

I try not to glance at his dome (which I mentally note resembles the roof of the Usher Hall) as he sits down, the hugging thankfully over. A voice in my head tells me never, ever to mention his condition. That would be pathetic, cruel and utterly utterly puerile. I make a solemn, silent vow to myself never ever to do so, no matter the circumstances or indeed the provocation.

My voice blurts out, completely of its own volition, I swear, 'Dave, you're going bald!'

And he just smiles pleasantly and in an unruffled way and says, 'Old age, pal,' and I feel a little childish and pathetic at my actions even though he doesn't seem to care, and I say to try to make things up with him.

'But you are looking great. Not beefed it up like me,' and I slap my belly.

'I work out,' he says, ordering a mineral water. 'And play squash.'

He tells me he was held up on a conference call to New York. 'Bloody Americans,' he says. 'Can't escape them. They have no idea of time differences.'

He's running the Scottish office of a multinational branch of an investment bank.

'Wanted the kids to grow up in Edinburgh,' he tells me. 'Out of the South East. So I've taken a job in the financial backwaters,' he laughs. 'But Edinburgh is a good place for kids to be brought up – as we well know. How are you getting on?'

I tell him. Of the house and the kids and the marriage, dressing it up a little to reduce the down side. I also fail to mention that I am on gardening leave – I do tell him that I'm up for a big job and am being interviewed tomorrow. On a golf course.

'Hope your golf's better than it used to be,' he jokes, in what I consider to be something of a cheap manner – I'm a little disappointed in him for that. A memory of him achieving a hole in one at the age of 10 comes back to me – the bastard always beat me at golf, too.

'So, where are you living?' I ask him.

'Cramond,' he replies.

We grew up near there, and used to cycle down by the river, through the yacht club. Memories of rare hot summers and carefree adventures. I've not been there for years, and have a desire to return.

He's bought, he tells me, one of the large old mansions we used to cycle past all those years back. 'Remember the turreted house on the left?' he asks, 'the one we used to reckon was haunted? Bought that six years ago. For the price of a semi in Hackney.'

'Lucky boy,' I say, remembering the house. In my mind it was a small French chateau – I'd see it from the top of the bus returning from school.

He's also an elder in the Kirk, he tells me. Seems to have swallowed the entire Edinburgh rule book, I note sourly – he's really taken to this growing up lark.

I order more wine. David has more water.

He tells me about his kids. Three of them: 16, 12 and eight. All at the best Edinburgh school money can buy. All uniquely talented in sports, music and academia.

He's still married to Kathlyn, his childhood sweetheart, a prim slim classically beautiful Edinburgh girl who, as I may have mentioned earlier, gave me trouserly stirrings on their wedding day. Daddy was a lawyer and lived in a pile out at Morningside – David made what would have been called a 'good' marriage, given that his folks were working class made good.

We chat on. He no longer follows football, but has

a debenture at Murrayfield, so sees all of Scotland's games, the long-suffering masochistic bastard. 'Any time you want to come up, call me,' he tells me.

I order another wine. I'm getting bored now. I need alcohol, and quite a lot of it, I decide, to dull the feeling.

And then something rather remarkable happens.

A group of six girls come in, mid-twenties, office workers, pretty and noisy and having fun, and David sees them in the mirror behind the bar and what he sees causes him to stop mid-drink of water and choke a little. I look at him to see if he is all right – the colour has drained from his face.

One of the girls, a very pretty, dark woman, tall and slim, comes towards him and without hesitation says, 'You bastard. Where have you been?' – no notion of my presence at all.

He replies awkwardly, 'Alison. Meet my friend Jamie,' and she says in a refined, Mary Erskine voice, again not even looking in my direction, 'Fuck Jamie. Why haven't you called?'

David is trying to regain composure. 'Not here, Alison,' he says. 'I will call you tomorrow. Jamie, I have to go. Squash game.'

I say, anxious for some dirt, 'I'll come with you. Need some fresh air,' and finish the glass of wine in a slug. 'Nice to meet you Alison,' I say, and smile. She ignores me.

'Phone me tomorrow, David,' she says, with not a

little menace in her voice.

Well, well, well, I think. Feet of clay. Size 13 boots belonging to Mr Wedgewood himself, or I am very much mistaken.

We leave the bar.

'Problems?' I say to David casually, as we gather ourselves on the pavement.

'You could say that, Jamie.'

'None of my business, but if you want to talk about it ...'

'I haven't really got the time. Just something silly. Last year ...' He tails off, obviously weighing up in his own mind the need to explain with the desire not to have me too curious about his private life.

'It was at a conference. In London,' he says, tentatively. 'I was under pressure at work, and Kathlyn and I hadn't been ... communicating too well.'

I interrupt solicitously, spotting a euphemism when I'm whacked over the head by one.

'David, this is nothing to do with me. We've all got our skeletons.' Though sadly mine are not under thirty and gorgeous – bastard even beats me at that.

'No, it's OK. Let's go for a pint and I'll explain,' and saying that he walks into one of the few real pubs left in the Grass Market. And orders a pint of strong lager.

'Fuck the squash,' he says, quaffing the liquid like a true pro. Bet he can't beat me at that, though.

'Alison was there, too. We got pissed together. I

knew that she liked me, but things just kind of got out of hand. Ended up in bed.'

'As one does,' I say, to give the impression that I often end up in bed with beautiful women 20 years younger than me.

'It was, Jamie, explosive,' he states emphatically

'I can imagine,' I say, trying not to.

'Screwed me up big time. I mean, when we woke the next morning ... '

'After having one for luck?' I ask and he smiles.

'We agreed that it shouldn't have happened. That it was wrong. That it wouldn't happen again. And we stuck to it for all of three weeks. I just couldn't stop thinking about her, and she made it pretty clear how she felt about me, too. But then I was working late, and she was there, and we just ended up ripping each others clothes off – in my office, for Christ's sake. Do you know how erotic that is, Jamie?' he asked.

I wasn't sure of the question – did I know how erotic it was to have my clothes ripped off by David in his office, to which the answer is obviously an emphatic 'no' – the very thought. But I don't think that's what he was meaning.

'And it went on, once, twice a week if we could manage it. I was mad for her. Honestly, Jamie, I never experienced anything like it before. Mad, mad passion ... '

Another mouthful and his pint is gone. I order

another.

'So, what happened? Kathlyn found out?' I say, passing him the drink.

'Yep. Stupid really. Message on my mobile phone came through from Alison, when I was out in the garden. And Kathlyn read it.'

'You presumably passed it off as a joke?' I ask.

'Couldn't,' he says. 'It was just too graphic.'

'Textual intercourse,' I say, knowledgeably.

'Yup. No, I confessed all. There and then.' Another swig, the pint's half gone. Christ, I think, he can pack it away for a slim guy.

'How did she take it?'

'How do you think?' he answers. 'Went ballistic. Tears, shouting, screaming, swearing ... It was pretty horrible, especially as the kids were in the house. She ended up slinging me out. I checked in to a hotel that night. Felt the end of my world had come.'

'Christ,' I say.

'Yep. Nightmare.' Pint finished. Another one ordered. Beginning to enjoy myself now – it is actually a pleasing experience listening to someone who's life is quite badly fucked up as well.

'Stayed there a week. Tried to sort myself out. Jamie, it was hell. I mean here was a beautiful, young, sexy, vibrant woman, and she wanted me. And yet, I had the kids, a home, an important job ... And what I was doing? I mean, adultery for fuck's sake ... It was unforgivable.' Another long swig on his pint.

'It happens, pal, it happens,' I say soothingly.

'Well, never to me before. At the end of the week, I decided I had to end it with her. Met up after work with her, and told her.' Swig. 'Most difficult thing I'd ever done in my life. We were both in tears ... And I went back to Kathlyn, and begged her to forgive me. Begged.' Swig. 'She took me back, albeit sleeping in the guest room. And insisted on discussing it with the minister. And getting counselling.'

'So she put you through the ringer?'

'And some,' he says. 'She was so cold. Didn't trust me to go to the paper shop on my own.'

'And Alison?' I ask

'She was great. She stayed away. She even changed jobs to avoid temptation. Saw her once in Jenner's with a guy – she didn't see me. And I tried at home, Christ I tried ...'

Another pint finished. Another ordered. I'm struggling to keep up here. Bastard beating me on my home ground.

'I moved back into the marital bed, but nothing happened there. She wouldn't let me near her. Fuck. It was awful.'

I look at him as he is talking, and the guy is in so much pain. It hurts, just seeing how miserable he is.

'So what was tonight about?'

'Two weeks back. Conference in Glasgow, and I

had to stay over. You know, dinner with clients. And I was just going up in the lift at the hotel, when Alison appeared. The lift door closed and we just fell on each other. It was drink fuelled desire,' he states, swigging. 'Woke the next morning and felt so ashamed, Jamie, I couldn't believe that I'd been through so much pain and all my good work was undone.'

'It's understandable,' I tell him sagely. 'Kathlyn cannot punish you for the rest of your life. Did you tell her what had happened?'

'Christ, no,' he says firmly. 'I knew it was a stupid, stupid thing to have done. So Alison and I parted that morning, and I told her I'd ring her ... and I couldn't. Didn't. I am a bastard. That's why she was so angry. Quite right too.'

I start to say something soothing and he cuts across me:

'I just destroy everyone around me. Chaser?'

I got to bed at four in the morning very, very drunk. The night had worn on, we'd stayed in the pub, then wandered up through the Old Town. I have recollections of some lap-dancing joint that David took me to, then a nightclub, but I was well out of it. And tired from the endless confessions.

It is nine o'clock in the morning and I feel lousy. I breakfast on bacon, eggs and a gallon of coffee to try to make myself feel human again. I need to work this hangover off somehow – I have another day of *temps perdu* to endure. A sucker for punishment.

As it is a pleasant late spring day, I decide to walk. I go down Lothian Road and end up at the Dean Bridge. I'm starting to feel a little like a local again. It's the small details that flood back. The yellow halogen street lamps. The noise of car wheels on the cobbles. The sandstone kerbs. Maroon buses. The stubs of metal embedded in garden walls where the railings were collected for armaments some 60 years ago. It all comes back. So what if there are new flats everywhere and unrecognisable affluence? Still my town – it's the closest place I have to feeling at home.

Over the Dean Bridge, remembering school swimming trips at Drumscheugh Baths. A memory of my first introduction to publishing entrepreneurship: Big Ally, selling nudey pictures individually, carefully cut from his elder brother's porn magazine collection. Think of the margin ... I remember a particularly unpleasant detention earned for playing cards in the back row of St Mary's when I should have been listening to the Founder's Day speech. I remember the trauma of haircuts with my father when I came out looking like GI Joe.

Am I having a breakdown? Every memory seems to be flooding back. Of shopping trips with my parents. Of games of football. Of bike rides. Of slights and hurts and insults and fights and fancies.

Of being headbutted by a gadgey (as the vernacular was in those days) at a bus stop. And my father's response – shock at the method of attack rather than how much it had hurt.

I walk into the school where I spent nine good years. It's a sandstone Victorian chateau set back from the main road fronted by huge rectangular lawns. I am 15 minutes early for my appointment so I walk around the grounds. There's been new build here, too. A sports centre, and swimming pool in one corner. A new junior block. A couple of tennis courts. Apart from that, it all seems remarkably the same only the scale is not as grand as my memory recalls.

I circumnavigate and end up back at the main entrance and reception. I enter and ask for Mr Haddon, the Headmaster.

It seemed like a great wheeze at the time. I had phoned and asked for a tour of the school as I'm apparently relocating from the South, or so I had told them. Only way to get into the place these days and a wee white lie won't matter that much. The absence of my children is something of an oversight. I sit in a reception area (new since my day) adorned with achievement. Photographs of smiling children under captions 'Year 12 trip to Vietnam', or Peru or Thailand. For Christ's sake, when I was there a coach trip to Burntisland was an adventure.

I pick up the brochure. More success. Under-15 rugby champions. Tennis doubles, badminton, cross-country, rowing ... everything. Except football of course, which is way too common. The offspring of the rich of Edinburgh are a talented sporty lot. And those that aren't are all musical prodigies: winners of piano, trumpet, violin, oboe, cello, glockenspiel – you fucking name it – recitals adorn the pages. Then there are the exam results. Stunning. Top 10 at all levels in the country.

I'm feeling rather pleased that I haven't brought my dullard children along with me to sully the good name of the family. Certainly it's all changed since my day when a kid was recognised as talented because they could piss higher up a wall or gob further than anyone else – and that was just the girls. But then they didn't advertise that in reception, either.

'Mr Gallagher?' a voice asks, stirring me from my recollections. I look up and see the sharpest-dressed, best-groomed guy I've seen for months. Immaculate Armani suit, Boss (I'm guessing) tie. Slim polished Churchills. Smooth, closely-shaved skin. Perfect hair, fashionably and shortly cut.

'Chris James,' he purrs in perfect Morningside Edinburgh. 'Marketing Director. Welcome.'

Trying to hide my amusement and vague shock that a school has a bloody Marketing Director and one so obviously suited to a career in a financial institution or fashion house, we shake hands. I can vaguely smell subtle aftershave.

He heads outside and we start to walk, following the same route I've just been on.

He tells me a little. Nothing I don't know. Co-ed. 5–18. Top results in Edinburgh. All-round success ethos. Children given the opportunity to excel. 'What about special needs?' I ask, not because I'm interested, more because I want to see how that fits with the success ethic.

'We have a special needs teacher, but I have to be honest and say that we don't encourage parents to send their children here if their children have, er, issues. We're looking more for high-end achievers. Children with, er … problems … get on better at schools which are rather less academically focused, we find.'

He burbles on. We're walking down the main corridor which has changed little since my time. It's adorned by splendid artwork. The bell rings and immaculately dressed and well-behaved children appear.

'First break,' says the mannequin.

I'm here for the Foreign Languages Department. I don't want all this other shit – but I cannot be that obvious. I start what I consider to be an amazing – and I think Hugo Fucking Boss agrees – assessment of my eldest son's supernatural skill at French. I'm in free flow. He's fluent given his mother – my wife – is the grand daughter of Sartre. Or Piaf. Or fucking Halliday – it doesn't really matter. I just feel this insatiable need to – in the vernacular of the time of writing – big the useless little bastard up. Not of course that he could manage a coherent sentence even in English. But still.

This stops our mannequin friend a little in his steps. I explain. 'My son is singularly talented in French, German and Finnish due to the multinational nature of his grandparents. At rugby the All Blacks under 15s' – of course I have no idea if such an organisation exists – 'have an option on him due to his maternal cousin.' I'm just making it up now. I'm in free flow bollocks mode – half-pissed still, I think. I talk so quickly and confidently that I can't be contradicted. This clown has got to me. I could tell him and his Yves St Laurent skin to fuck off, but I need him to guide me through the rest of the school. But I'd really like him to believe that my children are exceptional and beg me to send them here.

'Here's the science block,' he says. 'Built three years ago, there's three million pounds worth of new equip ...' and I've lost it. I tell him,

'It's the language department I want to see, please. Not science – I don't care about science and neither do my children.'

He looks a little startled. 'Mr Gallagher,' he says, 'we believe in a well-rounded education here. Arts and science.'

'It was biology that killed their grandparents,' I say dramatically, and not untruthfully, given one died of lung cancer and the other when a rubber plant fell on her. OK, you've got me. Another lie ... anyhow, I've always distrusted scientists and considered linguists and poets far better for the world than nuclear physicists – hey, am I not the little old hippy, still?

'Listen,' I say, as this prick is causing the escalation of my hangover with his eau de cologne words and soft vowels. 'My son Tarquin is seriously dyslexic and my daughter Chlamydia has only one leg after a tragic landmine incident when on our VSO holiday last year in Angola. Is this the right school for them or not, Mr James?'

I say all of this quickly and deadpan. He looks at me slightly – did he get the girl's name right? – suspiciously, then his professionalism kicks in. 'Well, Mr Gallagher, I think in those extreme circumstances it may not be, er ... appropriate for us to educate your children here. May not be, er ... best for them ...'

'Tarquin plays for the under-16 Kent rugby team and he's only 12 – the All Blacks are awfully cross lest he injures himself. Clammy is a violin virtuoso with a place at the Royal Academy. Their mother is Irna

Brewsky, the ballet star, and I' – here I whisper conspiratorially and wink, engagingly, I believe – 'am about to take a very senior job at the Royal Bank. I'd like to consider a donation ...'

This stops him. 'May we go in here?' I say, recognising the canteen of old. It's now the refectory and the blackboard offers three-course, fresh-cooked menus that put my memory of the stodgy shit they served us up to shame. Thankfully, though, the memory is stirred – the place still smells of custard and disinfectant and vomit. I have a recollection of Andrew Morris – a serial Olympian vomiter, the Mark Spitz of the vomitorium in my day – producing a spectacular plume of puke that bespattered the plates, blazers, hair and trousers of his adjacent classmates way back in 1970. I wonder if the lingering odour is dear Andrew's legacy to his alma mater.

I'm getting bored now. I've nearly seen enough. I want a peak at one more place – my old form room which was high up in a turret in the west of the building. As smarmy bastard waffles and talks about parental contributions, bursaries and Gift Aid, I automatically start heading up the well-remembered stairs. I keep going up to the second floor and stop outside what I recollect to be my old, indeed last in Edinburgh, form room.

'I don't suppose we could poke our heads round the door?' I ask. 'I'd just like to see a little teaching.'

'Of course,' smarm-bouquet says. He knocks twice loudly, turns the handle and opens the door. 'Do excuse us, Mr Morris,' he says, as we walk into the classroom. The children – I guess to be about 12 or 13 years of age – stand as one and drone 'Good Morning, Sir,' as one and sit back down amid the noise of scraping chairs.

I look around as Mr James introduces me, but I'm not listening. Little's changed in truth. Couple of licks of paint over the years and a few new posters but it's pretty much as it was. I feel a little strange at being cast back into this room, these walls that absorbed my breath and farts all those years back, but it's a rational rather than emotional response. I kind of hope for a wave of feeling, a sudden wellspring of understanding about youth and life and getting old and place and time. But nope, it ain't going to happen today anyway.

I then look more closely at Mr Morris, who's looking at me.

'Mr Gallagher? James? We were pupils together, were we not?' he says in immaculate Edinburgh brogue and advances towards me, his hand held out. I realise that it is none other than the 1970 World Vomit Champion, Pukey Morris (as I have just mentally nicknamed him).

What to do? I haven't come here on the grounds that I was a former pupil – I haven't mentioned it. To do so would probably mean formal deportation to one of the awful London FP get togethers that I've never attended but can richly imagine. No one pleasant, moderate, decent, entertaining or indeed, normal would be seen dead at those be-kilted gatherings at swanky London hotels for Burns Suppers or St Andrew's Day. You know the kind of thing: the great and the good of Scotland exiled in England and now running the country – business, financial institutions and the bloody government – dressed in their best Highland outfit whilst living in the Lowlands. Of Guildford and Hertfordshire. Not for me, the gathering of the clan McWank.

So, I deflect. 'Sorry,' I say, 'Must be some mistake. Schooled at Mill Hill. Father was a Scot, admittedly, but he was at Gordonstone. So, must be confusing me with someone else,' using my best posh English accent. It is an opportunity missed, I accept, to have a little fun. I'm sure the assembled class would love to hear of the bile-hurling exploits of their teacher – he may even be persuaded to re-enact some – but I don't want to spend any more time in this particular segment of my past.

'Strange,' he says. 'I'm very good with faces usually. Could have sworn you were my good, dear friend, James.' He turns to the class. 'We both played for the Scottish under-18 team you know, until my injury.' Here he grimaces and touches his leg. 'I thought this gentleman was my dear old friend and sparring partner. But obviously not.'

A wave of relief. No matter how anally retentive, screwed up, dissatisfied, embittered, envious and corrosive I may be, at least I have not had to reinvent myself in front of a classroom of twelve-year-olds. I mean, look at him. He's about 12 stone, three of them around his arse and gut – the only strongly defined muscles obvious are in his left arm and that is doubtless from years of sustained self-abuse. Even the Scottish Rugby Union – which has been at certain times since the War what could only be described as desperate – would draw the line at having this prize tit in one of their shirts, at whatever level.

I've had enough. I shake hands with Mr Morris, bid the kids good morning – suggesting that they check the SRU website for an archive team photo showing Mr Morris sporting the shirt – and leave the classroom. I head downstairs with Mr James gliding beside me. I want out.

'Thank you for your time,' I tell him, cutting across his well-rehearsed closing speech. 'I really am very, very impressed with what I have seen and I'll be in touch shortly, I'm sure. Next step will be to bring Tarquin and Clammy in, I guess. Entrance exams? Sure, no problem. Donation? I shall send a cheque.'

I'm practically jogging down the corridor towards the exit. When we get to reception I flash my finest smile, shake him by the hand, promise him that we'll be in touch as soon as possible, and fuck off out of there very quickly.

I'm sitting having a coffee. It's 11.30. The Castle looms large on the horizon through the coffee shop window. I sip a steaming cappuccino and consider ducking out of my next meeting. Lunch with an old school friend. I'm overdosing on the past but I'm aware that I have to consume as much as my mind will accept so that at the end of this period, I will be sated. I don't want to ever come back here again. So, although lunch with Johnnie will doubtless be tedious, it's probably necessary.

I finish the drink and walk. I cross Princes Street and go down through the gardens and start to climb the Castle Hill. There's a cold wind blowing from the north and it's bloody freezing. Every 50 metres or so I stop, ostensibly to looking back at the city as my ascent gives up a better view, but actually it's to try to capture some air in my lungs before my heart explodes due to physical exertion. I consider a cigarette just for the bravado but I don't think I would have the strength to make the lighter work.

Twenty minutes later I'm up on the High Street. I walk over the Heart of Midlothian which is no longer covered in spittle as it was in the old days – health and safety gone mad, I guess – and decide on a pint and a ciggy. I choose the Deacon Brodie only because I have never been in there before and because it seems to me that the old stories of tomb-robbing and body-snatching help desanitise the city a wee bit. And then of course I have to forgo the bloody ciggy.

Johnnie. He was a lad. A tough kid. Never scared – in a confrontation he did as everyone knew you should: aim a sharp kick to the bollocks or a punch to the nose while the other person is weighing up their approach or options. That way the fight was invariably over in an instant. He stood up to teachers, had a string of one-liners that he seemed to be able to draw on endlessly. He smoked, he drank, he bought porn magazines from newsagents and seemed so self-assured that he was never challenged over his age. He was, at the tender age of 13, the coolest kid in the class, if not the entire soft-as-shite school. Destined, we were convinced, to greatness, possibly of a criminal nature.

I had found his details on Old Pals, and indeed they were sparse. It looked like he'd had a series of dead-end jobs after being expelled from school. I'd be interested to find out for what. But the image I had from the details he provided was that life had kind of passed this once brilliant kid by. So, I have resolved to see him.

I decide against another Heavy as I have to drive this afternoon, and walk towards Chamber Street

Museum, my chosen venue. I suggested the cafeteria at the back on the grounds that if the meeting was excruciating I could eat my pastie, drink my tea and fuck off without having to sit through three courses with him. But also, Chamber Street, or more precisely the Royal Scottish Museum, has many happy memories for me and ranks in Jamie Gallagher's world as a Top Visitor Attraction. I remember as a kid the fascination with the big wooden revolving doors at the entrance, the goldfish and carp in the pools of the main hall, the endless rooms of animals caught in perpetuity by the skills of Victorian taxidermists. I loved the models of the great liners built on the Clyde and the working engines that sprang to life by the simple action of a child's finger onto a button. I queued for hours to see Tutankhamen and Moon Dust. Many happy memories indeed, and if the meeting's a disaster at least the venue won't disappoint. I turn right down Chamber Street and remember that the building has now been enhanced by a new wing. I walk towards Greyfriars deciding to use the new entrance just to get a feel for it.

It's a great building. I love the mixture of the old and the new, the bolting on of a brave architectural vision onto a Victorian building that in itself represents strength, Empire and omniscience. It's rare in this country. While the French stick a glass pyramid inside a seventeenth century royal palace, the British object to virtually any modern building on the grounds that it looks modern.

Anyhow, the museum, new and old, looks fantastic. I resolve to indulge myself a little in the history of Scotland once I have buried the spectre of Johnnie. I walk through to the cafeteria at the back.

Where processed-cheese rolls and pop once were, there are panini and cappuccino, and the place has been decorated in bright modern colours, and even I cannot get grumpy because a café has had a refurb in 30 years. I glance around – it's full of young mums with toddlers and babies and old folk on a day out. No one I could even vaguely recognise as Johnnie. I order a cappuccino and take a seat in the corner from where I can see all incomers.

I gawp, subtly I think, at a pretty dark-haired mum whose voice is pure Morningside and whose two-year-old son Rupert will turn, I predict, to parricide at the age of 20 after years of having the piss ripped out of him because of his name. And no decent legal system would convict him. She ignores me. Par for the course these days, I muse.

I'm beginning to feel a wee bit homesick, which is peculiar, as I thought I'd already established that Edinburgh was my home. But I rationalise that, in the last few weeks of nostalgia-fest, I think I'm homesick for the present. Though fuck knows why I should be.

Thus I sit with my coffee, Sartre-like (although obviously it's no smoking in the museum so my existentialist-philosopher-look-alike act is flawed by the Scottish Parliament, *les salauds*).

In comes from the street entrance a bedraggled, greasy-looking guy. You'd imagine he's sleeping rough – his clothes have a sheen of dirt about them, he looks like he's been to Halfords for his hair gel. He has a thick stubble on his face and his eyes have a slightly mad, staring quality to them. Of course, they alight on me and I realise with a sinking feeling that obviously this complete bampot is Johnnie. I've opted to spend time with an itinerant madman. He walks towards me – I stand to shake his hand, but he ignores the gesture and sits down in front of me. I take my place again as he says, simply, 'Jamie.'

'Johnnie' I repost.

'Jamie, you've no idea how good it is to see you, pal. No idea at all. When I got your email, I was delighted. Kind of kismet, ya ken? I wuz thinkin', I need a break. Need a stroke a luck. And up you pop, pal.'

All this is delivered in a colloquial but rather refined Edinburgh accent with the occasional working-class bon mot thrown in. I can't work out if the juxtaposition is deliberate.

He continues. 'Ya see, I think you can help me. You're an educated guy, you're in London and you're in publishing.' He's obviously read my brief biography online and seems impressed. 'I'm getting nowhere fast on my own. Rejection slip after rejection slip. The bastards don't even fuckin' read it, I reckon. I mean, how you meant to get started these days? Eh?'

With that he gets out a pile of paper from his inside jacket. 'This, Jamie, is my life's work here. Twenty years' worth. Twenty fuckin' years. And you can help me.' He pushes the papers over the desk towards me.

'Coffee?' I say, stalling, and get up to order him a cappuccino. As I queue I reflect simply that he's not dangerous, that all I need to do is to spend 20 minutes with him and then make my excuses and sprint like fuck to the nearest taxi rank and escape.

I take the coffee back to him and he starts talking again. 'Honest pal, this needs your help. Needs someone well connected like you ...'

'What's it about?' I ask, if only just to progress the conversation a little. He's scaring me a bit as I don't know what he'll do when I tell him I don't work in fiction and that even if I did I can't do anything with the literary ramblings of a mad hobo. 'Think the *Aeneid*, think the *Iliad*, son,' he says, leaning forward and I perk up, my shit classical education snobbery kicking in. 'This is an update. For Aeneas, we've got a second-generation Scot, based in the USA who comes back to Scotland to re-establish the kingdom.

His father's killed by terrorists and he meets a chick in Greenock who burns herself to death when he leaves.'

Oh fuck, he knows the *Aeneid* inside out and he's transposing the entire story to 1990s Scotland and sitting there and telling me about it word for word. I try to stop him.

'Great stuff Johnnie. No, really ... very interesting.' He tries to go on with the account of Kenneth's visit to the underworld but I fear for my safety. 'No, really,' I say. 'Don't spoil it. I'll take it – sounds brilliant. Can't guarantee anything, not my field Johnnie, but it sounds brilliant. Done anything else, or is this your first?'

At which point he regales me with his entire back catalogue. Short stories – Icarus and Daedalus transposed to Prestwich airport. Theseus and the Minotaur set in the Gyle Shopping Centre. And then the big projects – the *Aeneid* obviously, but Caesar's *Gallic Wars* at Tynecastle (God bless him) and Ovid's *Metamorphoses* set on a putting green in North Berwick.

The guy has become obsessed. It's his life's work. I ask him how he lives. He tells me: part-time work, spells in pubs, a few years on the rigs.

'I left that shithole of a school at 16 before the bastards threw me out. Only thing I liked was fighting and Latin. I left. Worked in a shop and studied the language properly. Travelled to Italy, spent time in

Rome and Pompeii and Calabria. Then visited all the major sites in Europe. All the time writing, all the time trying to make the beauty of the literature relevant. Working all the time. Don't care about the money. Just want others to enjoy the beauty.'

I realise he's harmless. And passionate. And doubtless barking mad – certainly two centurions short of a cohort.

'Listen Johnnie,' I say. 'I think what you're doing is brilliant.' I'm looking him straight in the eye, I have my Mr Sincerity hat on but – God damn it – I realise I partly mean it. 'You've got to keep going pal,' and here I touch him on the shoulder. 'Because you mean it.' We both nod. 'Now, I can't promise anything. You know what the publishing world's like. All celeb diets and fuckwit footballer biogs. True art – what you're trying to produce, unique work – could well just be ignored. In truth, it probably will be.'

'I'm working on Catullus transcribed to Barlinnie,' he counters, and I'm tempted to exclaim, 'Why didn't you tell me that before, that's got BESTSELLER tattooed all across it!' but in the face of madness I restrain myself.

'I'll try,' I say. 'I really will. But I have to go now. I've got your email address,' I say, rising from the chair. 'I'll be in touch.' I stick my hand out to shake his. I need to get away – I do genuinely admire his perseverance and unconventionality and in some way his different take on life, but I need to leave. Now.

'One last thing, pal,' he says. 'Can you lend me a hundred quid? Landlord's threatening to evict me. The bastard.'

I part from Johnnie at last, beside an RBS hole in the wall, considering my hundred pounds to be just about worth getting rid of the mad bastard. We shake hands, he promises me that this is just an advance against the advance that I am mystically going to achieve for him. Once I establish which way he's heading, I walk in the opposite direction.

Which fortunately takes me back towards the High Street and, carefully ignoring the Heart lest someone's deposited their TB-ridden phlegm on it, I am back shortly at the hotel car park and ready to leave the city. With just one more stop-off.

The area where I was brought up was a perfect environment for a child. On one side a long street of houses, on the other fields with woods at either end and old railway bridges from the time suburban Edinburgh was serviced by trains. Here I had what, when I think of it fleetingly, was an idyllic childhood, but now, as I drive towards it and specific memories – of fights and arguments, and new kids arriving disrupting the status quo – I now think of it as being a fairly normal upbringing. The usual fun and laughter interspersed with the usual teen and preteen angst. All of which contributes to post-teen, thirties and middle-aged angst, I guess.

I haven't been here for some 30 years being, prior to the events of the last month or so, pretty much a *carpe diem* sort of a guy (oh fuck, whatever neo-classical disease Johnie's got, I think he's passed it on to me).

My folks died a few years back, my Dad first then my mother quickly after from grief, and I've had no real cause to return. I guess up until recently I'd have seen such a visit as purely maudlin.

So that's where I'm heading, out towards the west of the city for the last Edinburgh hurrah before leaving town and on to new horizons.

I think of Johnnie and admire him a wee bit. Perhaps he is a great poet – who am I to say? He's obviously as mad as a drawer full of halibut, but there's a hippy purity about him and I resolve to try to do something with his magnum opus if only to try to recoup my hundred quid.

I pass once-familiar streets, and memories – of exchanges, of insults on buses or smoking surreptitious cigarettes, or bike rides or streets where friends used to live – the whole fucking city seems to be conspiring to absolutely do my head in.

I turn right through Davidson's Mains. The chippy's still there, with kids in school uniform queuing three deep out the door desperate for their traditional Scottish light luncheon of chips and more chips. There's the undertakers that looked after my ma and pa. The supermarket's been re-branded, there are new flats where the railway used to be and the Italian ice-cream shop is now a deli, but apart from that, it's pretty much the same as it ever was.

I head towards the sea and Cramond. The view across the Firth of Forth is still spectacular, with Cramond Island and the Fife Coast clearly visible in the early afternoon sunshine. Down the hill, round the corner along Gamekeeper's Lane, with its impossibly expensive beautiful town houses (didn't Johnnie's folks stay down here?) Nothing's changed apart from one generation or so of Edinburgh respectability. I'm sure these houses are now owned by financiers and footballers, whereas in my day it would have been lawyers and doctors, but the feeling of casual, safe wealth is pretty much the same.

Left at the end and there are various new builds and luxury flats where old town houses or woodland once were but in reality little's changed. It's still very familiar from the days when we'd cycle all over the area and I don't know why I'm surprised – the passing of 30 years can sometimes be covered in three lines of a history book.

I pass what I take to be David's semi-baronial pile and wonder quite how that is going to pan out.

And so, I pass the mock-Tudor splendour of the golf club. The shops have changed – a convenience store and Chinese takeaway having replaced a bakers and a boozer. I turn left again and head towards my street, past the place where I found a ten shilling note in a hedge (my parents insisted I hand it in to the police and that I swear was the last I saw of that), and around the corner where once was the power station.

This was a dangerous, eerie place full of deep pools and crumbling concrete. It was fenced off and being rather wimpy middle-class kids we only broke in occasionally. It stank, I remember, and always seemed sinister and full of strange shadows – I used to pretend with the rest of the guys that I was impervious to fear or the dark atmosphere of the place, but I was always secretly relieved to leave it.

The ground has now been flattened and a development of retirement flats has been build in a leafy surround.

The road emerges in front of me. 'My' side of the street is the same. Same houses, perhaps now extended, same clipped lawns and hedges. The other side of the street, where the field was, where – to quote from a particularly shit song popular at the time – we 'skinned our hearts and skinned our knees', is unrecognisable. Executive houses tower over the road, all brick driveways and 4x4s. Whoever's built them has been careful to ensure that architecturally they are all different – with the effect that they are all the fucking same.

I'm sad and I'm angry. I park up outside our old house, barely glancing at it, more concerned that the beech tree that we played under and climbed (well I didn't, but guess what? – David was really brilliant at climbing trees) – our, no my, beech tree is in some arsewipe financier's garden. He owns it, I guess, and I bet he curses it daily as birds sit and shit on his Seven Series and autumn's a nightmare with leaves falling.

I secretly pray for a colony of albatross to take up residence.

The houses, like some upper-class suburban planner's Coronation Street pastiche, stretch up the hill side by side for as far as the eye can see.

Bad move coming here, big boy, I reflect, and I turn to look at the house I lived in.

It's small and unprepossessing, '60s box design with a large front window, small front garden – pretty much as I remember it. It's looking a bit dilapidated now, as if in need of a lick of paint. I can see my bedroom window and wonder if the walls were stripped you'd still find the remnants of *Thunderbirds* wall paper, the application of which nearly drove my father to first, divorce and secondly, to a stroke.

The front room. I remember the fug of fags from my dad's chain-smoking, the kitchen windows steamed up with condensation from home baking or stews or roasts. It was safe. You knew where you were. Although there were few moments of parental induced elation, and money was not in abundance and had it been it would have been sensibly saved rather than squandered, my parents did a very good job at being parents. I don't think I realised that before.

That's because they kept their distance. Not aloof exactly, more restrained. Sure, you'd get hugs and kisses when you need them but without the EU hug mound and kiss lake that is deemed to be necessary for modern parenting. Dad was Dad. He was older and wiser and had absolutely no intention of, or interest in, engaging with me on a cultural level. The music I listened to was to him incomprehensible and loud, the language I used slovenly and the books I read, once I'd finished the acceptable boy's classics, incomprehensible.

And my mother – her main focus was my dad. I was secondary – Dad worked, she didn't, so he had to be looked after and fed and when he came back from working Saturday mornings – as he did in those days – he was not to be disturbed in front of a black and white television broadcasting *Grandstand* all afternoon whilst he chain-smoked. I never resented it, I don't today. They did what they thought was right, they did as their parents did.

The best thing about them – and I think most of the other parents in the street – was that they truly were a different generation. They might take their boy to watch the rugby or a latest Disney, but that was it. Had the iPod been invented they wouldn't have dreamed of sharing playlists. They were wise, old, in the main fair, and you knew where you were with them. They rarely rowed (except over *Thunderbirds* wallpaper) and best of all, to my young mind, they absolutely 100 per cent had Life Sorted Out. No angst, no middle-life wobbles, no depressions, no longing, no sense of better life missed. Just solid respectability and a sense of purpose. They were your parents, for fuck's sake.

What went on their dreams, I have no idea – it wasn't discussed. They must have made love together but waited until I was asleep as I have no recollection of amatory disturbances.

The line was clearly drawn between parent and child. They were enormously good at being adults.

And as a kid, your expectations were lower. You occasionally went abroad to France, but it was all costed out and you stayed in pre-booked budget hotels and you had your pocket money to spend and when it was gone, that was it – there was no more. You rarely went out to eat in restaurants. Dad's cars (Mum didn't drive) used to last five years and were nothing if not functional.

As for presents at Christmas and birthday, well, you had one big gift and that was it. Not the myriad of sacks containing must-have toys and computer games and TVs and iPods and all the paraphernalia that goes into Christmas and birthdays nowadays. Simple. A present or two – and no near-suicidal parents trying to pay off their credit-card bills for the rest of the year before the spendfest starts again.

And birthday parties – well you've got me on a theme now, dear reader – pass that soapbox and listen. When I was a kid you'd have mates round for a game of football, or maybe to see a film, then they'd all crowd into the kitchen where sandwiches and lemonade would go down a treat. Simple stuff. Nowadays the children's party is a competitive business. One child has a themed pirate party in the grounds of the familial home, using the swimming pool as a prop – the next hires the Golden Fucking Hind for the day. A coach is hired and they all spend two days in Eurodisney. Top that? 'Dear Tabitha – please come to Charlotte's four days trekking-in-the-foothills-of-the-Himalaya's party ...' Absolutely fucking ridiculous.

But thinking of it, in 1970, when I was ten, the Second World War had finished just 25 years before – half a paragraph in a history book. There was less money and sophistication, and conspicuous consumption was virtually unheard of.

Now every little bastard from a council scheme needs – not wants, needs – two hundred quid trainers despite the fact that he's too fat from a diet of pizza and chips to use them for the purpose for which they've been designed. I mean, what's the point of designer labels if every ne'er-do-well in the country's wearing the same fucking ...

My reverie (you'll be glad to hear) is disturbed by an aggressive tapping on the passenger window of the car. I look up and see an imposing looking woman, her fingers adorned in chunky, folksy rings (hence the sharpness of her knocking) staring at me. I press the button and the window glides open silently.

'Can I help you?' I ask, gathering my composure.

'I was just wondering why you've been sitting outside my house for 20 minutes?' she replies brusquely.

Silly woman. Do I look like a cat burglar (though perhaps cat burglary is now a middle-class occupation in these posh parts of the city)? I'm torn between telling her to fuck off and mind her own business or explaining accurately, pleasantly, and non-confrontationally what I'm doing there – and then telling her to fuck off.

It's then I realise I know her.

She's Mrs Beattie. She lived next door to us. Was into talking Gaelic, country dancing and breeding children with grotesque ginger hair and dressing them in hand-knitted shawls and taking them to Highland games. The father was a sociology professor at the university and hence a bearded leftie in my father's world view.

And here she is, looking like she's single handedly arrested the local paedo.

'I know you,' she says, and I have a split second to drive off or to tell her. Something about her makes me think she's probably taken a note of my number already and a swift escape will doubtless result in an APB for the Lothian plods, so I resign myself to five more minutes of swapping memories.

'I'm Jamie Gallagher,' I say. 'Used to live next door.' She smiles for the first time and actually she has a warm and open face, a little lined but hardly changed over the 30 years or so since I last saw it. Home-made oat cakes and cock-a-leeky soup are obviously good for the ageing process.

'James,' she says, delightedly. 'I thought I recognised you. You've hardly changed at all.' Silly, mad woman. 'How are you? What are you doing here? '

I explain I'm up on business and that I thought I'd just have a quick look at the old place.

'You must come in – Kirsty's home.'

I try to protest, blaming a tight schedule, but it's late in the afternoon and having spent 20 minutes daydreaming in the car it's a bit tough to protest pressing engagements. I get out and follow her up the drive to the house and into the front room.

It's an identical house to the one we had, unchanged in 30 years and there's part of me that feels I should go upstairs, change out of my school uniform and go and be ritually humiliated by David on the makeshift football pitch opposite.

I need to get a grip.

I glance around the chaos of their front room while Mrs Beattie goes into the kitchen to put the kettle on. There are tapestries on the wall of glens and crofts and lochs. There's a piano taking up half the living room and a cello, its bow discarded on the floor beside it. Everywhere is covered with reading matter – books, magazines (not a celeb one in sight), journals and newspapers are in precarious piles everywhere.

And I notice there's no television.

This is what happens to hippies when they reach 70. It's rather nice, this free-form chaos in amongst the perfect homes and gardens of the interlopers opposite.

I take a seat and Mrs Beattie appears. 'Kirsty will be through in a minute. She's home temporarily,' she says in a Tannochbrae accent I hadn't picked up on before.

Kirsty. I remember out of nowhere a fact. Kirsty

Beattie was responsible for the first erection I ever had out of doors and away from the more saucy of the bra adverts in my mother's weekly magazines. We used to play together, picking wild raspberries and strawberries in the fields at the top of the hill that are doubtless now home to busy young executives and their bimbo wives. She was a mate, forming an innocent cusp-of-adolescence friendship one summer when suddenly, out of the blue, when our hands touched as we both reached for the same berry, there it was. A bulge in my shorts that made me blush – in fact, it still makes me blush.

I don't think she noticed and if she had I wasn't sure if she'd know what it was. But I was mortified and turned my back slightly to try to hide its prominence from her.

My eleven-year-old penis obviously had a teasing, blackly comedic personality. The more I tried to distract myself, deliberately brushing against nettles or scraping my hands against briers, the firmer it stood out, proud and tall, my body's tribute to Arthur's Seat. It wouldn't go away. I smacked it and squeezed it when Kirsty wasn't looking. I felt in a moment of bleakness that I was stuck with it for ever. I dreaded shopping for a school uniform, the scrum at rugby and the subsequent communal bathing ritual – and as for riding my bike ...

I was wearing a Hearts shirt and I surreptitiously

stretched it as far as possible over the tumescence. Short-term that would have to do, I thought – long-term it'll probably be down the Western General for surgery. Now to get away.

'Erm, Kirsty,' I said over my shoulder, 'I think I'd better get home for my tea now. OK?' and with that I began to walk out of the woods in the direction of the house. My penis was beside itself with happiness now and seemed to sprout extra inches, while the mere function of trying to walk without being doubled over brought tears to my eyes.

I made it home without, I think, Kirsty knowing what was up. That something was up was obvious. Where before we'd amble, chatting, comfortable beside each other, now I was attempting to stride forward always three feet ahead of her, occasionally glancing back over my shoulder to check she was still there, my back protecting her from the awful sudden deformity that had sprung out of me – some perverted Pinnochio.

'Bye,' I had said over my shoulder, going up my path, walking sideways hoping that I wouldn't be responsible for shocking to death the old biddy next door as she pruned her roses.

It took an hour for me to be able to return to polite society.

Kirsty appears and I get up, unsure whether to

shake hands or kiss her.

'Kirsty!' I say. 'How lovely to see you,' and I go for the latter option.

I look at her as we sit down. She has the same face as I remember her mother having some 30 years ago. Not pretty, but striking, her blue eyes contrasting with her greying red hair which is pulled back off her face. Early wrinkles abound. She's dressed in post-hippy garb that does little to flatter an unpromising middle-aged body.

She looks deadpan at me, no smile, no sign that hey, it may just be fun to spend some time with someone you've last seen some 30 years back. She sits awkwardly in the chair as her mother starts to twitter on about how everyone in the street thought there was a 'wee romance' going on between the two of us way back when. I'm tempted to tell my tumescence story simply to shut her up but decide, probably wisely, to desist. But I do need to shut her up so I say casually, cutting across some reminiscence of a 1972 bonfire party,

'What do you do now then Kirsty?'

She looks at me as if I am something a tramp has just puked up.

'Kirsty's in the theatre,' says Mrs Beattie. 'In Manchester.'

'What do you do?' I ask, wondering how this sullen, sulky woman could be the same person whose warmth and loveliness had produced that monster adolescent hard-on all those years back. Christ she's hard work. I thought I was rude – I am, but a mere amateur compared to her.

'She's a director – very highly regarded,' chips in mum at which suddenly there's an ear splitting bellow from Kirsty as she yells,

'For fuck's sake mother will you give it a rest? It's a shitty little company that no one's ever heard of that puts on plays by writers no one else wants, that are seen by people desperate to be avant garde but who wouldn't recognise true avant garde art if popped up and bit them on the tits.'

I'm warming to the woman – a class act – but at that outburst she gets up and runs upstairs.

There's an unsurprising embarrassing moment during which I weigh up my options. I could feign disgust at the language and try to escape on the basis of offence, but Mrs Beattie's on her feet already saying, 'I'll just get the tea,' which she does quickly, bringing a teapot, some cups and a jug of milk back with her on a tray.

'Kirsty's been under some strain recently dear,' she says conspiratorially. '*Affaires de coeurs* I believe.'

'Oh?' I say.

'Yes. She seems to have fallen big time for one of her actor friends. Seems that they were very close.' She stirs the tea and starts to pour. 'Very close. And her partner found out and threw her out. Refused to let her see the children.'

'Poor girl,' I say.

'Yes. But it gets worse. Turns out the actor's married and has absolutely no intention of running off into the sunset with poor Kirsty. So it's not a very happy place at the moment. I thought you may have cheered her up, that perhaps you could have gone out together. You know – gone out for a drink or something. Taken her out of herself for a while.'

'What would the neighbours have said?' I ask her, mock seriously.

'That we were right all those years ago.' She laughs. 'Do you have children, James?' she asks.

And I tell her all about my dear offspring, making a rather impassioned speech, I feel, about how they are my very reason for living.

'Some advice,' she says, perhaps spotting my rampant, flood-tide bullshit. 'Do what you can with them, but don't set yourself impossible expectations. The truth is – whatever you do for them, however much time and care and love you give them, it's ultimately in their own hands whether they succeed or fail. I'm only glad Bill isn't around to see her so unhappy.'

Bill – Mr Beattie as I recall. 'I'm sorry to ask, but what happened to Mr Beattie?' I say delicately, wondering if it was cancer or heart problems that got him – he was a big guy, I recollect, and always seemed to be smoking.

'Oh, he ran off with one of his students years back. Lives in Perth. Australia – not up north.' She smiles. 'He's had nothing to do with Kirsty for about 20 years – barely keeps in touch.'

'I'm sorry,' I say.

'Don't be,' she replies. 'In the modern parlance, he's a total selfish prick,' and we both laugh. 'But I think that's why Kirsty has such disasters with men – it's kind of to get back at her father.'

'I can understand that,' I say. 'And what about ...?' I remember a younger brother with a mass of red hair again, must have been some six years younger than me but I can't remember his bloody name.

'Robert,' she prompts and I nod. 'We don't talk about him I'm afraid.'

'I'm sorry,' I say again. This family is a disaster zone.

'He's in the policy section of the Tory party, the bastard,' she says with venom, while smiling. 'Wants to be an MP. I knew Oxford was a mistake for him. Mixed with the wrong crowd. A child of mine – a Tory. I ask you. Bill has an enormous amount to account for, he really has.'

There's the final nail in the coffin of my 'perfect parenting generation' theory ...

'I have to go,' I say, actually a tad reluctantly. I'm

rather enjoying myself listening to this woman's problems which she faces up to without self-pity or much regret.

'It's been lovely,' I say and she smiles and says, 'You were always a terrible liar, James Gallagher.'

I smile back and kiss her on the cheek.

'Stay in touch,' she says.

'Sure,' I say.

I get in the car and drive off, heading out towards the Road Bridge. It's been quite a couple of days. Edinburgh has not disappointed – it's surprised, disturbed and indeed shocked me a little, but I'm glad I've come back. My parents died here when I had just started working in the South, and after that trauma I'd only been back fleetingly on occasional business trips. I think I now get it – the years of claiming to be a Scot, supporting the national team at everything in fervent opposition to the English when actually for the last 20 years I've sounded Surrey born and bred. I put it down to sheer bloody mindedness – it would have been easier to support England, sing 'Swing Low' and 'Rule Britannia' and get moist-eyed at replays of the glory of '66.

But you can't – it's in your DNA, it's where I belong but not where I will live. Edinburgh's not my city any more, I realise, but it is my home.

And in these days of Europe and unity and no more borders, I love the feeling of being a spy in the camp, of rejoicing when England lose at any sport to any other team – I love the smug smiles being wiped off the chinless upper classes and Volvo-driving middle classes when the rugger team takes a beating and the working-class anguish when the footballers underperform, as they always do. Give me the joy of one amazing, unexpected, Scottish victory every 10 years every time over following a team that a nation thinks has a divine right ('We invented the bloody game') to win at everything.

So I am in no man's land culturally, but I know where I belong.

And Christ knows it would have been easier to follow England, certainly at football. My life has been punctuated by overweening confidence at Scotland's potential to upset the big guys – think Ally's Army in Argentina, and their then debacle against Costa Rica, Zaire, Iran … Think 5–0 at Wembley. So much hope dashed principally through incompetence. And yet I could no more change my affiliations than I could make myself 6 feet 2, blond and hung like a beast of burden.

Well, that's that settled then.

I must get to St Andrew's, try to find a chemist en route for headache tablets and attempt not to make too much of a dick of myself on the golf course.

# 14

# (Just Like) Starting Over

I'm afraid the word dick does not begin to describe what happened yesterday, dear reader. It was a lesson in humiliation right up there with the first time I went skiing and an aerobics session at the local gym when the instructor suggested I had a nasty disease of the central nervous system – both stories for another time, I suspect.

No, this was simply awful.

I had stopped at a roadside hotel for the night and had rested well – I had eaten and drunk frugally and so was virtually without hangover. My instructions had been to meet Mr Womack at the reception of the Old Course Hotel.

I turned up five minutes early, and clapped eyes on Dick Womack, for the first time. He was a short, wiry man with full beard and moustache. His eyes were a little too close together for my liking, giving him the look of a hungry rodent. But he was an athletic rodent – not an ounce of fat and a permatan that suggested constant outdoor sport. He shook hands with me, crushing my hand in his, thus causing an insurmountable sports injury before I'd even started.

'James. Raymond,' he said. 'We can't play the Old Course – it was fully booked. We're on the Strathtyrum course – hope it's challenging enough for you.'

'I'm sure it will be,' I said enthusiastically, thinking that in this wind I'd be lucky to get round the local putting green in under a hundred. 'I have to warn you, I'm a little rusty.'

'You'll be fine James. Just a friendly game. Shall we say just ten bucks a hole?'

It would seem churlish and cheap to refuse – thank God for a strong pound is all I can say.

We changed in the plush locker room, he into a pair of check trousers matching his Jack Nicklaus golfing shirt and Pringle jumper. The highly-polished leather golf shoes, which looked like something you could wear to a society ball, finished the ensemble off nicely. I, on the other hand, struggled to do up the zip and buttons on my slacks. I pulled on an airtex shirt that last saw the light of day 10 years ago when I used (despite my central nervous system problems) to attempt to play squash, an old striped jumper that was two sleeves away from being the consummate tank top, and my old scuffed golf shoes with various studs missing.

I hadn't really thought this one through.

I went back to the car to get my clubs and trolley, which were cobweb-covered from years in the garage, agreeing to meet him near the first tee. My trolley was held together by a large elastic band. The wheels squeaked loudly.

Raymond was waiting for me with a bag the size of a World War One mortar, all leather and designer names, and clubs which shone in the sunlight like surgical instruments.

And off we went.

He teed off first, 230-plus yards straight down the middle. I followed him, and I too went down the middle. Twenty yards.

'Rusty,' I said, as he looked at me with disapproval.

I tried to divert him with shop talk. 'So this job – how does the UK office interact with the US?' and he shot me a look as if I had just accused him of having a sister who had entertained orally the entire US Navy.

'James. Golf,' he said. 'Business afterwards.'

I was chastened.

The next shot I hit went long and far into the horizon. And 120 degrees away from where it should have been, into rough that a dwarf would have perished in. Eight more hacks and I was on the green. And four-putted.

It got worse. Lost balls followed air shots followed scuffs 10 yards along the fairway. It was as if I had never played before. And a hangover I had no idea was there was kicking in – presumably a follow-on from the day before – and I wanted to just be away from there, in a hotel, to sleep and forget about this fucking stupid game with this fucking stupid man and his fucking stupid job.

I cursed foully, initially under my breath but latterly for most of Fife to hear. I mean, surely there is some tribunal that you can go to if you fail to get a job on the grounds of being shit at golf? If I were black, gay and disabled and I was refused all hell would break lose. But simply because I have the hand eye co-ordination of sea anemone meant my best chance of gainful employment was disappearing into the North Sea.

Raymond seemed hardly to notice my distress and heart attack-inducing anger. Head down, he was playing for himself, hitting consistently well, and staying focused.

Eventually it ended. We shook hands on the last green where I had achieved a jammy seven, he a five, and his face at last expressed emotion when it beamed forth a rodenty smile.

'Thank you, James,' he said, 'for taking me around the home of golf.'

'My pleasure,' I replied, resisting the temptation to apologise for playing like a quadruple amputee. I had managed to halve – somehow – two holes, so I was just down by what I felt to be a creditable one hundred and sixty bucks.

We cleaned up, changed and met in the bar afterwards. I wanted to order a litre of scotch, but thinking better of it asked for a pot of tea. He ordered a large whisky. I dug the last fifty pounds I had on me out of my wallet, promising to send on the remainder.

And we then talked about the business and the job. And golf. Then more business and a little golf. And a lot of golf and a little business and then he stood up, thanked me again and said, 'We'll be in touch,' and I was dismissed.

That was it – four hundred fucking miles across the rough landscape of my past for that: four hours of humiliation, a half-hour conversation, and that was it.

I went back to the car bemused, and drove south. Two hours later I checked into a roadside featureless lodge hotel and fell asleep.

I dreamed of attacking Raymond with my pitching wedge.

Early afternoon the next day, after a gentle drive down the motorway, I am in a coffee shop in a town outside Carlisle looking at every woman who enters, wondering if Vicky is going to show as she promised she would by email the day before I left home.

Let me tell you about Vicky.

I shared a flat with her at university for a year and we were in the same English tutorial group for two. She was a perfect natural blonde with a round, not typically pretty, face, and a tendency towards dumpiness. She was brought up in rural Northumberland, and had an incredibly sexy accent. To this day an educated Geordie accent makes me tingle. Indeed, everything about the woman was sexy. One evening after a particularly heavy dope smoking session, she told me of her adolescent sexual adventures in some detail and I went to bed that night with a hard on that lasted most of the night. From then on I longed for her, longed to make love to her, and yet, it never happened. I'd love to say that it was because we were too close as friends, that we respected each other too much, but no, we never got it on together because she didn't find me sexually attractive. And she had two other men in her life.

This sweet, innocent-looking girl was engaged to a guy she'd met in her first year when he was in his second. He looked like a Deep Purple roadie, long greasy hair and a face that when relaxed looked Neanderthal and the rest of the time looked simply simian. I could never understand what she saw in this ill-educated, thick bastard who smelled of oil and roll-ups, but she had agreed to marry him shortly before he had left to take up a teaching post

50 miles away. And she wasn't going to renege on this agreement for me, despite my best, if subtle, endeavours.

Then Steve turned up. Clean looking, well-dressed, cool, confidant, fashionable and popular. I hated the bastard. I hated him even more when I returned to the flat one wet Midlands winter afternoon following a particularly dull lecture on Milton and heard squeals of pleasure and groans of delight from behind her bedroom door, and I assumed she was in the act of ape lovemaking. I tried to do some work on an overdue essay, but the noise just went on and on and in the end I gave up, went to the sitting room, made some tea and turned The Clash up loud to drown the noise.

I was not a little puzzled. When Galen usually visited from his Planet of the Apes, the only noises to be heard were those of the two of them arguing incessantly. I don't think I'd ever heard more than a minute of grunting and then a satisfied exhalation from him. Nothing from her. Not that I made a point of listening, Of course. Often.

But here she was, performing the dubbing for a porn epic.

An hour later all became apparent. Steve appeared looking smug, said 'All right?' and walked out of the flat. Vicky appeared 10 minutes later, looking like what can only be described as 'loved up'.

That night, she didn't return at all, and from then on it seemed they stayed alternative nights in each other's rooms. When it was her turn to entertain him in her room, I'd drink myself stupid and smoke enough dope to fell an army of dope fiends just to ensure that I could sleep through it.

Then one day, John Lennon died and I lived through a Whitehall farce.

They'd been at it most of the bloody night, and I woke at 7am to a monstrous, hideous, hangover as the front door appeared to be being kicked in. I got up blearily and heard Galen himself shouting, 'Vicky! Vicky! Let me in!'

I opened the door slightly and, uncharacteristically for me, peered round and spat at him, 'It's seven o'clock in the fucking morning. What are you doing?'

'Where's Vicky?' he said, trying to see past me in to the flat.

'I think she's swimming, jogging ... playing squash. She's on a fitness kick at the moment. Think I heard her go out half an hour back. She's not here anyhow. Now fuck off,' I said very bravely, once I had shut the door on him. I heard him outside, breathing deeply and waited for him to kick the door down and beat the crap out me. He wasn't the sort of guy you told to fuck off, not if you planned on keeping your head attached to your shoulders. Then I heard him – thank the Lord –running down the stairs and out of the building. I watched him from the living room window as he crossed the courtyard and then, from my bedroom, saw him sprinting across the fields to the sports centre.

I had, I calculated, about 10 minutes before he realised something was wrong – the squash courts opened at eight, I believe – remembered I'd told him to fuck off and decided to return Vicky-less to beat the living crap out of me.

I ran to her door and banged loudly. Nothing. I stated kicking it, hammering on it. 'Vicky, for fuck's sake wake up. Galen ... er ... Ian's here.' Nothing. Christ, perhaps they'd shagged so much they were comatose. By this time, Pete and Joanna, our other flatmates, appeared bleary eyed from their rooms – to be awakened at this time of the day was indeed a sin against nature. I quickly explained what was happening. Pete said he thought he'd heard someone leaving earlier, and he went off to Steve's flat to see if they were there – perhaps the erotic symphony I'd heard had been drug-induced fantasy that evening.

I glanced out of the window and noticed Galen far in the distance heading back towards us. Five minutes.

Pete came back. 'No one there,' he told us.

'They must be in there, then,' I said and walked back towards the bedroom door. I kicked it and hammered it and screamed at the top of my voice:

'Vicky, Steve, he's coming back – get the fuck out of there,' again and again and again. Pete was at the window and yelled 'two minutes', and as he did Vicky's door at last opened and Steve was standing there in his underpants. A waft of sex escaped past him and I saw Vicky in bed, her blonde hair on the pillow and her body partially covered by a sheet and I wanted to push Steve out of the way and barricade myself in there with her.

'Ian – he's here – looking for Vicky,' I blurted out. 'Fuck!' they both said, suddenly scared, and then there was a hammering on the door and we all looked at each with what can only be described as fear.

'Here's Johnny,' I said wittily, anticipating an axe through the door at any moment. Time was frozen.

Then Joanna saved the day. 'In here,' she said to Steve, in a fierce whisper. He looked startled and she exasperated.

'Get all of your stuff out of her room, and get in here, quick,' she commanded. Which he did.

It struck me fleetingly that the good looking bastard would probably end up screwing both my flatmates.

The front door was still being hammered upon, and I sauntered towards it, trying to remain nonchalant. The radio was playing 'Help!' I noticed. I said, 'Who the hell is it?' and was responded to by a flurry of bangs on the door. As I heard Vicky and

Joanna's doors close I opened our front door and saw Ian confused, baffled and exhausted on the step.

'She wasn't there,' he said, pushing past me aggressively.

'Don't fucking push me,' I said bravely (did I mention he was a hard bastard?) whilst shitting myself, but I thought perhaps the minor distraction of him putting me into a coma might buy Vicky some time. Because I genuinely feared for what he would do to her if he found out what she'd been up to.

He marched straight to her bedroom door without even looking at me and banged on it. I put the kettle on and sat down waiting for all hell to break loose.

'Back in the USSR' was next up

I heard Vicky open the door, feigning surprise that Ian was there, and heard a muffled explanation involving sleeping pills – then, thank goodness, she appeared with Galen (the image of sloppy seconds flashed through my mind disturbingly) in the kitchen. He stared at me with hatred, as if I'd caused offence.

'Cup of tea?' I asked, and smiled. 'Imagine' was now playing.

Ian asked her, 'What was he talking about – swimming or squash? At this time?'

Vicky convincingly said she was trying to get fit and lose some weight, then with inspired hypocrisy, she added 'For the wedding.'

There was a silence as I waited for the kettle to boil. 'I am the Walrus' struck up, and they talked about nothing, then 'Strawberry Fields', then a marmoreal (funereal if you must) voice telling us that Lennon had been shot.

What a day. What a gal.


I am on my second cup of coffee and feel I have been stood up. For the second time, I remember. I had planned a meeting with her two years after university and she never showed for that. I smoke another cigarette and vow not to waste my time any longer – she has five more minutes.

After four, a small, dumpy, middle-aged woman in a camel coat and carrying a large shopping basket walks in, smiles shyly at me and walks towards me.

'Sorry I'm late,' she says, sitting down and I look at her with something approaching disbelief. She bears no resemblance whatsoever to the sex kitten of my memory. She looks like everyone's favourite grandmother. She takes off the ridiculous woolly hat she is wearing and that does lose her about 20 years, but still she's just about unrecognisable.

I order her a cup of tea. She seems distracted, not nervous exactly, just as if she's really rather indifferent to the whole situation she finds herself in. And I, I confess, am beginning to regret this arrangement myself.

She talks. She tells me of her child – who's 20 now. The father is Ian – she shows me a picture of a smiling girl who thankfully takes after her mother and doesn't look at all as if she belongs in Whipsnade. She divorced Ian when the child was five.

'Never should have got married,' she says.

'I would not have needed an industrial strength crystal ball to tell you that,' I say. And she smiles.

'I was thinking of the day John Lennon died,' I say and she blushes.

'I can never hear 'Imagine' without remembering it,' she says, a little coldly.

'Me too,' I say.

'I was a bad person then,' she says, sipping her tea.

'You were young – and alive,' I say.

'No – I was cruel and selfish.'

There's a pause. I don't know what to say to her, so I slurp my tea and she twitters on about her life now. She a freelance editor of children's books, and she works on her own in a cottage with cats and dogs and a challenging garden.

'Aren't you lonely?' I ask.

'Are you?' she replies.

'No,' I lie. 'I have lots of friends and family and work.'

'Well, James,' she says, staring me in the eyes. She starts to radiate happiness from her eyes and face and I think she is going to erupt when she says, 'I have Jesus.'

And for the next 20 minutes she tells me how Jesus has changed her life and erased her sins and that she is a clean, new person now, and that if I wanted to I could find peace too, because I am obviously troubled, she tells me. 'I can see it in your eyes.'

I don't argue. I smoke throughout her diatribe as she tells me how she has been born again through Jesus, how he has saved her, how she has been baptised to wash away all of her sins and how actually she always had unhealthy sexual feelings towards me all those years ago and could I forgive her for her impure thoughts?

'Why didn't you say anything?' I say, trying to hide my incredulity. 'Because you were too nice – it would have destroyed our friendship.'

'Oh but what fun we would have had,' I say.

'Ian always thought you and I were lovers,' she smiles, and for the first time she looks a little nearer her forty-something years. 'In fact, during a particularly horrible argument three months into our marriage, I told him that that morning – when John Lennon died – I'd been in bed with you. He said he'd kill you if he ever saw you again.'

'Thanks for that,' I say, hoping that Ian isn't an Old Pals addict. 'But what about Steve?' I say. 'You two always seemed very close.'

'I was a bad person. Steve was a very stupid boy,

but very good-looking – and fantastic in bed,' she said, as if reporting on her dahlias.

That shuts me up. I'm belatedly flattered that she felt attracted to me, but kind of let down, because she made the assumption – very probably correctly – that anything I could offer sackwise would be as nought compared to the Stud that was Steve. Fucking hell, this was nearly 30 years ago, and that knowledge annoys me?

I'm feeling very tired of all of this, and I want to get out of here – a recurring theme during this odyssey, I realise. But now she has grabbed hold of my arm and she's looking at me and she's saying a little bit too loudly for my liking (or indeed the liking of the other coffee shop customers, who have stopped talking to each other and are now looking at the two of us, mouths open in astonishment), 'James, you are unhappy – why did you want to see me after all of this time? Why are you so miserable? Let me help you. Open your heart to Jesus.'

Oh fuck, I think.

'You came here hoping that I'd let you take me, didn't you?' Her voice is rising, getting slightly hysterical. 'You did, didn't you?'

She goes on. 'You thought I was that Jezebel you lusted after all those years ago, didn't you?' Her eyes are those of a mad woman. 'You've the devil in you, James Gallagher. Cast him out!' And with this she stands up, points at me and screams, 'Cast the devil out of your sin-ridden body!'

The good people of the coffee shop are obviously enjoying this – a couple titter – and I get the impression that this will be the highlight of their rurally idyllic year. A soap opera in their local café!

She sits down, breathing deeply and puts her hand on my arm. I pull away from her, take a ten pound note out of my pocket and put it on the table to settle the bill.

I say, 'This is ludicrous. I am going now. Goodbye.'

And as I say this she snatches up the money and holds it in the air and screams, 'See. Satan is trying to buy my body. None of the Devil's currency can buy me back from Jesus!'

And with that she tears the note passionately and throws the bits in the air. They flutter down as she looks at me with the madness in her eyes. The café is silent, until someone stifles a laugh.

I return her gaze. My parsimonious nature makes me consider picking up all the pieces of the tenner, sticking them back in my pocket and reassembling them at a later date with cellotape (bear in mind my recent financial losses, please). But no, that would be foolish. This woman has obviously much more madness inside of her and she's not afraid to use it. I pull out another tenner and pass it to the waitress on the way out.

I walk back to the car – checking I am not being followed. I somehow expect Vicky to swoop down upon me from out of the sky, a feeling that follows me even when I am safely on the motorway, driving south.

# 15

# Tangled up in Blue

I check in to yet another anonymous roadside motel in the late afternoon and lie on the bed drinking red wine and smoking to soothe my ragged nerves. I decide that I had better phone home for the first time in a week.

Cameron (my son) answers the phone, and when he realises it's me and not one of his computer game/ skateboarding cronies, his voice loses all interest.

'Get your mother, will you?' I ask impatiently, after my enquiry about his homework output is met by silence.

As she comes to the phone, I hear her telling the kids to turn down the television. She picks it up. 'Where the hell have you been?' she barks affectionately at me.

She's right to be angry – I have been shamelessly AWOL these last few days. I don't lie exactly, I obfuscate, a word I don't personally think is in usage enough these days.

'I'm heading south now,' I say.

'Where are you staying?' she asks, suspiciously.

'In luxury, of course,' I say looking at the cheap

carpet and lousy autumnal prints of the motel room, 'and snorting cocaine off the taut bellies of Brazilian supermodels.'

She sighs, obviously attempting to resist telling me what she really thinks of me. 'You have to get back here and get a job James,' she says.

'Perhaps we should split up?' I say, and before she can retort I continue, 'Let's be honest, we're not happy together, we've nothing in common, I bore the pants off you and we haven't had a damn good shag for years. I mean, what is the point?'

I hear her taking another deep breath.

Then she spews out, hardly stopping to breath, 'If you grew up and knuckled under more, rather than moaning about your lot in life and mourning your lost fabled youth then things might be better between us. If you tried harder with the kids you might get more respect all round. And if you had stopped coming to bed pissed every night and lost some weight, we might have had sex more often.' Beautiful delivery, pacing and timing. A put-down master-class.

This is the most she's said to me for months.

'Well, if you ...' I start, and have a litany of complaints and criticisms to pour through in my speech of retribution, but the cow has put the phone down.

Good for her, I think.

I go for a meal of steroid steak and chips at the family Big Beaver restaurant or whatever the fuck it's called that's attached to the hotel and drink sweet, smooth, shit red wine which is like fruit juice and look around me at the families – balding dads trying to pretend that this is what life is all about and women, once pretty, who catch an occasional sight of themselves in their wedding day photographs looking radiant and wonder how and when they turned old and shapeless and dried up. And their kids have the genetic imprint to go exactly the same way as their parents.

Fuck, it's depressing. So depressing that I finish the bottle and sit in the bar and drink lager until I'm thrown out at closing time.

Seven o'clock. I can hear through the thin walls someone showering upstairs and someone shitting next door. A wonderful way for a hangover to break forth.

The hotel has a business centre – a room with a photocopier, a stapler, a wastepaper bin and a PC – so I decide to check my emails before breakfast and heading south to sort out my marriage, my career and my life.

I've not checked them for a couple of days. I have 68 emails, the usual junk that I begin to delete methodically.Then I stop.

There is an email from Lizzie.

Pathological, sex-mad, fuck-anything-that's-got-a-bank-balance-and-half-the-home-counties-attached-to-it, Lizzie.

I stare at the screen, unable to open the email. For a start, in this whole mad last fortnight, everything has been instigated by me. Seemingly, I hadn't made any impact on anyone's life enough for them to want to contact me. Until now. And it would have to be the acidic Lizzie of all people. Not some long-lost teenage girlfriend that I'd forgotten about, but Lizzie who'd betrayed me with a member of the landed gentry, or with the member of a member of the landed gentry.

Fuck. I was getting over this, I was ready to steam head first into the future with nary a backward glance at my unsatisfactory past. I was all set for my new life and this silly sex-mad cow appears on my horizon – come on, forgive the metaphor, I'm just a little flustered, dear reader. I'm sweating through anticipation, anger and alcohol without even having opened the fucking email.

I'm trying to be in control, to grow up. One thing I know I should have learned in the last few weeks is that you cannot go back. People from the past change, and all that happens by tracking them down is that your own disappointment and madness becomes intertwined with theirs dragging both parties further down.

I should delete Lizzie's message, ignore her, leave her rejected in hyperspace. So, I'm intrigued as to what she looks like – I remember her great body and fresh-faced English rose looks which I suspect are unlikely to have faded. And her insatiable sexual appetite. And desire to perform virtually any sexual act, no matter how base and possibly in those days technically illegal.

But she's probably dried up now, and judging from recent experience, in a nunnery, or on death row in Texas for having slaughtered her lesbian lover's entire family, and their pets. Or shagging her gamekeeper/gardener/cook/chimney-sweep/chauffeur – probably simultaneously – on Phil's country estate that is Wiltshire.

Nope, I am resolved, I shall not respond, I shall not take the bait, I am not interested, I have learned my lesson.

I hit the delete button with single-minded determination, and go for a Big Happy Beaver Breakfast served to me by a moronic teenager with repellent acne, a grimy shirt collar and a severe body odour issue. Delicious.

I start to think. She did give great head. And she had a lovely body and I remember a moment suspended in my erotic memory bank when I was making love to her and I looked into her sweet fresh face and she said to me filthily, 'Fuck me hard you fucking bastard,' and by jingo that's exactly what I did.

Shit, this image is causing trouserly stirrings, the likes of which I've not felt for months – even the occasional glimpse of Acne Child isn't dampening them. And I know I have an option – to relieve myself after breakfast by concentrating on that long-ago memory, or to leave the tumescence to take over control of my rationale.

Your delicate sensitivity, dear reader, will be pleased and probably not a little surprised to learn that I chose the latter option. I finish the edible parts of the Beaver breakfast, go back to the computer in the Business Centre, log back on and find Lizzie's email in the recently-deleted folder.

I open it, my heart and cock throbbing.

'Look me up next time you are in Cheshire,' she says and gives her mobile number. Nothing else, not an indication of what she's doing, or who she's with or for that matter why she should want to see me.

I check out, get on to the motorway, puzzled and bemused.


Three o'clock, I find myself drinking coffee in the lobby of a smart neo-classical hotel south of Manchester, built, it seems to me, exclusively to cater for sales meetings of insurance companies and envelope manufacturers. I tried to resist, God knows

I tried, I even drove up onto the moors for an hour or so, hoping that I would come to my senses. But like trying to give up smoking, there is always the allure of 'one last one then I'll quit,' and so I phoned her.

'Dahling,' she said, 'How wonderful!' and she gave me a venue and a time to meet.

I'm going to satisfy my curiosity, see what she looks like, give Lizzie a piece of my mind (the bit that's been festering for 20-odd years), then get into my car and head back home.

An hour later I am in a bedroom with Lizzie.

I'd seen a gleaming soft top Merc scream into the car park, loud music blaring. Then this woman, big hair, great body even at this distance, wearing fashionable sports gear had run through the main entrance, nodded complicitly at a couple of members of staff, seen me and rushed over. She put her arms around me and kissed me on the lips saying only, 'Dahling.'

She sat down and I took her in. She'd aged, obviously, but looked fantastic – subtly made up, big clear blue eyes looking at me affectionately, expensive but unobtrusive jewellery, and a subtle glimpse of tanned, sumptuous cleavage. She caught me looking (women always do) and started to talk as if we'd last met yesterday. Told me about her day, about shopping in Manchester, about the morning in the gym. I noticed the fat wedding ring on her fingers which glistened with half of Southern Africa's diamond output, and she stopped chatting and smiled at me.

'You look great, Dahling,' she said unconvincingly.

I refused to return the compliment.

'So,' I said, 'who's the lucky guy?' nodding at the ring on her finger.

She said, 'Perhaps you, Dahling,' looking me straight in the eye, brazenly.

'No,' I said, not responding, 'I mean, you must be married – is it Phil?'

'Phil?' she said, puzzled. Then she remembered. 'Christ no, Dahling,' she laughed. 'That thick rugger bugger? Christ no, rather die,' and she got a cigarette out and lit one. I joined her. 'Lasted about six months after uni,' she said. 'We did get engaged, I think … but God, I couldn't have spent the rest of my life with him. Whole family were inbred.'

'Thought he was your sort …' I said, sulkily enough for her to notice.

'God no. He was so so dull. Always preferred you, Dahling.'

'You could have fooled me,' I said. She looked puzzled and I realised that one of the defining moments of my youth, an incident that coloured, if not clouded, my entire view of women, had totally escaped her, as if it had never happened.

I decided to remind her. 'So, you don't remember me walking in on you and Phil in flagrante delicto? And me storming out and drinking solidly for three months to erase the image?'

'Vaguely,' she said, her composure slightly rocked. Then she smiled. 'But that was all in the past, Dahling. Years ago. We were young ... So what have you been up to then, Jamie Dahling?'

I gave her the edited highlights. I was utterly torn. I was falling for the big eyes and the amount of attention she was paying me and the tantalising glimpse of breast and I hated myself for being so shallow, so weak, so utterly led by the thought patterns of my cock. If only I'd had that breakfast time wank. She cannot be allowed to have this effect on me. I must resist.

She talked more. She told me about her husband, who is a partner in his own law firm. 'Does very well. Very, very well,' she said. 'Works all the hours God gives and when he doesn't, he's out with his little friends watching football or playing golf in Portugal. Hardly see him. Suits me, boring little bugger.'

'Why do you stay with him?' I asked and she laughed, shaking her jewellery. 'He has his good moments. We have a lovely house – you must see it, seventeenth century with a charming moat.' I flinched involuntarily. 'He gives me lots of money, I can do what I like, with whom I like, when I like and,' she winked conspiratorially at me, 'he asks no questions. I just have to turn up to dinners with him four times a year, flash my tits a bit at his boring clients and play the trophy wife.'

'Children?'

'No, thank God!' she laughed. 'Barely adult myself. Fancy a drink, Dahling?' she said and before I could answer she had summoned a waiter and had ordered a bottle of Pouilly Fumé. She jabbered on about the tennis club and the Harvey Nicks and her neighbours the famous footballers until the waiter returned with the wine in a bucket of ice.

'Cheers,' she said.

'Cheers,' I replied and we clinked glasses.

We drank. As we did, my resistance was ebbing. I was becoming increasingly attracted to her, excited by events that were unfolding. And sure that I was going to work myself up into a pre-coital frenzy when, true to form, she would screw me up by leaving.

I went to the loo to have a slash and pour some cold water on my face. Reality kicked in as I looked at myself in the mirror and saw a lardy guy staring back who was well past his sell-by date and with a sinking heart I told myself that I was imagining that a woman who looked as good as Lizzie, who had so much money she could have whomsoever she desired, was very unlikely to bunk up with a middle-aged, overweight guy from her past. I was resolved. A cup of black coffee and I would go.

I headed back to the table and she stood, saying, 'I've booked us a room, Dahling.' In the same voice as she might have said, 'I've made a cup of tea.' She took my hand and led me towards the lifts. She seemed to know her way about this place rather well, I mused. Perhaps, I surmised, Poirot-like, she'd done this before. As the lift door closed the voice, sister of lift woman at my much missed HQ, said, 'Lift going up,' and I was about to tell her of my fascination with the lift woman, when her mouth was on mine, and her tongue was gently licking my own. She tasted of wine. I reciprocated enthusiastically. Her hand reached for my groin and I caressed her left breast. She moaned – having first removed her lips from my face – and said,

'Fuck me Jamie.'

Do you now what, dear reader? Do you? No, you don't. I may be a nasty, snide, insinuating, lecherous bastard with a tendency towards the maudlin – oh for fuck's sake, I'll drop the self-effacing bit for a while – but what I feel, while being groped and stroked and on the cusp of possibly the best sexual experience since 1998 (just after the Hearts triumph in the Cup Final against Rangers, if you must know, when Adam scored that second goal) is – and please don't laugh – used and cheap. And a bit tarty. But very, very tumescent, admittedly.

'Third floor,' says lift girl and the doors open, and she hangs a left and walks confidently up a hallway of tasteful chintz paper and hunting scenes and she stops at 369 saying saucily, 'Almost my lucky number.' She takes the key card, inserts it in the door, turns the handle and pushes. And damn near breaks her shoulder. 'Fuck!' she says. She takes the card out, looks at it, noting the directional arrow, says, 'Try again,' and smiles at me, her lips wet and inviting. She reinserts it turns the handle and pushes simultaneously. 'Fuck fuck fuck!' she says to the firmly closed door. 'You try,' she orders.

I pull the card out, make sure it's the right way round, reinsert it fully, hear a click and see the green light. 'There we are,' I say, admittedly slightly patronisingly, and turn the handle and push.

Nothing. The door is, to use the vernacular of the professional locksmith, utterly fucked.

'Is it the right room?' she asks, looking at the little cardboard folder that has the number on it. 369 it says.

I try one last time, rather enjoying the bleak humour of the situation and assuming it is the work of a God in heaven who meant the commandment about adultery after all. 'I'll call reception,' I say and do so from a house phone near the lifts.

The first maintenance man pushes, then grimaces, then pulls, bangs smacks and swears, all to no avail. Number two turns up with a screwdriver. Lizzie has already shouted down the phone demanding to be given another room now, but she's politely informed that the hotel is booked. Re-insurance Salesperson of the Year Awards, Cheshire Branch, apparently.

The duty manager appears, apologising and appeasing. He's very sorry, nothing like this has ever happened before, please why don't we make ourselves comfortable in the bar.

Which we do for the next half hour, drinking more Pouilly Fumé supplied gratis by the hotel. And making small talk and catching up, and I'm sitting there thinking, 'I don't want to go through with this,' until the manager appears and, assuring us all is well, ushers us towards the lift and our room, which we're assured is now open and ready for us and will we accept a bottle of champagne on ice as further compensation for our ordeal?

It would seem churlish to fuck off now, given that they're so desperate to make us happy. And anyway, I've been drinking solidly for most of the afternoon and I'm too pissed to drive anywhere.

We reach the room and we assure the manager all's OK. He closes the door behind him and leaves us alone.

We look at each other. She smiles. I smile back.

'I'm not in the mood,' I say. 'Sorry. The moment appears to have passed. Let's have a drink instead.'

'Glad you said that,' she says and passes the champagne for me to open. 'Rather taken the wind out of my sails, too.'

And we both start to laugh.

Two hours later, with another paid-for bottle of champagne drunk, we're lying on the bed beside each other fully clothed, not even touching, but laughing and talking and laughing some more.

'I have to go,' she says and I protest.

'You can't drive like that – stay the night. I'll go on the sofa,' I say and turn my face to her.

'Ever the gent,' she says. 'Though a girl could take offence at not driving you wild with desire.'

'Oh come on,' I say. 'You still look great. You know you do. I'm just old and a bit pissed.'

'You angel. Thank you. But I'll leave the car and take a taxi – won't be the first time – and I do have to get home,' she says.

She looks back and I feel for the first time genuine affection for her. I touch the side of her face and kiss her mouth gently but firmly. She responds – not with the vamp queen stuff of earlier but with tenderness. It feels like the start of lovemaking, not fucking. Trouserly stirrings abound.

'You have to go,' I say.

'Yes I must,' she replies.

'Lizzie, I have had such a great time. Thank you.'

'I'm forgiven for Phil then?' she says and smiles.

'Well, he did own half of Wiltshire ...'

She kisses me on the forehead, says 'Stay in touch,' and leaves.

I lie there breathing her perfume and am torn between a certain smugness for resisting my adulterous desires and anger at having let her go, because I reckon that she would still be something special even after all these years.

I raid the mini bar of scotch and peanuts, watch some football and fall asleep.

# 16

# I Don't Wanna Be Learned

I'm on the last leg now of my pilgrimage, one more day left. Down the M6 to my alma mater for a nose around. I left early, having awoken at seven in great fettle. Despite shipping a shed load of alcohol, it was of good quality so the anticipated hangover hasn't arrived. And to make my day even brighter, when I went to check out, all the bill had been allocated to Lizzie's account. What a top woman. Wish she'd told me that – I'd have had another bottle and room service courtesy of her old man.

I reach the campus around 9.30 and am met by a security guard in a glass house and a barrier, neither of which were present in 1981, wanting to know what my business was. 'I just want to look around,' I say. 'I was here in the early eighties.'

'Sorry sir – I can't let you in. It's private property.'

In my day, there was open access to the campus. You could just walk or drive in and many of the locals did just that on a Friday night to try to pick up girls or failing that beat the shit out of students. And we'd protest that security was crap and someone would get killed and the lighting at night was a rapist's heaven and something should be done about it. My sense of relief that our protests possibly have borne fruit after all this time is dampened by the prick in a uniform who's stopping me from reaching a key, final, component of my pilgrimage.

'Actually,' I say, reaching into my wallet, 'I represent the Intellectual Property Corporation,' and I pass him my card with a fiver tucked behind it. 'I want to look up one of our authors – Professor Higgins. Expert on the Yanomami.'

All of which is true. The foremost expert on the Yanomami people is indeed to be found on this hillside campus on the edge of the Potteries.

This appeases the guard, who may not have done his youth training at Dachau after all. He gives me a card for the dashboard so that I can park with impunity, and I drive onto the campus.

And I am met first up by a business park where once open fields were. Then a science block, all glass and stainless steel. The road follows a different track to the one of old and I'm momentarily bemused. I then find myself reassuringly on the ring road again – I drive towards the union complex, a low-slung, sixties brutalist building in a dent on the hill. I park.

Nothing's really changed physically with the place – OK, the bookshop is now part of a high street chain and therefore probably reluctant to stock books on grounds of poor profitability, and the launderette has been modernised, but it's essentially the same.

Thinking about it, it was 25 years ago that I was last here – a reunion had been arranged some three years after we'd graduated. I went to it with a couple of buddies, long since disappeared from my life. Oh, I wonder what they're up to now. It was a depressing evening. The hip cool kids – mainly public school, with that easy confidence that comes with diminished chins – were still hip and cool and working in exciting industries like advertising or fabulously well-paid ones such as trading bonds in daddy's bank. And there was little old me, just embarking on a publishing career which involved a red Sierra and a territory of the Home Counties' book trade to go and sell academic books into. I vaguely recollect the night ending with me throwing up in the sink having consumed a prodigious, Olympian amount of subsidised beer and wine and vowing never ever to come back here again. I woke with a reassuringly awful – so it had been a good night after all – hangover, pointed the Sierra south on the motorway and never returned.

Until now.

'Twas ever thus at university – a lot of drinking, fuelled by the unlikeliest of drink promotional nights. I remember – just – reaching coma status after spending three pound eighty at a Pernod and cider event. Drink fuelled the whole three years. It was my way of dealing with the fact that I felt, from the moment I stepped on the campus, inadequate. Here I was, from a northern town no one had heard of, surrounded by impossibly trendy self-sufficient and glamorous kids who lived in Harrow or Hampshire and held a cigarette like a film star. And punk chic was the rage, and I tipped up with hair over my collar and flared jeans looking like something out of an extremely poor Lynyrd Skynyrd tribute band. So I drank. And made friends with some other social inadequates and gradually – halfway through my first year – began to enjoy myself.

I still didn't get the public-school bit, until much later. There was a gang of them – cool, confidant, witty, well-spoken and well-dressed. They had cars, money and it was rumoured, serious drugs, not the kindergarten dope that I hid in the toilet cistern. Nope, they did coke – a couple apparently were into heroin.

And of course they were accompanied always by impossibly beautiful girls. Thin, English-rose types, who looked like they'd stepped out of the pages of *Vogue* or some such. Not an ugly girl in the circle – they simply found their level, effortlessly. I was in awe – I longed to have that casual elegance, that confidence, that evident charm and wit. Most of all I longed for one – in fact any – of the girls to even give me a sideways glance, but of course they didn't – it was never going to be. Their class sensors picked up all interlopers.

But I got by – a few bonks, a couple of fairly serious relationships, some great bands and an ability to drink my own body weight – then, not so onerous a task – in subsidised beer.

And then it was all over. Just as I was starting to really enjoy myself, that was it – three years up, finals, moderate degree and out into the recession-hit early eighties that Mrs T. had created. And a vague idea that – because I liked books – a publishing job would be quite fun.

Anyhow, here I am again. I decide to explore – I start towards the Union.

There are a few students around, going in the newsagent or bookshop and I am overwhelmed at how young they look – they're babies. Did I ever look this young? Did my friends? My recollection – certainly of the trendy rugger bugger public-school guys – was how sophisticated and grown-up they were; must be part of the 'My, how young policemen look these days ...' syndrome – either that or the entire population has some fairly hideous portraits in their attic.

So, into the building, past the pigeonholes where letters from home were collected, up the stairs to the bar.

Two things reassure. The floor is as sticky from spilled beer as ever it was – your shoes squelch as you walk – and the juke box is playing 'Lola' by the Kinks. There are a few kids in having a drink, but not many – I suspect lunchtime boozing is something they'll grow into. I go to the bar and in solidarity order an orange juice. I sit and watch, and reminisce – of queueing twice a week at the public call boxes to phone home – a major hassle in those pre-mobile days. Of bands and balls, of how I – stupid fucking prick – went to see John Martyn with the rest of the hippies. Of fights – usually male posturing, caused by that heady cocktail of beer and testosterone and girls.

The juke box is now playing 'The Long and Winding Road' – Christ, don't these kids get contemporary music any more? – and I finish the juice and get up to leave, feeling like some sort of paedo in a play park.

Out I go, walking towards the other centre of the campus, the Old Hall. The campus was the country estate of a Victorian industrialist and the house – a Gothic pile of dark imposing stone – had become the Arts Faculty and consequently I spent much of my time there. Little has changed although there are now cars in the courtyard – bless 'em, you can't expect the students to walk from one side of the campus to the other. I go in the main door and ascend the large staircase to the Classics Department on the second floor.

Which is now Social Anthropology.

There's an office manned by an efficient middle-aged woman who tells me that the Classics Department closed 10 years ago, apparently through lack of interest.

'Gone to Manchester,' she tells me. 'Though Professor Corneil still lives on the campus ...'

Ah, Prof. Corneil. A real professor. Mad, incredibly clever, an expert on Samian Ware pottery. Smoked a pipe, wore a beret, a small frail man who from my memory was about seventy years of age when he taught me. He'd spent time in Africa and had a reasonable knowledge of Swahili and would seamlessly – in the middle of a Tutorial on Caesar's *Gallic Wars* – start speaking it.

He was an absolute gentleman. At one stage I was his star pupil – up for a first if I worked. Which of course I didn't.

I decide to visit him. The secretary very kindly rings his house to check that's OK – and I head off again.

There was a development of housing for the staff – we rarely ventured there as students as it was grown-up country, an estate of small sixties houses. It must have been incredibly claustrophobic living and working on campus, constantly bumping into students and colleagues. I guess it was a case of needs must – academic salaries being what they were and still are – so subsidised housing was grabbed with both hands.

I go round the back of the Hall, where the layout of the original Victorian gardens can be seen – formal hedges, flower beds and neoclassical statues and fountains. When I was here there was a set of rather incongruous pink Portakabins, their usage uncertain, deposited at the back of the hall on the edge of the ornate gardens. A friend of a friend had almost been elected as student president on the manifesto of painting the Hall pink to match the cabins. How we'd laughed, failing to recognise the onslaught of political disinterest amongst the young just 12 years after Grosvenor Square and the Rive Gauche.

It's all now slightly grubby-looking, as if garden maintenance gets the dregs of the budget – quite rightly, I guess. I'm surprised they've not by now built a mock Gothic extension where the gardens are and turned it into luxury accommodation for the really rich kids who are missing Daddy's stately pile and can't possibly sleep in normal box-like student rooms – not without wetting the bed, anyway. That reduces the gardening bill, and reduces further the local unemployment problem – you model this on an Oxford college, have septuagenarian porters designed to look after all their gentlemen's needs – et voila, you can put the fees up even more because you're offering a moderate education for the not very clever but very rich in an Oxbridge theme park. Brilliant. Kind of Open University meets Disney.

The lakes, the lawns, the rhododendrons sweep away and across the fields, the motorway purrs in the distance. I have flashbacks of romantic walks, seeing the sunrise whilst narcotically incapable, of picnics and sledging, of obscene snowmen and youthful abandon – all kind of redolent of Brideshead sans the foppishness, confidence, wealth and bottom sex.

I enter the small estate – it's called Larkfield, I remember. I'm a tad surprised that, considering it is housing some of the finest academic minds in the country (well, arguably), and indeed may well be where the world expert on the Kalahari bushmen resides, it has the look and feel of a slightly run-down, lower-middle-class suburban estate where upwardly mobile but ASBO-ridden families from really shit housing stock aspire to live. The first house – a semi – there's a Morris Minor in bits on the drive (OK, if this were downtown Toxteth it would be a turbocharged Sierra, but you get my drift). The house on the left has knee-deep grass. There's a motorbike and side car from the sixties further on – a weary-looking daughter of toil with a head shawl, knitted jumper, long hippy skirt and pink wellingtons is hoeing her flower beds looking for all the world as if she's tending the beet fields on the outskirts of Plovdiv. Kids play on the street, obviously socially deprived for the very reason that they have to play on the streets rather than with expensive Playstations going boggle-eyed indoors.

At the end of the cul-de-sac, I find the Professor's house, number 83. I ring the door bell with a little trepidation – despite years of working professionally with academics, I still have the feeling of inadequacy and intellectual inferiority towards them. Am I late with an essay? Have I used 'allergy' where I meant to say 'allegory'? Is it Simian or Samian? Will the fact that I ran out of time to read Ovid in the original language and cheated with the stodgy Loeb translation get me chucked out? (I had never heard of the term 'sent down' until much later.)

The door opens and the Professor is standing there looking through his wire-framed glasses at me, blinking in the gentle sunlight. He's resting his wiry frame on an appropriately wiry cane.

'Professor,' I say, confidently, as I shake his small, bony hand. 'Thank you so much for seeing me.'

'My pleasure,' he replies, beckoning me in.

We enter the hall, which is neat and tidy, coats hanging on hooks behind the door and a staircase leading upstairs.

'Come, come,' he says, 'this is my room, where the bloody cleaner isn't allowed. Bloody bitch.'

I'm slightly bemused by the outburst but follow him into the room at the back. He's barely changed – still a shock of floppy grey hair, a little thinner now, that cascades over his forehead, partially obscuring his sharp, intelligent, darting eyes. The thin moustache is still there. His face is a little thinner, and wrinkled, and there is – the result of an excess of testosterone in elderly men – a flourish of hair growing from his ears. He's wearing what looks like a plain old-fashioned school jumper over a checked country-squire style shirt and a pair of grey – what my father used to refer to as – slacks. Finished off by expensive looking brogues, he looks as I always remember him – like an archetypal, typecast old professor.

Only the brogues are clean. The rest of him – his jumper, his trousers – are covered in stuff. Hair. Dried egg. Soup. Ash. He's an absolute mess – a third-world family could live off the dried foodstuffs on his clothing for weeks.

'Sit down, sit down,' he says. 'Sherry?' and he reaches for the decanter and pours me a glass before I can reply.

I look around the room and feel pleased – it reflects his personal dishevelment perfectly. Books, newspapers and journals are everywhere, on the floor, on the desk, on the chairs – to sit down I have to carefully lift a pile of papers and create a cloud of dust. Half the carpet is taken up with what I assume is a site map of an archaeological dig somewhere.

Then there are artefacts everywhere. There's Simian – sorry, Samian – pots on the carpet, a box of coins, a small bronze head of what I assume to be an emperor, and a marble head of a young girl. The walls are covered by pictures of temples and forts, and steam railway trains, and mountains and wildlife and seascapes and sailing ships. There are masks – Asian, African, Latin American. And books and books and more books, and dust that rises and hangs in the sunlit air to our motion.

'*Santé*,' he says, energetically passing me the sherry. Which, on first sip, is marble dry and very fragrant.

He sits himself down and looks at me. 'So, how is your work?' he asks. 'Did we train you well?'

His voice is cut-glass English, powerful and somehow old fashioned in its precise enunciation of every vowel and consonant – he sounds for all the world like a 1950s radio announcer.

I smile and start to tell him a little of what I've been doing. Distractedly, he reaches to the table beside him, which seems to contain half the west wing of the British library. He picks up his pipe, his tobacco pouch and after a little packing lights it with a Swan Vesta. Even his matches are classic. He sucks and exhales just as he used to in tutorials.

The whole department smoked. Rollups, untipped Senior Service, Rothmans – they all had their distinctive tobacco habits – and we'd join them; remarkable when you think of it now, where you can barely smoke in a field without an ensuing law suit from a farmer for secondary smoke damage to his livestock.

He swigs his sherry and asks, 'So how did it go down in Orange?'

I have no idea what he's talking about and hesitate.

'Of course, load of old bollocks, those big digs – sponsored by the local tourist boards rather than a desire for real archaeology. Fuckwits. I ask you. All of them.'

He swigs the sherry back, emptying the glass. I love the way he swears – it's so incongruous, this perfect toned and modulated English accent saying the word 'fuck'. He stands and refills it.

'Why they don't fucking excavate some interesting places is beyond me. I mean, we all know what a fucking amphitheatre looks like don't we? And we know what went on there whether it was elephant, giraffes, tigers,' swig of his drink, 'or fucking hamsters. Ridiculous. Waste of fucking money. So where are you working now, David?'

I try to explain. I am not David. I am James. I have not worked in archaeology for nearly 30 years and even then I was simply doing it as part of my degree – it never featured, as far as I can remember, as a career option.

But he continues with more sherry and another effusive pull on his pipe. 'What are you working on now? Is *Gallia Narbonensis* still of interest to you and the team?'

He's obviously seriously deluded about who I am. Maybe that's what a sherry habit does to you, or maybe it's Alzheimer's. I tell him again, gently, that I'm a publisher. I tell him I publish the leading academic authority – his former colleague – on the Kalahari bushmen.

'Absolute cunt,' he says.

I tell him we also publish the definitive, bestselling guide to the place names of Roman Britain, too, to which he yells,

'That idiot! He was my student. He was terminally stupid and a fucking cunt!'

And then he starts. How archaeology has been hijacked by TV celebrities with big digging machines. 'I mean, for fuck's sake, old boy, what's in the soil that those fucking JCBs clear? Does anyone ever check? Cunts, all of them!'

Another swig of the sherry, another pull on the pipe. He coughs a little as he does so and a small amount of ash joins its co-frères on his jumper and his trousers.

'So, how long where you at Arles for?'

'Professor,' I say, becoming rather pissed off and not a little frustrated at his inability to grasp some basic facts here. 'I did a six-week course in archaeology, graduated in classics and joined a chain of booksellers that no longer exists. I have just lost my job as Vice-President, Marketing, for the eighth largest academic publisher in the world. I am not and never have been an archaeo ...'

'Splendid,' he cuts me off. 'Archaeology – terrible fucking career choice. Want to know why?'

He looks at me with something of an evil twinkle in his eye as he grasps the decanter, leans forward with it towards my glass which I proffer through politeness, and tops me up with the urine-coloured liquor.

'Want to know why, eh?' he asks me again. Without waiting for my response he continues. 'Because the women are all so fucking hideous. Your average female archaeologist has a face like a bulldog's arse. Trust me. You'll never find a good looking archaeologist. Never. If they're good looking, they aren't archaeologists.' He sucks on his pipe with something approaching satisfaction, his message delivered.

I don't really know what to say. It's all a bit sad this, the foremost expert on Samian pottery and the owner of an obviously massive intellect spouting this abject, sexist nonsense.

'Believe me,' he goes on to say, 'the sixties, when I first moved here, were terrible. We had a sociologist on one side and a psychologist the other and as far as I can tell all they used to do was bring their students back for a fuck – we could hear them. Sitting in our front room we could hear them. Audrey and I used to marvel at their cheek and the girls' stupidity. Rumours were rife of who had to arrange for an abortion for their first year undergrad and who had the clap – oh, the sixties. It was like Nero's palace here. And there was I, in my forties, teaching smelly boys and ugly girls about the glories of the Roman Empire when that little fucking shit of a professor in applied psychology was accepting fellatio on his back lawn from a Home Counties' nineteen-year-old Marxist – without even knowing the derivation of the word fellatio.'

He sank back into his chair, puffed on his pipe and stared silently into the distance.

I'm a tad overwhelmed by too much information and there's something of an awkward silence, broken suddenly by the Professor shouting, 'Pornography!' He goes on. 'Look at this,' and he passes me a dark red Samian bowl. It has been reassembled from six or so pieces and glued neatly back together. There, clearly, you can see the etched images of people having sex. Big penises penetrate ladies every which way you can contemplate.

'Ah, he says, 'when Audrey and I used to want a bit of stimulation, my pots used to do it.'

I feel a little ill. I remember meeting Audrey once – a then middle-aged, thin, sexless woman with straight, grey hair, big glasses and sensible shoes. Nothing at all sexual in Audrey, I was sure.

'That was the trouble,' the Professor goes on, 'with teaching classics. I mean, the girls – they were all so fucking ugly. Dumpy, dull things from the Home Counties with fringes and spots and big backsides and glasses.' My memory concurs. 'And the bastards around here – the sociologists, criminology, psychology johnnies – well, they were lucky buggers. We'd see it all. Over the back fence, the bastards fucking lovely undergraduate girls on the promise of a 2:1.'

He sighs regretfully and finishes his sherry. He refills the glass and offers me the same. I decline.

'I mean, Audrey and I were happy enough – she was a lovely old stick – but a man needs a bit of excitement. Of course he does. And Samian Ware is all well and good, but not the same as a beautiful twenty-year-old undergraduate. Audrey understood that.'

I'm getting restless now, as the professor is getting more animated. 'You have to take your chances in life when you can. Of course Cicero could stand there talking his *tempora et mores* stuff and nonsense, but what the fuck is the point of high-mindedness if you're offered just one night – just one hour – with a delectable young woman and you're 42 years of age? Eh? I mean, morality, stoicism, monogamy, for fuck's sake, can all go flying out the fucking *fenestrae* as far as I am concerned.'

He puffs on his pipe and I sit there like a nineteen-year-old ignorant and nervous undergraduate in awe of the Professor, not knowing what to say, how to interact. He has just bared his soul to me and I don't know what he's talking about. Indeed I don't want to know.

'It was just the one girl,' he continues. 'But you know, you remember. 1972. Laura. Beautiful. A beautiful girl. And me, a middle-aged professor and she a fragrant young Helen. And you, you stole her from me.' He looks at me now with venom and I notice his hand is shaking, possibly through alcohol, probably through rage.

'There's a mistake,' I say. 'I was 12 in 1972. I was here in 1978. You've made a mistake, Professor. I never knew a Laura when I was here. Or a Helen for that matter.'

'Oh your youth stole her from me,' he says. 'And I hated you, hated you for taking my one chance of happiness. I drew all the ancient curses down on you' – this he is saying seriously, deadpan and it's a little unnerving, 'wanting you dead, wanting you to shrivel and rot so that Laura would want me, would want to nurture my intellect against my impending old age, and Audrey – she wouldn't have minded. She'd have understood that a man needs youth and beauty to survive – she'd have let me go. But you, you utter petit bourgeois, intellectually-void bastard, stole her away from me.'

He looks at me with pure venom and I realise the denouement of this crazy story of mine of the last few weeks, how it is all meant to end. I am about to be murdered by an obviously mad octogenarian classics Professor in the front room of a semi-detached academic's home, and no one except for him will be there to hear me scream. Oh fantastic, I think, my own pilgrimage ends at the hands of a deranged classicist who will doubtless cut my throat using a replica of a centurion's sword and a fucking strigil.

He's still looking at me as though I've defiled something precious. Which I suppose in his fetid mind, I have.

'Erm,' I say, far from bravely, expecting a renewed outburst of murderous geriatric energy, 'I came here in 1978, I don't remember a Laura. Really. It must have been someone else.'

'Of course you don't, you fucking bastard.' And with that he picks up a large Samian Ware bowl and throws it at me with all his might. It arcs through the air towards me and I pluck it easily from its trajectory. I put it gently, unharmed, on the table beside me and say casually, 'I have got to be off now.'

He sits there somewhat bemused and says, 'So soon? Stay for some supper. I so rarely get guests now.'

And it's obvious he's forgotten what has just gone on and what he's accused me of. It's gone, disappeared.

'Professor,' I say, standing and holding out my hand, 'It has been my pleasure. Thank you so much – and don't get up, please,' I add, as his frailty and the half pint of Amontillado suggest he would stagger, possibly nosedive. 'No, please, don't get up.'

And as I go to leave the room I take one look at his wrinkled, noble, old face, and I see a tear in his eyes.

I march head down, resolutely, towards the car. I don't glance up, I don't reminisce internally, I focus simply on putting one foot in front of the other as quickly as possible without actually running to get the hell out of there. I resolve never ever to return. Ever.

I get back to the car, start it up and, pausing only to lob my iPod onto the back seat and set the sound system to Radio Four, I head south and home. I'm purged, I'm exorcised, the Grail has been found then buried in an enormously deep hole and I am ready again for normal adult life.

Honest I am.

# 17

# Wha' Happen?

Iam on the train, dear reader, heading toward London, surrounded by the usual chinless City types. I muse that, like the Royals, perhaps the chinless should travel on separate trains. If there was a fatal train crash – which I guess is inevitable these days – the entire chinless gene pool would be wiped out in a one-er, causing distress and dismay to someone somewhere, turning lots of little chinless financial wannabes into orphans at a stroke. Anyhow, I'm showing solidarity these days in second class, still reading *The Guardian*, and heading off for the New Job.

Oh, how times have changed, my friend, since last we spoke. Guess there's a bit of catch-up needed here.

First off, I was about an hour from home following my near decapitation at the hands of the mad Latin Prof, when the mobile chirruped – the number was withheld, but I took the call anyway.

'Hi – Ray Womack here,' an American voice drawled.

My immediate response was to assume that he was phoning me to taunt me for the one hundred and fifty odd strokes I had taken at St Andrews.

But no, that was not the reason. He was phoning – fuck me – to offer me a job. Global Vice President of International Marketing Communications, Africa, Middle East and Europe – I'll need a metre-long business card with that job title, I mused. Starting? Monday. Salary? Twenty five per cent over what I was on before, with a company helicopter flown by large-breasted Bulgarian peasant girls eager to please, and an expense account to make the most profligate African dictator weep with envy ... you get the drift. The silly bastard was offering me The Job. Fuck knows why, after my crimes against golf, but I had cracked it.

I played cool, of course. Asked for the job offer in writing and for 48 hours to consider as – it goes without saying, Ray – I've got quite a few irons on the table and cards in the fire, you know how things are.

We agreed to speak the day after tomorrow.

I considered ringing Helen to tell her but decided against it. The good news would distract her when I got home and hopefully mean I wouldn't have to answer too many questions about what I'd been doing, where and with whom, over the last week.

That is indeed the plan I formulate through the motorway traffic as I return homeward. I feel upbeat about the future, purged and confident. I'm ready for battle. I'm going to clean myself up, quit the drink and the fags, drag my children screaming from surly adolescence into intelligent young adulthood, make an effort with Helen – I don't know, take up a hobby with her, shop (oh fuck) occasionally with her, fuck (oh shop) occasionally with her, show an interest in the new bathroom blinds, consider now the moated manor house options – fuck knows exactly what, but I am resolved to get, if not happy, then normal.

It's past, it's gone. Look forward – this is my life, it's what I've chosen, it's what I do, what I've done, it's what grown-ups do. Grown-ups don't want to be 19 again – well, not every minute of every day. They are fascinated by pensions, ISAs, bank charges, second homes, ride-on lawnmowers, gym membership, new sofas, dinner parties, moated manor houses and gardening. Seriously, they really are.

And I will become fascinated, too.

Of course the one hour from home, a little like dog years, turns into seven fucking hours of sitting in traffic on the M25, so by the time I arrive at the house, I'm feeling exhausted and in need of a drink. I pull into the drive, grab my bags from the back, open the front door and with a cheery 'I'm home!' head to the kitchen and the wine rack. A good glass of Barolo to celebrate is called for, I believe.

I take the bottle out of the rack and feel a little disappointed not to be surrounded by sobbing family members, relieved at having me home, eagerly planning sacrifices to the gods in thanks for my safe return.

Nope, the house is silent, but as the lights were all on when I entered, I am a little puzzled as to where everyone is.

I take an enormous mouthful of wine, and feel the complex flavours, then the alcohol, flood through me. I top the glass up and go into the living room.

Helen is sitting upright, looking a little worried and not a little scared. The first thing that strikes me is that for the first time in living memory, the television is off.

'James,' she states, deadpan.

'Hi love,' I say enthusiastically, heading towards her to kiss her, when the second thing strikes me. I realise she is not alone.

Edward is sitting in the armchair, my armchair by the way, looking quite a lot worried and quite a lot scared.

'Time to renew the insurance already?' I quip, taking a slug of wine and sitting myself down. 'Well then,' I say jovially to Helen. 'Have you missed me darling?'

You see, I know what's happened already. I can just sense it, the awful English middle-class guilt bit.

I'd actually have preferred to have walked in on them in flagrante on my fucking armchair. At least there may have been some pleasure for them. But this way, this awful strained sterility which will, sad for them I think, dictate the terms of their shitty little relationship is not an auspicious start for them.

However, I'm not going to make it easy for them.

'James,' Edward starts, trying to be authoritative but sounding very nervous. 'Helen and I are in love.'

I laugh and a line from an Ian Dury song enters my head. 'Have I, Edward,' I say, 'my oldest mucker, come home to find another gentleman's kippers under the grill?'

Edward looks confused.

'Christ, James,' Helen says. 'This is serious. I'm leaving you for Edward. I'm taking the children and leaving you.'

I sip my wine and look at her, smiling amiably.

'Fucking hell' – she rarely swears, and Edward looks a wee bit shocked – 'I am leaving you and taking the kids and moving in with Edward. Do you understand?'

'And what does your wife make of this Edward?' I ask him pleasantly.

'She's in a bad way, actually James. Gone to her mother's. It has all come as a bit of a shock.'

'Poor woman,' I say, and he looks up at me. 'I mean, for being upset that such a boring cunt as you has left her. Any normal woman would rejoice.' I smile sweetly again.

'Well, if you're going to be personally abusive ...' he begins.

'You'll what?' I ask quietly. 'Take my darling wife away this very moment? Well, fantastic old fellow, please do, don't let me stop you.'

Now before, dear reader, you begin thinking that your old pal Jamie is losing his cool here, let me reassure you – all of this is delivered by me in a butter-wouldn't-melt-in-my-arsecrack way. I'm positively purring it.

This is the most fun I've had in this living room since the Hearts–Gretna Cup Final on satellite. The two of them want me to explode, threaten violence, throw wine in Edward's face (no chance of that at twenty quid a bottle), be hurt, weep, beat my breast and ululate. But I won't – simply because I don't give a fuck. This is a perfect resolution. They're welcome to each other.

And I, fear not my friend, do not give a flying fuck. I don't feel hurt that I've been deceived, I don't feel cheated upon or cuckolded – I just feel mild amusement. I mean, for God's sake, why not some firm-flanked toyboy? Why dull, boring, methodical, insurance Edward?

I'm a little intrigued and break the momentary silence saying, 'So when did you two lovebirds get it together, eh? Did you fall for each other over the herbaceous borders?'

'You sarcastic prick,' she says. 'We tried to do this gently and all we get is this pathetic, childish response. And to think I was feeling guilty ... I was worrying about you. I wanted to help you get through this. And as usual, all I get is your smart-arse comments that you obviously think are so clever and funny. Grow up, Jamie. This is real.'

'Very sweet – the language and the sentiment, I mean,' I say, and she raises her eyes to heaven in a kind of 'see what I mean?' gesture. 'But no, I'm genuinely interested – how did you two link up? I mean, who made the first move? Where was it?'

Edward says to Helen, ignoring me, 'I see now what you mean. He really is an unpleasant fellow.'

'Unpleasant, you say? This isn't unpleasant. Unpleasant would be,' (this, still light-hearted, not a hint of threat) 'coming over there right now and breaking your fucking nose. That would be very unpleasant. Glass of wine now?' I ask seamlessly as I empty my glass.

'Yes please,' they both say, and I go into the kitchen, drain the Barolo into my glass, grab two more glasses and the bottle of Chilean Merlot and return to the mildest of domestic mêlées.

'So', I say, passing them a glass each. 'What are your plans? Who's place will provide the love nest?'

'Neither,' says Edward. 'I've bought a new house out in the country. Had a bit of coup money-wise with the business. So, we're moving in there. The kids will like it – it has a pool.'

'I assume,' I say, sipping Piedmont's finest, 'it has a moat?'

So, my friends, it has come full circle. My marriage is over and I rejoice in my bachelor status. I have no desire to start dating or joining singles clubs – I am too old for that. Middle-aged people shouldn't be allowed to date. It is too stressful and embarrassing all round.

I am working hard and that's where all my energy goes. Helen and Edward are not as yet forcing through an onerous divorce settlement, being very reasonable with maintenance demands. The house is on the market, we'll split the proceeds and I will buy an apartment. And for the next five years I will work my little bollocks off and succeed in adulthood – indeed, a successful divorce is something of a prerequisite for a normal adulthood these days.

Strangely, considering we don't live together anymore, my relationship with the children is much better. They have to talk to me now as they see me every other weekend. We do the usual things distance fathers do with their children – cinemas and shows, interesting places and pizzas, so we do talk much more than ever before. Most entertainingly, we royally rip the piss out of dear Edward. He is, according to my kids, and entirely unprompted by me, the most boring man in re-insurance.

Helen seems happy enough. Edward's credit limit is probably twice mine so she'll be able to indulge in her preternatural shopping sprees without causing him too much anxiety. Occasionally when I go to collect or return the children we exchange what I think could be meaningful glances and I wonder if she too occasionally reminisces about the great sex we had in the early days of the relationship. I know, despite my desire to live in the present, that I do, and consider it would be quite cool to have an extra marital affair with your ex-wife.

The train arrives in the City – oh, I work in the City now, which Unesco has declared to have the highest concentrated population of twats in the western world – and I walk the 10 minutes to the sparkling tower block that is the HQ of the World Knowledge Corporation, who are ironically on the cusp of buying the Intellectual Property Corporation, thus making Wayne Simpkins report into me – oh, how I will enjoy the three days before I sack the bastard.

Up in the lift to the sixth floor and out to the sleek leather and ash reception and the even sleeker Fiona, the receptionist. Now, obviously she's not in Janice's league for demure sexuality – who could be? – but she does make an old man very happy at 8.30 in the morning, with her slight showing of cleavage, her wide smile and estuary vowels.

Seated behind my Centre Court-sized desk, I log on – there's an email from Johnnie. I'm publishing his Catullus in North Berwick book in our new Classics series, which will gain us academic kudos because it will lose money hand over first. I sent him an advance of £5K and he's happy enough. He's working on Plautus set in Peterhead Prison now. I have yet to see my hundred quid, though.

Life feels good. I have a challenging job that I am taking seriously, I have freedom, I travel and I can indulge my intellectual passions at least until, as inevitably will happen, I am unceremoniously booted out by another New York City accountant in three years' time.

I then do something that I have not done for five months – I log on to old-pals.net. I don't know why – perhaps it was a touch of rebellion from the Jamie of Old.

I have four emails, apparently.

Two are from Lizzie, telling me she's coming to London – unfortunately, or possibly fortunately, that was last month so she's bound to have found a new flame in the interim.

One is from David telling me he's getting divorced.

And the last one is from Madeleine Walker, a girl I dated in 1976 for one week only.

My fag-free, slimmed-down heart skips just a teensy-weensy little beat as I remember Madeleine Walker. Big eyes, I recollect, perfect teeth and a fine, firm young body that I never got anywhere near because she chucked me within a week to go out with a boy in the upper sixth who had, I recall, a rather natty red Ford Escort complete with sunroof. I was rather pissed off about her, I remember, but was nearly instantly consoled by the voluptuous Barbara.

Apparently Madeleine thinks fondly of me often. She lives in North London.

Perhaps we could meet for a drink?

# What Jamie Did Next

# David Grant

# Chapter 1

# The Book I Read

The alarm clock shrieks inches from my ear. This time it has awakened me. I glance at it remembering that I had set it last night – Sunday – for 9.30 am.

9.30am? I hear you ask, on a Monday morning? Whatever is the matter? Why is our dear Jamie Gallagher, captain of industry, publishing (or as we call it now Content) magnate not awake hours sooner? Why is he not battling for his place on the 7.15 with all those other sad fucks? Could it be a bank holiday? Might Jamie be poorly?

Oh no, you think. Has Jamie, consummate bullshitter, finally been found out and fired? Is this new indolence the result of recent but not entirely unexpected unemployment? Has the alarm gone off thus simply to give our hero the chance to wash his oxters prior to a meeting at the DHSS or whatever the fuck the dole people have been re-branded as now?

Well dear reader, thank you sincerely for your concern. No really. It's greatly appreciated. And I know in the past I have lavished the self-deprecation on you, my only friend, and so you would be right to consider incompetence, incontinence or unfortunate sexual harassment proceedings, the obvious and most likely cause of my tardiness.

But you'd be wrong

And let me tell you why.

Think back to when last we met. My formerly trophy, now atrophied, missus had run off with Edward, he of the reinsurance empire. My trip around the UK, my various brushes with unfaithfulness rendered inconsequential compared to what I had now become – a happy, nay delighted, cuckold. Hip hip fucking hip hooray, I sang as I left the two of them together, already resembling a middle-aged couple who had spent their entire adulthood together and now were frankly regretting it. I was free. I was out of there. I even began seeing eye to eye with the children again, laughing, joking, spending time outside of the house away from the prole shit TV that seemed to be constantly on.

I was back from my round Britain quest to discover quite how I had become such a miserable, fat, cynical, perma-pissed knobhead. Well I didn't really discover why in truth but I did have the satisfaction of finding out that just about everyone I had ever known was in the same if not worse position than me. I was not the freak. I was one in amongst a whole shoal, flock, parliament or school – what is the collective noun? – of freaks. I, through a process of self-discovery and self-diagnosis had come through it with flying colours.

2

And I had been offered the job from heaven. More money than I knew what to do with now that my missus was restricted as to how much she could legitimately mug me for. Apparently she now had an account at Harvey Nicks – something that somehow I had always managed to avoid. Poor Edward I mused – I wonder if you could get insurance against that.

I worked hard. I focused – I stopped questioning everything about the life I was leading and just frankly got fucking on with it. I wasn't a windswept poet, or indeed any sort of poet. I didn't live in the North, I wasn't teaching talented but disadvantaged kids to express themselves through the medium of modern dance. I was me. I had made my choices early on to follow this life of business and responsibility and an existence in the crowded, twat-infested, South East of England, commuting, worrying about profit margin and how to play the political games that one has to master to succeed in Big Business.

I hope I don't disappoint you dear friend with such a display of cynicism. Don't see it as such, please. Don't think ill of me. It's harsh reality I am afraid. It's what happens – OK, inside of me there still beats the heart of an existentialist philosopher/ trawlerman/pantyhose designer – or possibly a combination of all three – what a fantastic South Bank Special that would make, eh Mr Bragg? – but I have accepted my lot.

3

Why? Because it's the world I know as an adult. Because I don't want to live in a croft. I quite like having a smart car. I rather like being (fuck knows how – it just shows the criminal levels of incompetence amongst every other fucker in this business) quite good at my job. And of course I have two children who – maybe naively I believe – need a father around to restrict just how screwed up they become as adults.

Self-justification over I believe.

Business went well. We hit our numbers. We set up an independent online company that exceeded all expectation and I got the credit for it rather luckily. So, while our competitors were sitting scratching their arses bemoaning the state of the economy and blaming student debt on poor textbook sales, we were flying. The American masters were delighted, they gave me chunks of export markets to sprinkle my magic dust over.

And then Jimmy hit the big time.

I had been at school with Jimmy and he had been a mad bastard in those days. He was expelled at 16. I had found him on old-pals.net when I was doing my round Britain tour of every miserable screwed up fuck I had ever met.

I had met him in the café of the Royal Scottish Museum, surrounded by Yummy Morningside Mummies with their ridiculously named, twenty-years-away-from-jobs-in-the-Bank offspring all having simultaneous tantrums. Jimmy had turned up looking for all the world like he had stepped out of the front cover of *Tramp and Hobo Monthly*. Long, greasy hair, a beard that had enough food attached to it to feed a Darfur refugee camp for weeks and clothes so dirt-incrusted that I suspect the museum staff burnt the chair he had been sitting on the moment we'd departed.

Now, Jimmy had a passion – no, not for park benches, cider and baked hedgehog. It was for the ancient world. He was mad for the literature of the Romans and spent his life translating the works of Plautus, Terence, Virgil and Ovid and putting them in contemporary settings.

Complete fucking lunacy of course, I had been rather struck by his passion – it resonated for me in the light of the passionless world I was living in at the time – and I gave him a contract for four of these works. The usual deal in these cash-strapped times (unless you're a breast-enhanced supermodel married to a Manchester United footballer whose IQ is expressed by the number on the back of his shirt) – tiny advance but huge upside on the royalties when the book hit thirty thousand units. Which of course, these never would and Jimmy didn't care anyway – he was doing it for love, for the thrill of seeing his life's work in print.

The TV production company made an enquiry. They were interested in a six-parter of the *Aeneid*. It happened, we repackaged the book as TV tie-in and sold two hundred thousand copies around the world as the programme was sold to some twenty countries. They snapped up Plautus, Terence and the rest, and suddenly we had hot, hot property. Jimmy's first royalty payment was enough for him to put a fifty per cent deposit down for a flat in the New Town.

Hollywood bought the rights.

Bastard still owes me the hundred quid I lent him the day we met, but it now seems churlish to remind him.

I was hailed as the most prescient publisher of the moment who had single-handedly reintroduced the Classics to the masses.

My salary increased. My share options increased – options that I had barely paid any attention to when I started working for the business.

In two short years, they were worth millions. Literally.

Then a takeover war ensued as a major US media conglomerate decided they had to buy us. I sat for period of months as rumours flew about valuation. I could never bring myself to believe that any of this was going to happen. That Jamie Gallagher could soon be a wealthy fellow.

It did happen.

I am a wealthy – very wealthy – fellow. So wealthy I now use the services of a Private Wealth Advisor, a humourless bastard who wouldn't recognise a good penis joke if I told him one but does, I suspect, frot excessively when a new tax saving initiative presents itself.

The Americans wanted me on a three-year earn out. I told them to fuck off. I said six months. We agreed a year. I have agreed to be a publishing consultant for them two days a month for which I am paid royally.

Now, dear reader, to cut a seemingly very long story short, today is the very first day for me of freedom. Hence the alarm clock, the lie-in, the feeling of mild elation.

So what does Jamie do next?

I lie in the bed for 10 more minutes wondering what I shall do with my day. I get up, make a cup of tea come back to bed and continue to wonder what I shall do with my day.

I must get the papers delivered. It will be nicely decadent to lie in bed drink tea, and read the papers, I muse. I have never liked a TV in my bedroom – there's something just a little council flatish about households that have a TV in every room, including the bog.

I get up and ablute. I am feeling good.

One thing you should know old friend is that I – Jamie, he who single-handedly kept both the distillers of Speyside and the viniculturalists of Piedmont and Bordeaux in ass's milk over many years, paid for their children's education and second homes – has sobered up.

In the last year, I made some rules. No booze Monday–Friday except if a) abroad b) faced with a lunch/dinner of such appalling tedium that it was a straightforward toss up between alcohol and insanity – and certainly no drinking on my own. Ever. Consequently I have lost a couple of stone. I sleep deeply without the need to wake at four o'clock, visit the toilet and put what remains of the inshore fishing fleet in the South of England in deep deep peril. People tell me I look years younger. The red boozer's cheek and accessorised nose have all but gone. My teeth are no longer stained by red wine and fags – yes, the fags have gone, too. Never even tempted.

So you find me in the rudest of health. I have just joined a trendy – now don't laugh – gym.

There may be ulterior motives for that, I confess.

I get up after half an hour of light slumber, draw back the blinds in the living room and note that, for early May, the sun is indeed shining brightly. I pick up the remains of last night's supper – a cup and plate and take them through to the kitchen.

I like this flat, I muse. When Helen and I split, I moved here. It was the first place I saw, it was just about in my price range and it was in the centre of town near to the pubs and restaurants that I envisaged using in my solitary bachelorhood. It had a spare bedroom so the kids could stay if they so wished, it was low-maintenance, reasonably soundproofed and quite light and airy.

Despite the change in my circumstances, I no longer own property. I could virtually buy the entire block now if I wanted to, but to be renting somehow makes me feel free, young and slightly unconventional. Stupid, I know, pouring money down a landlord's throat monthly with nothing coming back for it.

But fear ye not – I do have a plan in this department too.

I make a cup of coffee and out of curiosity I switch on the television – I have heard tell of the horrors of daytime TV, but have rarely ever experienced it for myself. It's not boredom driving me to do this – of course not. I can't be bored on the very first day of freedom. I can't imagine Mandela, his first morning out of Robben Island, asking Winnie if she's switch on 'Boer Supermarket Sweepstake' as he was bored. No, this is part of the beginnings of my new life, it's something I have to experience for myself, just to acclimatise.

There's a programme on there featuring a fat bloke and his fat knockers-hanging-out wife who have made their fortune in pies in Wigan and who now want to move to Spain. The Spanish are welcome to them I think switching channels. The Moors obviously fucked off through clairvoyance.

Kids cartoons and adverts. I flick. Ah – here we are.

I've come in halfway through a reality

confessional TV show – I have heard talk of such things. There's a lot of shouting. A woman in leisurewear too awful even for Maidstone Town Centre is pregnant and crying. Oh and about 18 stone and hideous. There are two blokes being restrained by shaven headed bouncer types as they are obviously determined to beat the shit out of each other for the cameras. The smug middle-class presenter tells me that they're going to calm things down while they go for a commercial break.

I'm mesmerised as I sit through adverts for debt consolidation businesses, Pot Noodle and celeb magazines. What targeted advertising.

Soon they're back on and I listen fascinated as Fat Woman tells Dim Boy 1 (shaven headed, large fake diamond earrings, tattoo and all the native intelligence of a red mullet on the fish stall at Tesco) that it was very likely her daughter – their daughter – had indeed been fathered by Dim Boy 2, who was very similar to Dim Boy 1 on account of they being brothers. Apparently when DB1 was on remand for theft, then DB2 would pop round for a little TLC.

There's a fight brewing again as the two Dim Boys start swearing (thankfully bleeped out for the delicate ears of the audience) at each other and threatening to slit throats, kill, maim, etc.

And then the twist – I kind of knew that this programme needed some extra piquancy to keep it going for the next 15 minutes and so I was anticipating a further denouement. And by jingo we've got it.

On walks George. George looks early fifties. Earringed, tattooed, shaven headed. He's wearing a vest as you so obviously do on national TV – what were you thinking of Mr Dimbleby? – that show big arms and much greying chest hair. He's short, squat, muscular and looks like a psychopathic armed robber.

Turns out he's a psychopathic armed robber. And the father of DB1&2. Oh, and in a brief window when DB1 was on remand and DB2 was hiding up in Carlisle because he'd been a bit naughty to a local villain, Daddy had come out of prison after a ten-year stretch and found his sons' bird rather accommodating.

There's mayhem in the studio as the credits roll and I am absolutely hooked. I wonder if the poor daughter has to buy three Father's Day cards every year.

What is it with these people that they cannot behave in a civilised manner – but also want to parade their semen splashed dirty laundry on national television? It's appalling, fascinating, revolting and marvellous.

I shake my head in mild desperation at the ways of the world and decide to take advantage of the sunshine. I shall venture out.

# Chapter 2

# When I was cruel

Washed, shaved and dressed I leave the flat. I have a plan. I shall walk to a pub on the outskirts of town that serves good food and wine. Yes, I know, I don't drink during the week or on my own, but today feels like a day of celebration and frankly I can do what the fuck I like.

The first part of the journey takes me through the shopping centre. I am not a shopper, I rarely visit this place unless absolute necessity demands that I do. And I never visit midweek.

It's busy. There a young mothers, some yummy, some less so, everywhere. The town is socially divided. Middle and upper-middle-class mothers, husbands toiling in the City starting affairs that will eventually break up their marriages, push babies in designer buggies while shopping casually and meeting their friends for coffee or lunch. And then the fun starts – the gossiping, the boasting, the leaving-the-car-keys-of-the-new-Porsche on the table accidentally so everyone notices and comments. The Caribbean fortnight this summer, the Paris surprise for the wedding anniversary – that actually was assuaging the husband's guilt for shagging his secretary rather poorly at that conference in Dusseldorf a couple of weeks back.

The less yummy are but kids – anything from 14–18 year old girls who should still be in school but who are suffering for accommodating their condomless – now absent – boyfriends. It's leisurewear, hooped earrings, gum, swearing and midriffs on view. Strangely the buggies that their children are pushed around in are identical or superior to those of the yummy mummies. Presumably bought from The Catalogue and paid for monthly out their dole money.

Which my fucking taxes are paying for. Makes my blood boil. Get a fucking job. Or put something in the water to stop their fertility. What has happened to personal responsibility? Everything is everyone else's fault – you get up the duff in the park at fifteen after too many alco-pops and the state will care for you.

Makes my blood boil.

And also scares me to think I am capable of such middle-class, middle-aged Victorian-values rage. What has happened to me? What is happening to the man more Liberal in his views than Gladstone himself, who believed in the empowerment of the Working Classes (although he wouldn't want to share a lift with them), who believed in Society helping the Unfortunates?

I remember as a young man at university briefly toying with the idea of teaching. I wanted to promulgate knowledge. To work with working-class kids brought up on *The Generation Game* and Little and Large, so that they would weep at Lear and Othello, love Austen and the Brontës and melt at Keats.

OK, so my career path changed when I realised how shit the money was, but the passion for equality was there. I marched for the miners, I demonstrated against Thatcher, I read *The Guardian* – and not just the sports pages.

Now my views seem to have become so right wing I'd be deemed too extreme for the letters page of the *Daily Mail*.

I pass the recently opened Ann Summers shop and think how different the world is today – dildos on the high street. Sex everywhere. A bloke of my age has to be careful when the weather turns. There's so much flesh on display you can easily face accusations of being a dirty old man – girls young enough to be my daughter walk around town centres as if they've just popped off the beach in Ibiza. I have a rule in these situations – despite my innate ability to ogle (particular penchant for bosoms), it's eyes ahead, don't fall for the obvious and keep yourself out of trouble.

I am going up the escalator. Half-way up is a blond woman in tight jeans with a bottom to die for. I stare safe in the knowledge that I cannot be found out unless she turns round.

She walks off the escalator and I follow still staring at her backside when suddenly she does turn around. She's obviously remembered something. I feel immediately guilty – caught mid-lech, then I feel confused.

It's Helen. My ex-wife Helen. She looks at me and smiles. I have been ogling my ex. Yuck – that's kind of unnatural. A sort of incest, surely?

I haven't seen her for a couple of months, but something has happened to her. She looks amazing. I walk towards her and kiss her on both cheeks. 'God' I say 'You look fantastic Helen. What's happened?'

'Meaning I never used to, Jamie?' She smiles. She looks like the girl I met some twenty years back in London.

'You look – different. Younger. Sorry, Helen, I'm just a little stunned.'

'It's nice I can still stun you James Gallagher,' she says, slightly coquettishly I think. 'Oh and you look pretty good yourself.'

Is she flirting with me?

We chat a little then she says 'If you buy me a coffee I'll tell you my secret.'

It seems churlish to refuse and we plump for one of the 563 fair trade *maestro barista* establishments within 200 metres of where we are standing.

We get our coffees and sit. She tells me her secret.

It's not much of a secret. She had felt that she'd let herself go a little, started taking Edward somewhat for granted. So, she'd employed a personal trainer and dietician. She started feeling better, then treated herself to a week in Poland. At a plastic surgeon's clinic. New arse, tummy tuck and she said, seductively I am certain, 'New boobs' as she pushed them out towards me. 'So, what do you think?'

'Lovely' I say, uncertain how to respond to a flirtatious ex-wife. 'But more importantly, what does Edward think?'

'Oh he's thrilled. Dear old stick. When he remembers to look.' And she gave me a strange sideways glance.

Oh I get it I think. Oh I really get it. She knows.

'So how are you then Jamie? How is life? How is the Corporation?'

'It's fine,' I say, non-committedly.

'Still in the flat?'

'Yup.' She knows all this. She's fishing.

'Not working today?'

'Day off,' I say.

'I heard,' here it comes I think 'that you'd had a pay out?'

'Helen' I say, 'the divorce settlement is done and dusted. There's nothing more there. I maintain the kids. There's nothing more to it.'

She looks hurt. 'Darling, I'm not after anything more from you. I just hope you're enjoying your success. You deserve it.' She smiled sweetly then sipped the coffee.

I am a cynical deeply-flawed bastard I think. She means it. She's happy for me.

I think what is troubling me is that I am finding her attractive. The top two buttons of her blouse have opened *comme magique* and there's not a little cleavage being shown. Oh and it's firm cleavage. And despite myself I take a glance.

Trouserly stirrings.

She catches me. I feel as if I have been apprehended in an aunt's knicker drawer.

'Take me for lunch, darling,' she says, naming the most expensive and frankly overrated restaurant in town.

'I can't' I say. 'I have business to attend to.'

I drink my coffee and tell her I have to go. 'Tomorrow night,' she says, 'I shall be in George's. Meet me there at eight.'

'OK' I say if only to get rid of her. I'll phone and cancel – I just have to get away from her and that Lorelei cleavage. Now.

I kiss her on cheeks and virtually run from the coffee house.

Fuck fuck fuck fuck and thrice fuck I think as I walk away and head out of town. Oh – and bollocks.

# Chapter 3
## Cars and Girls

Well let me give you a little lesson in success, dear friend.

Let me show you a little glimpse of what goes on inside the mind of a fabulously successful creative bloke like me.

I'm in the pub –obviously. I needed shelter and sustenance after my lunchtime walk in the valley of death with my ex-missus. Thinking time. Space.

Five pints of strong ale and a couple of cigars later you find me having sorted out this potentially messy problem . I have analysed the facts, I have worked out what the issues are here.

I have another beer whilst I put the finishing touches to my theory.

Fact 1 – I have, in the four years since Helena and I split, not had a significant other. I've worked too hard. There have been a couple of near things, a casual grope and snog with a New York woman in a hotel lift after a long flight and a boozy meal, but in terms of sex, forget it. I have not been interested in the involvement. I have never been able to multi-task and I wasn't going to put myself off my game whilst building my empire and so I resolutely kept my cock out of my day-to-day life.

Fact 2 – Helen must know something of my new financial situation. There were press releases about the various stages of the sale and my subsequent employment and she probably could work out with Edward, who's many things but isn't financially retarded, the kind of figure I ended up with.

Fact 3 – She left me originally through (in no particular order)  a) my mild midlife crisis b) Edward's superior financial capabilities c) my boorish constantly pissed dissatisfied-with-my-lot behaviour.

Fact 4 – She saw a father figure in Edward who would look after her. She could not ever, ever find Edward more attractive than me.

The break up didn't bother me truly. I was not hurt, distraught or in any way pained at her unfaithfulness. We'd run our course. The mediocrity of my marriage to Helen was now replaced in my mind by the mediocrity of her marriage to that boring old fuck Edward. If anything I felt sorry for them.

The settlement was fair, I willingly agreed to support the children and took provision to pay educational costs. Helena went off and lived with Edward in their moated house. The kids lived there but visited me virtually every weekend and royally took the piss much to my delight out of Edward and his fuddy-duddy ways. Cameron is now at Cambridge in his second year and Ailsa is mid A

19

levels planning a gap year. They receive from me the financial support I originally committed to.

No way the children will or need to know of their father's wealth. What would motivate them to get out of bed in the morning if they know they're set for life? Absolutely bugger all. So, it's student loans for the both of them, a degree of financial responsibility at this time for them and I'll settle their debts when they've graduated.

It's all worked out. I will not be responsible for producing yet more spoilt brats. Helen must not be allowed to mess this grand plan up.

That's that decided. I have another drink. I'll worry about cancelling her tomorrow.

I think about my future. It might, just might get a little lonely. Now I've always enjoyed my own company – there's none better in my humble opinion. But for the next thirty (God willing) years? Should I start to look for someone with whom to grow old?

I've avoided it, not needing the involvement, too busy. Also there's something slightly repulsive about the language that is used. It's all so borrowed from teenagers. To hear middle-aged people talk about dating, their boy friend/girlfriend – it's just so unseemly. Perhaps this is a throw back to my Scottish Presbyterian upbringing – where as previously discussed, your parents acted as parents not as slightly older siblings and fucking behaved themselves.

A couple of people have suggested internet dating or speed dating. Yuck. Humiliation obviously lies down that route. I have no real interest in any of the women who I have worked with except of course for darling Janice my former receptionist who I tracked down and made my PA. She was without doubt the least-effective PA in the history of that particular function, but her smile and tight sweaters and firm calves made my days even more bearable. But that was never going to be anything more than mild office flirting on her part and lust on mine.

Why this self analysis? It's fucking obvious why. I've just been hit on by my ex-wife who has defrosted my gonads by flashing her Warsaw-manufactured tits at me. And I liked it being a shallow, hollow arse. I was flattered and let's be honest – tempted to cuckold Mr Reinsurance in the same way he cuckolded me.

No, I tell myself finishing the beer and paying the tab. No. No.

I start to walk back towards town. I feel disappointed about how the day has panned out. My first day of liberation has soured.

Put simply as I am nothing if not a simple fellow – I thought my life was sorted out. It fucking isn't.

The outskirts of town where the industrial estates are reminiscent of a medieval city. In those days you'd have the furriers or candlemakers together in one street. Now you've the electrical and plumbing suppliers, the DIY superstores, the car dealers all in similar enclaves.

I walk past the Mercedes dealership and stop. There's a car on the forecourt.

I think I've fallen in love with it.

I stare. It's a lot of money for a car. But it's beautiful, small black compact designed convertible sports car.

I stare.

I have a nice car already, I think – my big BMW. I don't need another car. And not a sports car, not at my age. What do they say about sports car and middle-aged blokes? – oh yes I remember. They are bought by rich middle-aged blokes chasing their youth and compensating for their slackening libido.

I walk past the little piece of tarty Germanic engineering – determined not to fall for its sleek lines.

But I could just go in and enquire. Ask for a brochure. Where would the harm be in that?

I walk into the glistening reception area and approach a pretty dark-haired girl behind the desk. She looks me up and down and asks not very convincingly if she can help me.

I can see her point. I have just walked a couple of miles in spring sunshine after consuming beer and cigars that she can probably smell from where she's sitting. I've just walked in to this establishment. My shirt is hanging out and I'm rather sweaty – she has me identified as a pissed tramp.

22

'That black sports car out front – I'd like some details please.'

'With a view to...?' she asks.

'Buying the bloody thing, actually,' I say a little aggressively then change my tack. 'Did you think perhaps I wanted permission to sketch it in charcoal on your forecourt?'

She bristles, picks up the phone and obviously whispers rather more to a colleague than just 'You've a customer.'

'Take a seat – sir', that last word uttered reluctantly. 'Someone will be with you shortly.'

'Shall I help myself to coffee?' I say nodding at a machine and cups and saucers.

She ignores me. I pour a cup of black coffee and sit down. I pick up the *Daily Mail*. It's enough to make you walk out.

'Sir,' says a snappily besuited young man of about thirty-five. 'How can we help you today?'

I tell him about the black car on the forecourt. He mentions a name for it that sounds like a chemical compound to me.

'It is expensive sir. Seventy-five thousand'.

'I noticed that. Tell me what it does please.' He sighs, looking me up and down. In a bored voice he tells me about horsepower and torque and  pistons and I stop him. 'Sorry Mr ...? 'He offers his name, Peter. 'Peter, I don't want to be rude but I know nothing about cars. Just tell me basics. Top speed?

Automatic? How many seats? Servicing? Miles per hour?'

He tells me all of this in a bored voice.

'Thank you,' I say. 'Now, if I pay cash is there a discount?.'

He is looking at me thinking he's been had. 'Cash? Seventy-five grand? Come on mate, you're taking the piss. You've obviously had a few to many and you're having a larf. I have to ask you to leave.'

'OK Peter,' I say affably. 'You're right. I don't have that kind of money on me obviously. Sorry to mislead you.'

'That's OK, Sir,' he says wearily shepherding me to the door. I shake his hand. Reaching for my wallet, I take out my Platinum Amex card and hold it up to him.

'You my young friend, should learn not to be judgemental.'

My shitty first day of my new life was made somewhat better by the purchase of the beautiful black sporty Merc. For £65K. Pick it up on Friday.

I walk back through the town centre. Via the off-licence. I revisit my vow of abstinence and remember a caveat.

It only ever applied to Speyside Scotch.

I treat myself to a bottle of Islay's finest and return to the flat.

*To be continued...*

*What Jamie Did Next will be published by Refreshing Words in Spring 2023. Available as an ebook and paperback*

*The author enjoying a small tipple of Irn-Bru*

REFRESHING WORDS has been set up to help authors tackle the independent publishing process.

One thing above all that will help to sell in a crowded and competitive marketplace is quality — readers demand that their books are as well-written, well-laid out, and as well-edited as ever.

Whether it's your novel, family history or poetry we can turn it into a book your friends and family will cherish — and a wider audience will appreciate.

So if you're thinking of self-publishing and want that all important support then visit us at:

## www.refreshingwords.co.uk